"[A   es.
Sop   iice
job   ssion
at the end."   —*RT Book Reviews*

"This mystery had me completely stumped until the end. With corruption and bribery between the town council and local developers, everyone had secrets and everyone looked suspicious. I can't think of a more delightful way to spend an afternoon than with a cup of tea, a scone, a copy of this book, and a cat . . . of course!"

—*Melissa's Mochas, Mysteries & Meows*

"The mystery was complex and well plotted, and I enjoyed trying to fit the clues together."   —*Book of Secrets*

"In *Tempest in a Teapot* we are introduced to a charming and quirky cast of characters. This includes our feisty protagonist, Sophie Taylor . . . This lighthearted mystery becomes a page-turner of a read that I could not put down. It is well plotted and kept me wanting to find out whodunit."

—*MyShelf.com*

"Amanda Cooper writes an engaging mystery in her first book in this new series. With intriguing characters and a delightful setting, I can already tell this series is going to be a firm favorite. For tea drinkers all across the world I highly recommend this series."   —*Cozy Mystery Book Reviews*

Berkley Prime Crime titles by Amanda Cooper

TEMPEST IN A TEAPOT
SHADOW OF A SPOUT

Shadow of a Spout

Amanda Cooper

BERKLEY PRIME CRIME, NEW YORK

THE BERKLEY PUBLISHING GROUP
Published by the Penguin Group
Penguin Group (USA) LLC
375 Hudson Street, New York, New York 10014

USA • Canada • UK • Ireland • Australia • New Zealand • India • South Africa • China

penguin.com

A Penguin Random House Company

SHADOW OF A SPOUT

A Berkley Prime Crime Book / published by arrangement with the author

For information, address: The Berkley Publishing Group,
a division of Penguin Group (USA) LLC,
375 Hudson Street, New York, New York 10014.

ISBN: 978-0-425-26524-6

PUBLISHING HISTORY
Berkley Prime Crime mass-market edition / April 2015

PRINTED IN THE UNITED STATES OF AMERICA

10 9 8 7 6 5 4 3 2 1

Cover illustration by Griesbach Martucci.
Cover design by Diana Kolsky.
Interior text design by Kelly Lipovich.

This cozy mystery is lovingly dedicated to all the grandmothers—and grandfathers!—out there who introduce their grandchildren to tea (liberally laced with milk, of course) and the lovely ritual that attends the beverage. I hope you know your grandkids will cherish the memory of the time you spent with them having tea parties.

In memory of my own grandmothers Tena Phillips, who gave me my first tea mug, and Charlotte Simpson, who always had a strong pot of tea on the stove!

A Cup of Tea

by Anonymous

When the world is all at odds
And the mind is all at sea
Then cease the useless tedium
And brew a cup of tea.

There is magic in its fragrance,
There is solace in its taste;
And then laden moments vanish
Somehow into space.

And the world becomes a lovely thing!
There's beauty as you'll see;
All because you briefly stopped
To brew a cup of tea.

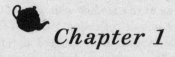

Chapter 1

The dark-paneled meeting room of the Stone and Scone Inn was full on the first afternoon of the annual August convention of the New York State division of the ITCS, the International Teapot Collectors Society. Rose Freemont should have been listening to the speaker, but instead she examined her treasure. It was a homely thing, the metal teapot, battered and beaten, like a raggedy old man who has been buffeted about by the elements and fallen on hard times. But like that raggedy old man, it had a past, a purpose, and meaning. She turned it over and over in her hands, examining the patina, caressing the dent on its round belly and hugging it to her. There was something about the size of it and the intricacy of the decoration that hinted at a noble history.

That was what had inspired her to bring it to the convention in Butterhill, New York. She wanted to know more about it, and hoped to find some answers. In the past Rose had to attend without Laverne Hodge, her best friend and sole employee at her business, Auntie Rose's Victorian Tea House, because someone had to keep the place open. They alternated years going to the convention and never got to enjoy it together, as such good friends ought. But this summer she and Laverne were attending with some of the other Silver Spouts, her teapot-collecting group in Gracious Grove, a small town nestled in the Finger Lakes region of upstate New York. She could thank her sweet granddaughter, Sophie Rose Freemont Taylor, trained restaurateur, for this time with her friends.

Sophie was still feeling the sting of the failure of her New York garment district restaurant In Fashion, but helping her grandmother at Auntie Rose's was proving to be just the elixir she needed. It had put the spring back in her youthful step, and in return she had brought a zest and vigor to the tearoom that was dragging it, as Laverne said, kicking and screaming into the twenty-first century. She had added items to the menu that were bringing in a new crowd without alienating the old crowd, an ideal situation for the tearoom.

Though some of her nonfood ideas were radical, like redecorating the entire chintz-and-roses tearoom—Rose cringed at the thought of the expense and work and business days lost—she liked her granddaughter's enthusiasm. When Sophie first came back to Gracious Grove, Rose worried that the girl was too beaten down by defeat to care. But she was rebounding, and it was a revelation that having Sophie around was putting the spring back into her *own* octogenarian step.

She sighed as the voice, a background to her wandering thoughts, droned on. The lack of effective air-conditioning meant the room was getting stuffy, and she was far too old to go without air-conditioning for long on a hot August day. She nudged Laverne, sitting next to her. "Do you think she's *ever* going to stop talking?" Rose whispered. The "she" who had monopolized the meeting so far was Zunia Pettigrew, president of the New York State division of the ITCS.

"Never," Laverne snapped. "Loves the sound of her own voice too much."

"So in short," Zunia finally said, straightening to her whole five-foot height and completely missing the humor inherent in her words, "welcome to our annual convention."

"That woman wouldn't know short if she ran over it," Laverne groused.

Laverne's father, ninety-something Malcolm Hodge, who sat on the other side of his seventy-year-old daughter, snorted. "If she wants to know what short is, she *could* look in the mirror," he murmured, in his dry-as-dust tone.

"I would like to introduce at this time Walter Sommer, our distinguished International Teapot Collectors Society president!" Zunia finished, and led a round of applause that was brief and scattered, as Walter stood, shook the creases out of his trousers and approached the dais.

Josh Sinclair, wide-eyed and at sixteen the youngest member of the Silver Spouts and likely the youngest member the ITCS had ever had, smirked at the exchange among his elders, but then pressed his lips together and sobered immediately. Rose smiled at his earnest demeanor. It was his first convention and required him to take a day away from his summer college courses, but how could his mother say no when he was a straight-A student? He not only kept up his grades but was in an accelerated course at high school, was the recording secretary of the Silver Spouts, and held down a part-time job editing digital content for the Gracious Grove newspaper.

He was one of those rare souls who knew from the age of five what he would become: a historian with a specialty in object conservation. He had already begun writing on the topic for the *Gracious Grove Gazette*, with a piece on the history of the Sinclair crest he found on a teapot left to him by his great-grandmother. Sophie had a lot in common with him in having an early determination to pursue a particular line of work. She had always known she wanted to be a chef. She called Josh an old soul in a new body and they had become somewhat unlikely friends.

As always deliberate and measured in his pace, Walter cleared his throat, examined his notes, collected them together into a neat pile, harrumphed and cleared his throat again. He then tapped the microphone, which squealed in dismay. The mic was hardly necessary, since the conference room of the Stone and Scone was a mere thirty feet long and twenty wide, more than adequate for the twenty-five or so attendees at the conference, but Walter liked to make a production out of his yearly appearance.

Walter Sommer, tall, slim and slightly stooped, had unusual green eyes and a thatch of white hair that lay obediently in a wave across his forehead. He was the president and one of the founding members of the ITCS, which had grown to include twenty-five regional or state divisional chapters that were in turn made up of local groups. Walter and his wife, Nora, another founding member, lived in Schenectady, and the New York State convention was considered by some as the "home turf" for the entire society. The only collectors club from the state that wasn't there was the New York City society, Big

Apple Teapots, whose membership was too big to stay comfortably at the Stone and Scone. They boycotted the convention every year, preferring to hold their own chapter convention in New York City. Walter would also attend that event, since he was originally from the city himself, along with Zunia, state division president, and her husband.

He began to talk, welcoming each and every attendee and setting out the plans for the weekend. There would be three seminars, two the next day and one Sunday morning, on the history of tea, silver hallmarks as they pertained to silver teapots, and the development of tea vessels, form versus function. Saturday evening Walter and Nora would guide a group through a local art museum where art depicting teapots was on display. Sunday afternoon the convention would draw to a close in time for folks to get back to their homes before dark. Informal group gatherings over dinner in the inn were optional, with some folks preferring other area restaurants.

After introductory remarks he launched into the meat of his talk. He blathered about his year, traveling to the different chapter meetings of the ITCS, his and Nora's trip to England to visit a teapot enthusiast with a vast collection, and his continuing passion for the hunt for new treasures. He launched into a detailed explanation of what the next year's meetings would look like, how they would be organizing future conventions to coincide with special events in the upstate New York region.

The crowd was restless, but his wife, Nora, shot a warning glance at those who checked their cell phones, rustled around in their purses for a mint or chatted quietly. It was a silent look, but effective. A hush fell once more, a kind of drugged, weary stillness as Walter droned on and on and on.

* * *

Thelma Mae Earnshaw shifted in her seat and pulled her polyester dress away from her legs, where it stuck to her diabetic stockings and overheated skin. A late August heat wave and an under-air-conditioned conference room had her grumpiness ratcheting up to dramatic levels. Why in the good Lord's name had she wanted to join the danged Silver Spouts so badly? Until three months ago she and Rose Freemont hadn't spoken more than a few muttered words in sixty-some-odd years. Maybe she should have kept it that way, but now here she was a member of the teapot-collecting group. This little excursion took valuable time away from her tearoom, La Belle Époque, and forced her to leave the business in the inadequate hands of her sole employee, Gilda Bachman.

She looked around. There was Rose, beau stealer, one row ahead of her. Even though they'd made up, Thelma would always contend that she'd seen Harold Freemont, Rose's late husband, first and had dibs. Sitting next to her was golden girl Laverne Hodge. Thelma wished sad-sack Gilda could be more like Laverne, who was steady, smart and a workaholic, even if she was on the shady side of seventy. Thelma's granddaughter, Cissy Peterson, said she was too hard on Gilda, but Cissy was what the youngsters called clueless. Clueless; what did that mean? Without a mystery board game? She snickered and caught a dirty look from some frumpy-dumpy woman who put her finger to her lips like a librarian.

Her attention drifted to the others. Distracted once again, Thelma surveyed the group, wondering how she'd gotten mixed up with such an oddball assortment of folks. Who would think so many people in their small town of Gracious Grove would collect teapots? Her own collection wasn't near as big as Rose's, but she didn't pay the earth for them, either, not like *some* folk with more money than brains—not naming names, of course, but if the flowery name fit . . . She tried to get her achy back more comfortable, and the chair creaked and squawked. Every eye in the place fixed on her, so she mumbled an apology as that Sommer fellow droned on. Back to teapots . . . Thelma figured if a spout was chipped or a lid was cracked, you just turned that side of the teapot to the wall.

She sighed. This place was hotter than a bordello on nickel night, like her daddy used to say just before her mama shushed him. Thelma wished she were up in her room lying down on the clean white coverlet with the window open. Most of the Silver Spouts club had decided to come and she was stuck rooming with that SuLinn Miller girl, a Gracious Grove newcomer and barely thirty, if she was a day. All she did was text on her phone and listen to music on her headphones. No conversation at all, so far, in the few hours they had been here. Except now she was sitting up bright and perky listening to that Walter Sommer fellow drone on about who knew what.

To distract herself from the boredom of listening to a fellow with the voice of a bumblebee, she examined the other Silver Spout members in attendance. There were the two old men—Laverne's father, Malcolm Hodge, ninety-plus but still full of spit and vinegar, and Horace Brubaker, a vigorous ninety-seven. Rounding out the group was that young fellow, Josh Sinclair, who had a little single room down the hall. Since Thelma had just joined it was all new to her, but Rose and Laverne had explained that there were three other collecting groups besides the Silver Spouts in attendance at the New York State divisional convention: the Niagara Teapot

Collectors Group, the Genesee Valley Tea Totalers and the Monroe Tea Belles. There should have been another but they were mysteriously absent, so far. Some were staying in the inn, while others were rooming with local collectors.

Thelma shifted in discomfort as Sommer groaned on. The room had rickety seating, dark paneling and no ventilation to speak of. If things didn't get going soon at this danged convention she'd call Gilda and tell her to bring the car and pick her up. She regretted not coming in her own vehicle, but Cissy was beginning to make faint noises about Thelma not driving by herself anymore, so she had come with SuLinn. As if a couple of fender benders were such a big deal. Or a traffic ticket for going too slow—how stupid was that? Too slow was better than too fast. And who didn't have a parking infraction or two? Or three. A ticket for parking facing the wrong way on a street? It just seemed silly to her that the driver had to park so they had to get out of the car into traffic. Why shouldn't she park so she could get out of the car on the sidewalk, like a civilized person? What difference did it make on a quiet side street in Gracious Grove?

A couple of the folks were whispering to each other. Looked like a sweaty fellow in the front row and the New York division president were arguing about something. Thelma strained her neck to see, but was blocked by Rose and Laverne and the rest in front of her. Darn it, but they had stopped. That Zunia woman, the chapter president—Rose had pointed her out as they took their seats—had moved to sit away from the feller she'd been arguing with, but now she was shooting poisonous glances at a pretty red-haired girl who sat near the door, all alone and lonesome. She was Irish-looking, with that reddish hair and freckles all over. Poor kid sure seemed downhearted.

Thelma glanced ahead at Rose again, still clutching that dumb metal pot that she had bought at some dealer's shop in Ithaca. You'd think it was solid gold or something, the way she mooned over it! Rose had told them all that there was going to be a "Stump the Expert" portion at the end of today's talk; she was presenting her new prize to be looked over by Zunia Pettigrew. Rose said the Ithaca antiques dealer had told her it was likely Chinese, but Sophie, Rose's granddaughter, had done some research and didn't think it was.

Rose wanted to know if Zunia Pettigrew, who had a PhD in historical objects identification, could tell her about it. Thelma could have saved her the trouble and told her it was a hunk of junk, but everyone would get their unders in a knot if she said that. Folks just didn't want to know the truth.

Walter Sommer wound up his lengthy speech by giving the floor back to Zunia Pettigrew, a sour-faced, dark little elf if ever Thelma had seen one. Zunia minced back up to the dais in her five-inch heels, thanked Walter effusively, and said, "And now we come to the most interesting part of the day! We will soon adjourn to the dining room for afternoon tea, but I see a few folks in the audience who have brought teapots for me to look at."

A fellow in the front row stood and applauded, shouting, "Bravo for Zunia!"

"Who in tarnation is that fool?" Thelma muttered.

"Shh! That's Pastor Frank Barlow; he's a member of the Niagara Teapot Collectors Group, Zunia's club," Laverne whispered.

Pastor? Looked more like a crooked accountant at an audit, and sweating just as bad, too.

"Who's first?" Zunia chirped, looking around. She smiled thinly at Pastor Frank, but it looked more like a grimace to Thelma.

Rose, who was excited that she was finally going to learn something about her teapot, was about to stand, but one of the Monroe Tea Belles was quicker and approached the lectern holding out a teapot in the shape of a cottage. Zunia took it, turned it around in her hands, then handed it back. "Well, of course, that is a Price Brothers teapot . . . Ye Olde Cottage. Very common. It's cracked, almost worthless. Next!"

The Tea Belles member returned to her seat among her friends, her face slightly red and her shoulders slumped. Rose felt for her and eyed Zunia with distaste. The woman was voted New York State division president just a year ago. Laverne had attended that convention with her father, along with Helen and Annabelle, two of their friends, while Rose stayed behind to look after Auntie Rose's Victorian Tea House. So though Rose knew Zunia slightly from her attendance at the convention the year before, she hadn't been there when the choice was made to elect her with no opposition.

"Is she always like this?" Rose whispered to Laverne.

Her friend, dark eyes narrowed with anger, nodded. "Drunk on power. Only reason everyone voted for her last year was they were afraid not to. *And* there was no one else standing against her! Ran a smear campaign against Rhiannon Galway. Poor girl withdrew and Zunia was elected just like that."

Rose nodded. She knew some of that from their discussions

when Laverne came back from the convention last August. Rhiannon Galway, of Galway Fine Teas in Butterhill, was her supplier, making up packets of Auntie Rose's Tea-riffic Tea Blend in bulk for her, a black tea blended with Chinese and Kenyan leaves, creating a strong yet mellow brew. But the girl was reserved and Rose didn't know her well.

She glanced over at Rhiannon, who sat alone near the door, her lips compressed into a thin line and her gaze distant. Sophie had struck up a friendship with Rhi, as she called her. They were close in age and refugees from New York City, where Rhiannon had tried to open a shop to extend her mother's tea business. It had failed miserably. Poor girl had been through a lot, it was rumored. No one quite knew what it was that Zunia had against her, but she had hinted at scandals that would hurt the image of the ITCS if they got out. According to Laverne it appeared that Rhiannon had backed down rather than force a confrontation, as if Zunia had some kind of hold over her.

She didn't actually belong to any of the groups but was still a member of the society and acted as its tea supplier. That was a lot of business, when you considered that the ITCS had over a thousand members, many of whom ran tearooms or bed-and-breakfast establishments and so bought a lot of tea. As they arrived Rhiannon had handed out gift bags with various tea-related items, donated by her shop. However, it had been whispered among the groups, as they gathered before the meeting, that Zunia was going to try this year to oust Rhiannon as the official tea supplier to the ITCS, thus severing her only real connection to the society, since she was not a teapot collector, nor did she belong to a collecting group. No one knew why other than their run-in at the last convention the previous summer.

Amanda Cooper

One of the Tea Totalers approached the dais and held out a bird-shaped figural teapot. Zunia took it and turned it over and over, her dark eyes pinched and her brow furrowed. "This is . . . uh . . . well, it's definitely English. Victorian. Worth a couple of hundred, perhaps. Next!"

"Excuse me," the woman, a tall, gaunt, gray-haired senior, said. "I believe you're mistaken. The pot is clearly marked on the bottom 'Bavaria'—in other words, German. I'm not asking the country of origin, I was merely wondering what era the pot might be from, and if you'd ever seen the pottery mark before."

Zunia's face, framed in a dark bob, reddened. She pushed the pot back into the woman's hands and folded her arms over her prominent bosom. "If you're going to argue about it, you can just sit down. Next!"

The whispers became a steady murmur. Even Walter looked uneasy, though little fazed him, Rose had observed at past conventions. He exchanged a glance with his wife, Nora, who sat in the front row of the audience. From Rose's angle it appeared that she didn't meet his glance, instead remaining stone-faced and unresponsive, staring straight ahead at the wood-paneled front wall. Zunia's husband, Orlando, appeared anxious, scanning the crowd. His daughter, Emma, a sullen teen, tried to get up but he held on to her arm firmly with one hand, while he pulled out a handkerchief, flapped it open, wiped his red eyes and blew his nose.

Laverne nudged Rose. "You going up there or what?" she muttered. "Come on, old friend, you can best her."

No one else appeared to have anything more, so it was now or never. Though she no longer cared what Zunia Pettigrew had to say, nor did she have much confidence the woman knew what she was talking about, she was not going to back down without even doing what she came to do. Rose stood and approached the lectern with her teapot presented.

Zunia stared at it, squinted, frowned and seemed reluctant. She finally took it from Rose and turned it over and over in her hands. She was a small woman, but with a big attitude. Rose had seen her quicksilver changes in temperament, from smiling and laughing to lashing out in anger. She looked sour in that moment, but perhaps the previous trouble had made her cautious. "What can you tell me about it?" she asked, glancing over at Rose as she thumbed the elaborate silvery braided decoration that overlaid the copper belly and spout. "I'd like to see how much *you* know."

"I bought it from an antiques dealer in Ithaca. He thought it was Chinese, but my granddaughter doesn't believe that's so." Rose hesitated. Sophie had done a lot of research, and believed that it was not a teapot at all, but a Buddhist holy water vessel. Rose had decided that she would have a teapot "expert" evaluate it, but now she thought she might not know anything more when Zunia was done than when she had begun. "One thing I do know is, it's old. Silver over copper, we think."

Zunia turned it over and over, squinted over at Rose, then picked up her jewelers' loupe, examining the bottom closely. She then made a noise between her teeth. "Hah! Not an antique at all. The hallmarks are fake, even the patina is fake. It's a cheap repro made in Hong Kong." She shoved it back at Rose and looked around the room. "They're designed to fool unwise collectors who don't know what they're doing. Is that it?" She looked around, as Rose stood stunned, with her piece cradled in her arms. "Then we can go to the dining room for afternoon tea."

"Wait just a minute," Rose demanded, arresting the crowd as folks obediently stood, with a rustle and murmur. The noise stopped, and it was as if the group collectively held its breath. "I may not have a degree, but this is no reproduction," she said to Zunia. "It's at *least* a couple of hundred years old, maybe more!"

The murmuring of the group began again, whispers and mutters of interest.

"Rose Beaudry Freemont, right?" Zunia said, eyeing her. "You always were a know-it-all."

Rose heard Thelma snicker and shot her a look. As Zunia Pettigrew turned away, Rose snapped, "Don't you speak to me like that, young lady!" and grabbed her arm to keep her in place.

"Ow, *ow*!" Zunia cried, jerking her arm away. "You *hurt* me! I won't be manhandled. Orlando, will you behave like a proper husband and help me out here?!"

Orlando Pettigrew leaped up from his chair and moved toward the pair as his daughter, Emma, began to laugh. It was an unpleasant sound filled with malice, ugly from such a young girl. Rose caught Josh's expression as he stared at Emma. He came from a happy family and seemed puzzled by the resentment Emma apparently had toward her stepmother.

"Zunia Pettigrew, I did *not* hurt your arm!" Rose said, refocusing on the chapter president. "For heaven's sake, I'm eighty, and you're fifty. I'm not strong enough to hurt you!"

"Fifty?" Zunia shrieked. "I'm thirty-eight, I'll have you know. *Fifty!* Of all the insults . . ." She reached out, grabbed Rose's shoulder and gave it a shove.

Rose staggered but found her footing as the room buzzed with shocked conversation and even an outcry of distress.

Laverne stood, moved swiftly down to the aisle and then strode forward, saying, "Zunia Pettigrew, you calm down and don't you *dare* lay your hands on Rose again."

Walter Sommer stepped up to the embattled trio, stuck out both hands, palms outward, and cleared his throat. "Ladies, tempers, tempers!"

Rose, clutching her teapot to her chest, said, "Walter Sommer, as ITCS president, why don't you tell Zunia Pettigrew to stop being such a petty tyrant?"

Walter shook his head, reached toward Zunia, then stopped, cleared his throat again, surveyed the chattering group with a sweeping glance, and said, "We will now adjourn to have tea and everyone will calm their nerves with the bewitching brew, as poets call it."

His mixture of pomposity and oily solicitude was grating. Zunia tossed her head and stormed off, grabbing Orlando's arm and dragging him after her as Emma followed, snickering at her stepmother's anger.

Chapter 2

The dining room at the Stone and Scone Inn was across the small, dark lobby from the conference room. Though about the same size, it was lighter and brighter, paneled in white wainscoting and with dusty gilt chandeliers dangling from the high ceilings. It would be set for dinner in just two hours, but in the meantime the inn serving staff had set it up for afternoon tea for the conventioneers. Round tables layered in white-and-pink damask tablecloths dotted the room; fresh flowers in bowls adorned the center of each table. The tea ware was restaurant-quality Villeroy & Boch, but at least it was patterned in green and looked fresh against the pink tablecloths.

The dining room, cooler than the convention room had been, was abuzz with chatter. Zunia and the other members of the ITCS national executive committee, which consisted of Walter Sommer, his wife, Nora, and other ITCS members from different chapters, sat at a table in the center. Penelope

Daley, a large blonde woman with frizzy hair in a cut that emphasized a long jaw, was bent toward the pastor, talking at him. He cleaned his glasses and watched Zunia, who chatted with a pair of sixtyish twin sisters.

Rose and her group sat at a big round table near the back, her grand teapot, or whatever it was, on the table in front of her. Laverne examined a scone then spread it with fruit preserve and bit into it. "Not bad," she mumbled. "Not as good as ours, but not bad."

The tea, a strong mix of black teas, was excellent, of course, a special ITCS blend from Rhiannon Galway's shop. It should have been refreshing but wasn't doing the trick for Rose, who was still upset about the confrontation with Zunia. She tried to soothe herself by people-watching, a favorite pastime of hers. For the most part the groups stayed within their own tight circles. Rose knew many of the members but it was a superficial acquaintance, revived only every two years. It seemed that many of the members she had known for years had drifted away, canceling their memberships just in the past twelve months.

"I know it's just Friday afternoon and that more will arrive tomorrow, but it seems to be a smaller gathering this year," she said, and sipped her tea. "We're missing at least ten or twelve ladies who used to arrive for the Friday introductory meeting every year. And one entire club is missing in action; where are the Catskill Collectors?"

"Remember I told you about the trouble Zunia had last summer?"

Rose nodded. Laverne had given her the whole scoop: Zunia Pettigrew, her sights firmly set on the chapter presidency, had taken over every meeting as if it were her due, even though she was a relative newcomer to the ITCS.

"I guess I forgot to also tell you that the CC group was especially critical of her, since their club founder was the outgoing chapter president. They threatened to quit en masse if she was elected and I guess they did just that."

Saddened by the fracture in a formerly peaceful and fun-loving group, Rose scanned the room. One bad apple really did spoil the whole barrel, sometimes, she supposed. SuLinn Miller, a newer member of the Silver Spouts, was sitting at a small table near the door into the lobby chatting with Rhiannon Galway. SuLinn, who had recently moved to Gracious Grove with her husband, architect Randy Miller, had started out shy with no local friends. She now seemed to be getting into the swing of living in a small town, as opposed to New York City, where she was from. Sophie and SuLinn had become fast friends over the last couple of months. Rhiannon was in that same age group, which was perhaps why SuLinn gravitated to her in a group of mostly older folks, middle-aged and beyond.

Rose was grateful that her granddaughter had friends her own age in Gracious Grove. No one knew as well as Rose how Sophie had been shattered by the closure of her beloved restaurant. It had been the dream of a lifetime, and she had put every bit of her bountiful energy into it, as well as all her saved cash and every waking moment of her time. When it went belly-up, the other investors refused to do a thing to save it. Sophie's own efforts to make the changes she felt In Fashion needed to survive the difficult New York City food climate weren't enough and it crushed her. She had limped back to Gracious Grove and Auntie Rose's Victorian Tea House with a wounded spirit, like a beautiful bird with a broken wing.

SuLinn and Rhiannon, as well as Cissy Peterson, who was an old friend from the summers Sophie spent in

Gracious Grove as a child and teen, and Dana Saunders, another friend from that time, had given Sophie back the camaraderie that she had lost while working too hard and long on a doomed dream. Rose glanced over at Laverne, who was surveying the group with dark, intelligent eyes. Friends were the glue that held a lifetime of memories together. Rose would never have survived the loss—many years ago now—of her husband, and that of her son in the Vietnam War, if not for Laverne.

Her thoughts drifted back to her granddaughter and Jason Murphy, a local boy and Sophie's first boyfriend when she was just sixteen and he eighteen. Rose never knew what went on between them when Sophie's mom, Rosalind, came to get her to take her to boarding school that August, but she and Jason broke up on bad terms and were just now, thirteen years later, making amends. Rose had a feeling her granddaughter still had a soft spot for Jason, now a professor of English at Cruickshank College, but Sophie didn't talk about it much. As far as Rose knew they were just friends.

"Excuse me, Rose Freemont?"

Rose looked up to see the woman from the Tea Belles, the first to be put down by Zunia. "Hello! We've met here before, have we not?"

"Yes, two years ago, my first year at the ITCS convention. I'm Jemima Littlefield."

She was a plump woman, in her seventies, Rose judged, with a lined, round face, a worried expression and a habit of wringing her hands. "Why don't you sit for a moment, Jemima; rest your bones!"

She sat down next to Rose and said, "I was so happy to hear you put that *awful* woman in her place!"

"I don't feel like I put her in her place," Rose said. She looked across the room, where Zunia, with her circle of fellow committee members, was holding court, gesticulating and shooting malevolent glances around the room. "I should have held my tongue. No good comes of talking in anger."

Laverne murmured, "Some women *need* to be told."

"I wouldn't have had the nerve to say what you did," Jemima admitted to Rose.

At that moment the other woman who had brought a teapot to the talk joined them. She and Jemima greeted each other as old friends, with air kisses and pats on the shoulder, and she hovered over them as serving staff brought around urns of hot water to heat up the individual pots of tea at each table. "That woman is a poisonous menace," she said, after introducing herself as Faye Alice Benson. "I know for a fact she is the sole reason the Catskill Collectors quit the ITCS. Zunia Pettigrew makes a bad enemy, though. I was not going to stir that particular pot, even though I *had* to say my teapot was clearly German porcelain. I don't know if she is missing her glasses or her medication," she finished, acidly.

"Certainly odd mistakes to make for someone claiming a PhD!" Rose said.

"PhD! Hah! Maybe a doctorate in faking it," Laverne said, with a snort of derision. "She was never actually clear about what discipline the PhD was for, or where it was from."

"Why don't you run to replace her next year, Faye Alice?" Jemima asked.

"And have to work with that letch Walter Sommer? I don't think so."

"I think we would be safe from him at our age, dear," Jemima said, suppressing a smile.

Laverne said, "Some men don't care about a woman's age. They just can't help but try to lure the female of the species!"

Rose chuckled. "Speaking of age, is Zunia Pettigrew really thirty-eight?"

"No, you had it right," Jemima said. "I know for a *fact* she is fifty-one, the same age as my eldest, Lesley. They were sorority sisters. When my Lesley heard the name Zunia, she knew *just* who I meant. How many folks have that name, after all? Said Zunia was always spiteful and not too bright. Constantly has plans and plots, but they never work out."

While the crowd babbled, Thelma worked her way laboriously around the room, sitting down in a chair every once in a while to rest her feet. She had been sitting with the other Silver Spouts but had tottered away, working herself up into a righteous snit. Rose was doing her usual thing, gathering a group of folks who all hung on her every word and doted all over her. How she did it, Thelma would never know. She wasn't *that* fascinating! But Harold Freemont, the best beau at the Gracious Grove Methodist Church picnic, sure thought so sixty-some-odd years ago and didn't give Thelma another look once he saw Rose Beaudry, as she was then.

However . . . *forgive and forget*, Thelma repeated to herself like one of those man trees the young folks were always babbling about. Man tiaras. Man-whatevers. She hobbled through the room and listened in on a conversation among the group that called themselves the Tea Totalers. Dumb name. Did they even know what a teetotaler was? Nothing whatever to do with tea. With a low groan for her poor old feet, she sank into a chair near the table.

"Well, I say bravo to Rose Freemont for standing up to Zunia," a thick-waisted middle-aged woman exclaimed. "If even *one* of us had the guts to do that last year, we wouldn't be stuck with her as division president now."

Thelma made eye contact with the speaker, and winked. "Zunia Pettigrew better watch out, you know," she said, with a knowing nod. "That Rose Freemont, she's a dangerous one. I've known her for over sixty years. Looks like a fluffy old lady, but tell *that* to the woman who died at her tearoom!" She clapped her mouth shut. She hadn't meant to lie, but it was out before she thought twice. In fact, she had promised Cissy she wouldn't lie anymore—the woman had died in *her* tearoom in May, not Rose's, after all—but old habits die hard. She was so used to trying to sink Rose's business it just slipped out, even though she had vowed to stop.

Six pairs of eyes widened; various painted-on or natural eyebrows rose. The speaker grabbed her sleeve and tugged her to sit closer, pushing out a chair so Thelma could shift over more easily. "*Do* tell! It sounds simply fascinating. I heard about a murder in a tearoom in Gracious Grove."

All six women watched her and awaited her next words. She should correct the impression she had given, but, drunk with the interest of so many at once, she couldn't help but go on. "Oh, I could tell you a thing or two about Rose Freemont," she said, dropping another wink, like she had a fluttering eye problem. "Still waters run deep, you know!"

Across the tearoom Rose and Laverne were soon alone at the table; Josh was off talking to one of the young bus staff, SuLinn was still chatting with Rhiannon Galway, and Horace and Malcolm had gone to their room next to the conference room, after which they were going to take a walk—their daily constitutional, as they called it. Laverne yawned. "I *am* tired!" she said. "You wouldn't think this would be more wearing than working all day at the tea house, but it is."

"I suppose you get used to the work, but this is something different." Rose glanced around, uneasy. "Laverne, I'm getting an odd feeling."

"Not your heart, is it? Angina? Indigestion?"

"No, nothing like that. I mean, look around. Folks are staring. And whispering. What's going on?"

Laverne scanned the gathering. "You're right. *Something* is going on, and I don't have a good feeling about it."

Uneasily they both glanced around the room, alone in a sea of chattering folks.

Some were just plain busy with other mundane things. Orlando Pettigrew was swallowing a couple of tablets while arguing with his daughter, Emma, who had her arms crossed over her chest and her lip jutted out almost as much as her hip. Zunia stormed over to them and began to argue, too, gesticulating and waving her arms around, but Orlando just took out a kerchief and blew his nose. Pastor Frank was now sitting alone with Penelope Daley; he cast anguished glances toward Zunia, while Penelope earnestly talked at him, plucking his shirtsleeve and patting his hand to get his attention.

But the other collector groups were clustered together in one knot, and in the center was Thelma Mae Earnshaw. Rose got a troubled feeling in the pit of her stomach.

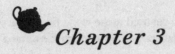

Chapter 3

"What do you think Thelma is up to?" Rose asked her friend.

They watched the gazes cast toward them. When the other convention goers saw Rose and Laverne watching, they bent their heads back toward Thelma.

"I can't imagine," Laverne said. "That's the scary part. I just *can't* imagine. With Thelma it's always something unexpected. That time she posted the notice in the *Gazette* that we were closed for renovations . . . Who would have expected that? Or the time she managed to imply that we had an E. coli scare."

"Thelma's problem has always been that she is impulsive. She was that way as a girl, and it never got better. But she's promised to behave," Rose said. Should she march over and find out? Rose wondered. That was ridiculous; she knew these people and Thelma didn't. Surely nothing her irascible old friend said would be taken seriously. She sighed wearily; at any rate, she'd handle it tomorrow.

Over the last two months it hadn't been easy bringing Thelma into the Silver Spouts, Rose reflected, and there wasn't consensus when she proposed it. Two of their friends, Helen and Annabelle, were sitting out this year's convention because Rose had invited Thelma to attend. Annabelle, in particular, found her upsetting; Thelma needled her constantly about her two late husbands, calling her the Black Widow and making insinuating remarks.

It had been too late to uninvite her at that point, and Rose regretted that her two old friends had stayed home. She didn't quite know how to handle the trouble with Thelma yet, but would soon have to figure out what to do. She wouldn't let her go on sowing dissension in the Silver Spouts, and she was afraid that might mean pitching her out of the group. "I think I need to go lie down," Rose said.

"Do you want me to go over there and find out what's going on?" Laverne asked, her striking face set in an expression of concern mingled with anger. Though they were as different in appearance as any two women could be—Laverne was tall, robust, dark-skinned and still dark-haired while Rose was short, round, pale and white-haired—they were similar in the ways that mattered. Both were hardworking, with a strong moral outlook, loved their families and were as close as the sisters neither of them had.

"No, Laverne, let it go," Rose said, putting her hand on her friend's arm. "Whatever it is, we can handle it tomorrow. Patience. Do you have the room key?"

"I do." Laverne handed it over, a thick brass key on a numbered key tag. No newfangled key cards for the historic Stone and Scone Inn! "You go ahead and take the elevator and I'll meet you up there. I'm taking the stairs." Laverne climbed the stairs whenever she could, and claimed it was that same dedication to physical exertion that kept her daddy still relatively hale and hearty well into his centenary decade.

Rose grabbed her handbag, picked up her teapot, and they left the tearoom. The staircase was to the right of the check-in desk. Laverne headed to the stairs while Rose started toward the elevator, which was on the *other* side of the desk. A door slammed and the inn's owner charged out from behind the check-in counter and crashed into Rose. Her teapot went flying and hit the floor, bouncing and rolling several feet.

"Oh my gosh, ma'am, I'm so sorry!" Bertie Handler, a short, fussy, fidgety man, raced after the errant teapot. He picked it up and rushed back to Rose. Laverne, who had paused to see if Rose needed help, started up the stairs as Bertie thrust the pot into Rose's arms. "But it's dented!" he mourned, touching the dimple with one finger.

"Don't you worry about that," Rose said, catching her breath. "It already had that dent in it." At least she hoped it was the same one. Despite Zunia's disparaging comments, she was still convinced the teapot was old and worth money; a new dent wouldn't help its value. Although she had never been one to collect teapots because they were worth a lot, but because she liked them. This one gave her a sense of serenity when she held it, like it had poured a million cups of tea—or holy water—and heard a million prayers.

She put one hand on the inn owner's arm and examined him with concern. She had known Bertie for a long time, but this year he seemed excessively nervous and looked like he was aging rapidly, his sparse hair changing from the sandy brown it had always been to gray. His pocked face was ashen, like he needed sunshine or iron pills. "You need to slow down, Bertie. Take it easier!"

He shuffled and shook his head. "No, ma'am, Mrs. Freemont, I can't slow down. This is my best weekend of the year, when the tea convention is in town, and I need to make sure everything's okay. *Some* people want to move the convention to Buffalo or Rochester! Or even Syracuse." He sniffed. "*Syracuse!* I can't afford to lose this. It would be that straw . . . you know, the one that broke the camel's back."

"Who's talking about moving the convention?" Rose asked, alarmed, as the elevator dinged. She ignored the opening doors, which closed again as it remained riderless. She was sorry to hear someone was agitating to move the convention. It would certainly not be as convenient for her group to come to the convention if it was moved from Butterhill.

"Who? Well, you know I've always been friends with—"

"Mr. Handler, I'm done for the day." A young woman in jeans and a tank top strode up to him and handed him a key. She shifted a shoulder bag over her body and lifted her long hair, twisting it into a bun and fastening it with a clip. "Brittany was supposed to come in today at three, but she hasn't shown up yet. *Again.* Do you still want me early tomorrow?"

"Melissa! Thank goodness," he cried, clasping the key in his palm. "I'm so glad I caught you before you left. I'll need you extra-early tomorrow, and if you could get that friend of yours who helped you clean rooms last summer— what was her name?—I'd appreciate it."

"She doesn't work anymore. She hurt her back and is on disability. If you want to replace Brittany, I'm on board. I could look around for you, if you like."

"Oh, I don't know . . ." He paused, and looked at Rose. "I'm sorry, Mrs. Freemont, I have to talk to Melissa about the schedule."

Just that moment a rumble of thunder echoed through the old inn, shaking the walls slightly. "Sounds like we're in for a summer storm," Rose commented, looking out the front glass doors. The day had gone from sunny to dark.

"I hope not," he said, his tone fervent. He listened for a moment as thunder rumbled long and low, like cannon fire, his gray eyes wide, his mouth twitching. Trembling, he took the girl's arm—the chambermaid having handed in her master room key for the night, Rose assumed—and tugged her back past the check-in counter and into the office as he babbled about Brittany, and getting someone new, and what he could do.

Rose, feeling even more weary after noting the inn owner's tension and jitteriness, headed to the elevator and stepped in as thunder rumbled through the old inn again. She rode up the single floor and stepped off to head to her room. She was getting older, no doubt about it, and the first sign was that she needed a nap before dinner.

S ophie Freemont Taylor sank into a chair and curled her toes inside her sensible waitress-type shoes. It had been years since she had served tables, and running both the kitchen and taking care of the customers without the aid of Nana and Laverne had been a challenge. Luckily Dana Saunders was helping her out at Auntie Rose's Victorian Tea House on a day off from working at their friend Cissy's store, Peterson Books 'n Stuff.

Dana locked up behind the last customer. "Whew!" she

said, leaning back, resting her head against the door and looking up at the ceiling. "*That* was a day! I'll have to go back to work at the bookstore just for a rest. How does your grandmother do it?"

"You would not believe those two," Sophie said, with a weary laugh. "She and Laverne are like a well-oiled machine, working in tandem. Couple of workhorses for a seventy- and eighty-year-old."

Dana, gorgeous as always in turquoise walking shorts and a crisp white blouse, with turquoise-and-silver earrings dangling from her ears, crossed the floor and sank into a chair next to Sophie. She put her white-sandaled feet up on another chair, a no-no in a restaurant, but Sophie didn't have the heart to correct her after her friend had been so helpful.

"Who all did we have, anyway?" Dana asked. "Among the groups, I mean."

On her fingers, Sophie counted them off. "Okay, so we had a lot of drop-ins and some smaller groups, like the Gracious Grove Businesswomen's Association, for late lunch. But not counting them we had, let's see . . . three bus tours, a Sweet Sixteen tea party and a Little Princess birthday party."

Dana groaned and shaded her eyes with one hand and flapped the other, languidly. "Don't remind me. Ten little girls on a sugar high with only two moms to wrangle them!"

Sophie chuckled. "The worst part was when they got the bright idea to storm the gift nook and a couple tried to eat the maple sugar candles!" She sighed. "I worried about Nana's teapot collection mostly," she said, eyeing the shelves that lined the walls and the sideboards and bureaus that held a collection of figural, silver, chintz and antique teapots, many valuable.

"The moms were good about keeping the kids from touching them, anyway," Dana said.

"I guess. After a day like this I wonder, did I do the right thing moving back here? Nana's come to rely on me, and how will I ever leave and go back to NYC?"

"You worry more than anybody I know. Stop! Give it some time. Just enjoy for a while. Everyone is so pleased with what you've done here . . . spiffing up the menu, trying fresh new ideas. And they're glad your grandmother and Laverne have help. It's really going well."

"Except when ten six-year-olds rampage and demand cupcakes. Only cupcakes! Nothing but freaking cupcakes." She sighed. Vanilla cupcakes were all well and good, but a chef did like a bit more of a challenge.

"Those rug rats sure were cute, though," Dana said, with a wistful tone. "I liked the littlest one, the brown-haired girl with the fairy wings and a tiara set in her curls."

"She was a doll. Do you want kids?" Sophie asked, curious about the woman she had barely known when they were in their teens. Dana had admitted being jealous of Sophie's privileged upbringing back then, and that explained why she had remained aloof, while Dana's best friend, Cissy Peterson, had gone out of her way to be friends with Sophie. The sad thing was, Sophie would have traded places with Dana in a heartbeat because Gracious Grove, with her grandmother, was more of a home to her than any of the places her mother and father lived, whether it was the New York condo, the Palm Beach condo or the Hamptons "cottage." Sophie had wanted to stay with her grandmother and go to high school in town with her friends, but was always dragged back to boarding school.

"Doesn't everyone want children?" Dana asked, turning to examine Sophie. "Haven't *you* ever thought about it?"

"I guess I've been too busy." Culinary school and a double degree in cooking and hospitality management had kept her on the go. Then several jobs at once, catering, cooking, managing, and finally her own restaurant, In Fashion, which had consumed her from then on. She had found investors easily because of her family ties, she supposed, but nonetheless, those fellows had turned tail and run last winter when the going got tough, and by March they were bankrupt and shut down. All the restaurant had needed was some tweaking, shifts in direction, something she was confident she could undertake, but no, they pulled their support and took the loss, preferring to use it as a tax benefit.

"Someday, maybe," she finally added, trying to imagine Jason Murphy and herself as the parents of a brood. It was weird to think of him in that light, since she was just getting reacquainted with her long-ago teenage boyfriend.

"Well, start thinking. We are none of us getting any younger!"

"I just turned thirty!" Sophie protested.

"And neither you nor your eggs will ever be in their twenties again."

Sophie chuckled and shook her head, then heaved herself to her feet. "You go on home, Dana; you have to work at the bookstore tomorrow. I'll clean up here."

"No way. I told you I'd help and I will. Where do we start?"

They both looked at the wreckage that was once a tidy and pretty tearoom and laughed. "Anywhere!" Sophie said.

The place was pristine by the time they were done. Dana was going home to have a frozen dinner, she claimed, and read a book. Sophie forced her to take some of her own homemade soup and a couple of cheese tea biscuits with her, then sent her on her way. Pearl, Nana's gorgeous Birman cat, followed Sophie around, chirping relentlessly as she locked doors.

"Now, Pearly-girlie, behave," she said, using her own pet name for the cat. "Nana and Laverne have only been gone for a few hours. You can't tell me you miss them already." Pearl chirped and Sophie headed up the narrow back stairs, followed by the cat, to Nana's spotless apartment on the second floor. "Aha, your food bowl is empty. You've eaten all your crunchies."

She played with Pearl, trailing around a blue feather toy as the cat bounded and attacked, over the furniture and across Nana's bed, until the beautiful chocolate point Birman finally just sat and stared at her, then turned her back and leaped in one elegant motion to the top of her cat tree.

"I guess we're done," Sophie said.

She ascended to her third-floor attic apartment and looked around, eyeing the shelves of teapots in the living area—her own collection, mostly art deco and art nouveau. One of the things she enjoyed about teapots was how the design of them really reflected the artistic themes of the time. She loved art deco teapots for the clean lines and beautiful shapes. They should be dusted after the past few hot, dry August weeks, but she was too tired. She needed something not related to work, nothing to do with teapots or tea.

What to do, with the house to herself? She was restless, the late-summer heat building and an electric feeling in the air, like a storm was going to break. They could use the rain, so she hoped it poured. She ate a salad left over from the day's luncheon crowd, read an e-book for a while, and was about to settle in for an evening-long marathon of true crime shows, her new obsession, when her cell phone buzzed. She eagerly picked it up and clicked on a text message.

"*Come to the window*," the message from Jason Murphy read.

She assumed he meant the one overlooking the street and raced over, threw open the sash and leaned out.

Jason lounged against a fire-engine-red sports car parked at the curb and waved, grinning. "Look what I borrowed from Julia!" he said, naming a colleague. "Want to come for a ride to the lake?"

"I'll be down in two minutes," she said, holding up two fingers and then ducking back, shutting the window. This was exactly what she felt like doing, she thought, as she raced around her tiny, slant-ceilinged apartment. She changed into cute plaid shorts, a tee and sandals, and on her way out the door grabbed her bag and a hoodie.

The ride was invigorating, the wind pulling at her dark ponytail, flipping it around. It ended in the parking area by the dock where they used to swim on the eastern shores of Lake Seneca. It was private property, but the owners were Jason's cousins, and he used the spot whenever he wanted.

By mutual consent they walked down to the end of the dock and sat, draping their feet into the water as the sun descended close to the hills on the opposite shore, the sultry heat unbroken even by a breeze. Swishing her bare feet through the refreshing water, Sophie wondered . . . did he remember a little over fourteen years ago when on an evening just like this they had kissed for the first time? This was the exact spot, this wooden dock, with the family's motorboat bobbing gently in its slip, buffeting against the rubber tires that protected the boat against damage from the dock. Crickets chirped this time, unlike last time when it was birdsong that fluted through the air. It was June, that long ago evening, the beginning of a golden summer she had never forgotten, when she was Jason's girl and thought they'd be together forever.

"How are preparations for the new school year going?" she asked.

"I haven't even thought about that much; suppose I have to get going on it," he replied. "Working on my doctorate has had me so busy this summer. I'm lucky that Cruickshank is really generous about teaching and pursing your doctorate at the same time, but it's exhausting." He glanced over at her. "I would have liked to spend more time with you this summer, Sophie, but work comes first, right?"

That was the mantra she had always chanted, but coming back to Gracious Grove had made her question the priorities of the last ten years of her life. "I suppose. It's so nice right now for me to just do my job at Auntie Rose's and then have time to catch up with old friends."

"Like Dana and Cissy," he said. His hand clutching the edge of the dock was so close she could feel it brushing against her bare leg.

"And you," she said, bumping her shoulder against his, and smiling up at him.

His brown eyes were warm and lit by the sinking golden sun, and those rays found highlights in his shoulder-length hair. He had always looked a little like a seventies hippie, with hair longer than the current fashion. On this warm evening, wearing khaki board shorts and a bleached-out tee, he still looked like the teenager he had been that long-ago summer, except that he was leaner and not as tanned.

Shadow of a Spout

The air was close and humid, the water refreshing and the company wonderful. She was content, an odd feeling for her because contentment had never been a part of her makeup. She had been driven by ambition, fighting every day against her mother's wishes for Sophie to attend a top-notch college and find a wealthy, socially acceptable husband. Getting her culinary degree had been barely tolerable to her social-climbing mom, but actually working in restaurants as a sous chef and then pushing to open her own restaurant at an unfathomably young age had horrified her mother, almost breaking the fragile bond between them. Her two older brothers had both gone the business-school route, and now were working in two of their father's businesses. Her mother would have preferred if Sophie had done that, because at least she would have had a chance to meet eligible men, but she had gone her own way.

She knew in her heart that her mom wanted what was best for her, or what she *deemed* best for her only daughter: a quality husband, a gracious home and babies. As hard as Rosalind Taylor worked at staying astonishingly young-looking at sixty, she still longed for grandchildren. Maybe Sophie would want kids eventually, she thought, remembering Dana's wistful comments, but . . . not yet. It was her older brothers' turn first, she always reminded her mom.

Still, how would her life have been different if she and Jason hadn't broken up so abruptly before her senior year? She stifled the melancholy when she thought of the missed opportunities. It just confused her, though she had long ago stopped worrying over her mom's part in that, the way she had talked Sophie into breaking it off and then dragged her away to head back to boarding school early. She had now convinced her mom to stop interfering in her life, and so she'd forgive and forget the past.

She straightened and turned her thoughts away from those memories. "So I haven't had time to ask, seeing you so little this summer, but what *is* your doctoral thesis?"

"You sure you want to hear it?"

"I do," she said.

He took a deep breath. "Okay, here goes: when I was a TA I did a course on poetry from the sixteenth through eighteenth centuries. It made me think of the way literature was so a part of everyday life in the past. The Tudors, the Stuarts, the Georgians, the Victorians: politics was talked about in their poetry, and allegory was used to explore the important movements of the day. So because that was a period of intense global exploration, the imagery in the poetry reflected that."

She had followed him so far, but as she listened on and he connected world exploration to the social and political movements of those centuries, and how that came together in literature, her mind wandered. He had changed over the years, and she felt a little intimidated. She was straightforward; she loved food and cooking. The ultimate expression of that was to be a chef in her own or someone else's restaurant. But Jason spent his time thinking and writing and musing and pondering. His journey in life so far had been internal. He had left her behind academically, and perhaps he had left her behind emotionally, too.

She missed the rest of his explanation of his doctoral thesis subject as she fretted about the miles between them intellectually, and after she had asked him about it, too! Gloomily, she wondered if she would even have understood it. She shivered.

"Are you cold?" he asked. He picked up her folded hoodie.

"Not really. I guess I'm just a little tired." She wished she could find a way to talk about her concerns, to explain how she felt. She worried that with Jason having become a professor, being surrounded by the kind of people he was every day—like Julia Dandridge, his beautiful, intelligent department head—Sophie would not be able to share the things with him that he needed from a woman he would consider dating. Nothing came to her, or at least nothing that didn't sound like she was fishing for compliments or asking him if he wanted to get more serious.

Thunder rumbled in the distance, the warning of a summer storm to come. She looked up at him, his stubbled chin, his lips so close. Though they had hung out on occasion in the last couple of months, it was always with others. She wanted to kiss him. Or she wanted him to kiss her.

"Jason," she murmured softly. "Do you—"

Just then a crack of thunder crashed above them. She jumped, and then rain began spitting down, dotting the lake with little rings. A gust of wind came up, sending waves scudding across the dark surface.

"Shoot, the top is down on the car," Jason said. "Julia will kill me if I let the leather get wet!" He leaped up, took her hand and hauled her to her feet as he shoved his wet feet into tan deck shoes. "Last one back to the car gets soaked!" he yelled and took off, sprinting ahead of her.

"Darn," she muttered, eyeing the sky. "Couldn't you have held off for just a few more minutes?" She grabbed her sandals and trudged barefoot back along the dock to relatively dry land and up the hill to the lane where the car was parked. Jason was already in the car, raising the top, but it was a soggy drive home.

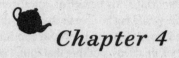

Chapter 4

Rose and Laverne had dinner in the dining room, all the Silver Spouts at a single small table, since SuLinn had gone with Josh to the coffee shop for a light meal and Thelma was nowhere in sight. Laverne, Rose, Horace and Malcolm chatted, but all were tired and had called it a day.

It was later now, about nine. Laverne was going through her habitual night routine of taking a shower, then slathering moisturizer over every joint. *No ashy elbows for Miss Hodge*, Rose thought, with a smile. She'd put cold cream on her face, leave it for exactly three minutes, then gently wipe it off. That was the virtue of getting older, Rose supposed; if you were smart you knew, by then, what was best for you and established a routine. Her own routine (other than the hygienic necessities) consisted of gentle stretching, finishing by reaching down to touch her toes. Like Laverne's father, who climbed the stairs, she reasoned that if she touched her toes every day, she'd never stop being able to do it. Maybe that was unrealistic, but so far, so good.

She had already checked her daily list of things to do—she had made it a habit to check every night to be sure she didn't forget anything important—and had tried to finish the list off, but found that impossible. If she had only caught Rhiannon Galway at the convention tea she could have asked if the tea purveyor could bring her a case of her special blend, Auntie Rose's Tea-riffic Tea Blend, for the gift nook back in Gracious Grove. She had mentioned it before the convention and had just tried calling the girl, but there was no answer on her home line and Rose didn't have her cell number. She left a message on the machine but she'd definitely have to follow up the next day. She jotted a note to herself on a fresh page to do just that.

Rose was tempted—*so* tempted—to call her granddaughter and see how the day had gone at the tearoom, but resisted the urge. Sophie was a bright girl and had shown good sense by calling in Dana Saunders to help, given the heavy schedule the tearoom had as folks tried to get in some last-minute fun before school started in a couple of weeks and everyone got back down to business. Laverne had been set on staying in Gracious Grove to work with them, but Sophie appeared insulted at the notion that she couldn't handle it on her own. She was still a little prickly. Rose felt it was up to her to help rebuild her precious grandchild's fragile self-esteem, so when Sophie insisted that Laverne and Rose go together for the very first time to the ITCS convention, Rose agreed, and maybe she was right. At their age it was time Rose and Laverne got to enjoy a few outings together. Laverne was her best friend in the world, after all.

She just hoped they actually *did* enjoy the convention, starting the next day. She grunted a little as she bent down to touch her toes one more time.

"Careful, there, roomie," Laverne said. "Don't you bust anything."

"I've done this every single evening for fifty years. I think I'll be okay."

Someone hammered on the door and Laverne yelled, "Come on in!"

Thelma shoved open the door, clumped in and slumped into a chair. She looked around the spacious room, nineteenth-century elegance expressed in high ceilings, tall windows, and furnishings that were a compromise between Victorian style and modern utility. For the Stone and Scone Inn, that meant there were wing chairs and dressing tables, as well as a flat-screen TV and decent mattresses.

"Figures you'd get a better room than me and *that girl*," she said, referring to SuLinn Miller, her roommate for financial purposes only.

Poor SuLinn, Rose thought. "This is thirty dollars a night more than yours, which is the only reason I have it and you don't. I offered it to you, but you said no."

Laverne suppressed a snicker as she continued her moisturizing routine; face, neck, elbows, knees and hands.

"Some people don't mind throwing money around like they've got a million bucks stashed in their mattress," Thelma retorted. After a pause she went on with her grumbling. "*That girl* is in the bathroom again! Doesn't she know that an old lady needs access to the toilet at all times? Can't she do some of that fussing somewhere else?"

"Fussing? You mean like she could shower in the hallway?

Bathe in the elevator?" Laverne eyed Thelma, eyebrows raised.

Thelma sniffed. "*You* try rooming with a thirty-year-old and see how you like it, Laverne Hodge."

"Your other choice would have been Josh Sinclair," Rose said, and exchanged a glance with Laverne while they both tried not to laugh.

Thelma gave her a squinty, purse-mouthed look.

"Since you decided to invade our room I feel free to ask," Rose said, "what in heaven's name were you talking about so intently with all the other teapot collector groups this afternoon at the tea?"

The woman shuffled her feet together and examined her nails, frowning in intense concentration. "Nothing much," she said. "Just, uh . . . you know, collecting teapots and such."

Laverne stared at her through narrowed eyes. "It's funny that when I went down to the desk to get some postcards to send to my nieces and nephews, Jemima Littlefield came up to me and asked if I was nervous, rooming with Rose."

"You didn't tell me that!" Rose exclaimed.

"Didn't want to worry you, but since Sally Sunshine is here I've thought better of it."

Thelma shrugged, the movement shuddering over her from her tightly permed silvery curls to the tips of her sad-looking shoes. As usual, she wore a flowered muumuu, this one a pattern of poppies in an eye-catching red, white and black. Her ankles were swollen, and the sides of her orthopedic shoes were broken down, Thelma being too cheap to buy shoes more than once every three years or so. "She just thought you were a little forceful with that Pettigrew woman, you know, when she told you your pot was fake."

"Really? Jemima seemed to be cheering me on when she spoke to me personally, before she joined your little clique." Rose sat down on the end of her bed and watched her old nemesis carefully. A rumble of thunder added an ominous sound track to her comments.

"You know how folks are. Strange, all of them." Thelma licked her lips and tried on a smile. "Anyhoo, isn't that Bertie Handler an odd duck? Kind of a weirdo, I say."

"He's perfectly nice," Rose said, a little cross that Thelma was clearly avoiding something. But what? She dreaded to think on it, but she had a feeling she'd find out the next morning when she went down to join the others for coffee.

"Maybe so, but I think he's having a fling with that teapot president's wife."

"Nora Sommer?" Rose exclaimed. "Proof, Thelma? You can't go around slinging accusations like that without proof."

"She was alone with him in his office! Saw it with my own eyes just now."

"That's not *proof*," Laverne said. "Doesn't mean a thing. She helps her husband organize the convention every year, and so she has to talk to Bertie about seating arrangements, the daily tea, that kind of thing."

Thelma harrumphed and stood, shifting on her feet, an expression of pain on her lined face. "None so blind as they who will not see," she intoned, with a priggish sniff. "And now I'm tired. Going to see if *that girl* is out of the bath yet so I can do my business in privacy."

Thunder rumbled, rattling the windows. Rose and Laverne exchanged a look after Thelma hobbled out of their room.

"She was being shifty," Laverne said.

"That's no change. I've known that woman for sixty-five years, since we were girls, and she's always been shifty."

"I know, but still, it worries me. I don't know what she's done, but I sure hope it doesn't come back to haunt us."

"Especially me," Rose said. "I thought we were tolerably made up, but now I'm not so sure."

Laverne yawned and capped her moisturizer bottle. "I am plumb wore out!" she exclaimed, climbing into bed. "And there is no lovelier bed than one that I didn't make, and for which I won't be responsible tomorrow!"

"Amen," Rose said.

"Don't say 'amen.' I won't be at church on Sunday, and I don't like missing!"

"Well, I'm sure the Lord will let you off a week, and I'm glad you're here," Rose said.

"Now, that is very sweet."

"Otherwise I'd be rooming with Thelma," Rose added, with a chuckle.

"You are just too *bad*! G'night, Rose."

"Good night, Laverne."

Rose had been asleep, that she was sure of. But a commotion out in the hallway made her sit up with a start, for a moment forgetting where she was. Laverne's moan of irritation reminded her.

"Who is that making a racket?" her roommate mumbled.

"I don't know, but I'm going to tell them to pipe down!" Rose clambered out of bed, pushed her feet into mule slippers and shuffled to the door, beyond which she could hear voices raised in anger. She paused, but then decided she just *had* to know what was going on, a trait her Sophie called the snoop gene, which she had inherited.

Laverne followed, hovering over her as she turned on the overhead light and threw open the door. Down the hallway near the elevator there was an altercation. Two shadowy figures were clutched together, swaying back and forth.

"Get off me, you idiot!" one man grunted.

"You've got no right," the other howled. "You don't deserve her!"

"Orlando? Frank?" Rose had recognized the men in the dimly lit hallway. "What's going on?"

There was more grunting, and the sound of a scuffle, but the hallway was dim and they were a ways from the commotion. Just then the elevator doors opened and Bertie Handler hustled toward the two. He shrieked, "Frank Barlow, what the heck do you think you're doing?"

Others poked their heads out of doorways. Josh staggered sleepily out of his room and toward the fray, rubbing his eyes.

"Josh, you go back; don't get involved!" Rose said, worried the young fellow would get mixed up in the fracas. How would she explain to his mother that he went to a teapot-collecting convention and got beaten up?

Walter's stentorian voice came from the crack in his doorway. "What is going on? Stop this, this instant, before you awaken Nora!"

Bertie had hold of the pastor and dragged him toward the elevator, as he said, "Go back to bed, everyone. Nothing to see here. Sorry about this, Orlando." He grunted and struggled some. "Frank, you come with me or I'll call the cops."

A couple of doors shut, but Thelma had hers open and

leaned out, watching with glee. "More excitement than I've seen for ages," she said.

The pastor was sobbing. Rose could see that his lip was bloody as they passed under a light sconce. Bertie dragged him along the hall to the elevator and punched the down button.

Orlando Pettigrew, hand over one eye, called after them, "What in God's name is wrong with you, Frank?"

The pastor pulled away from the innkeeper and straightened. Glaring back at Pettigrew, he said, "You don't deserve love, you pathetic piece of sh—"

"Enough!" Bertie said, and stabbed the down button again.

Penelope Daley, one of the Niagara Teapot Collectors Group, popped out into the hall, housecoat on over a filmy nightgown. "Poor Frank. I must go to him!" she cried, clutching the neck of her housecoat with one hand and flapping the other.

"Miss Daley, please go back to your room!" Bertie said, struggling with the pastor.

"You're out of your mind, Frank!" Orlando shouted after him as the elevator doors opened and the two men got on. The doors closed. Orlando glared around at the watchers. "What do *you* all want? That guy's crazy. Drunken fool." He slammed his door.

Thelma chuckled and went back into the room, where SuLinn could be heard drowsily asking what was going on. Penelope Daley dithered for a moment but then retreated into her room, as did Rose and Laverne. A low, distant rumble of thunder shuddered through the old inn. Laverne turned out the light and the two climbed into their beds.

"Where was Zunia during that little dustup?" Rose asked.

"I can't imagine. Standing behind her husband, working Orlando's mouth, I'd imagine," Laverne groused.

Rose chuckled. Laverne's imagery was apt, since Zunia did seem to speak for her husband more often than not. Orlando wasn't always like that. She had known him with his first wife, Dahlia, and he had seemed much more decisive. "Did Frank seem drunk to you, Laverne?" Rose asked, glancing over at the digital clock on the nightstand. Just about midnight.

"I know for a fact that Frank Barlow does not touch a drop of alcohol."

"That's what I thought. What got into him, I wonder?"

"I don't know. Maybe we'll find out in the morning."

Chapter 5

It was much later. The room was pitch-dark, and then it was filled with a sudden flash of brilliant light, every piece of furniture in the place throwing shadows. Rose sat up with a cry, as did Laverne, as more lightning flashed. An alarm went off in the hall, then swiftly after, a woman screamed.

"What the heck is going on now?" Rose staggered from bed and pulled on her cotton housecoat.

"I have no idea," Laverne grumbled. "What time is it anyway?"

"About three. One of those nights, I guess. Wonder what that alarm is? We'd better get up in case there's a fire." Rose once again slipped her feet into her mule slippers and started toward the door, as Laverne switched on a bedside lamp, pulled a flowered cotton housedress over her head and followed. As Rose jerked open the door she could hear voices. It seemed like everyone else had the same idea, to investigate what was going on. She followed the chatter, as someone cried, "Call nine-one-one!"

"What's going on? Is there a fire?" Rose asked of Josh Sinclair as he, she and Laverne followed the crowd. SuLinn followed, too, as did Thelma, crabbing about the worst night's sleep she'd never had.

"Don't know, but I'm going to find out." Josh, dressed in a T-shirt and boxers, pushed through the people in front of him.

Moments later, as Rose and Laverne reached the pack of people near the elevator, they heard Josh yelp and say, "I know CPR; let me help."

"What in tarnation is going on?" Laverne demanded.

Rose, who was slightly in front of her, peeked through the gap left by taller folks and could see. Her heart thudded and she clutched at her chest, the pang fearfully like angina. "It's Zunia," she said, her voice weak with horror. "There's blood. I think she's dead!"

Laverne made a pathway for them to the front and tugged Rose after her as the alarm mercifully stopped. Penelope Daley, gowned in a frilly pink nightie, stood, eyes wide, huffing and puffing and staring down at the floor. Zunia Pettigrew lay by the elevator with her legs crumpled beneath her. She was indeed bloody, streaks over her face and matting her dark hair, eyes wide and staring straight up at the ceiling, a puzzled expression forever etched on her face. She was dressed as they had seen her the day before, in a skirt suit. Lying on the carpeted floor beside her crushed, bloodied head was Rose's antique teapot, one side completely dinged in, and a dark patch stained the carpet.

Penelope Daley finally found her voice and cried, the words echoing in the hallway, "That's your teapot!" as she pointed at Rose.

The crowd parted and some of the teapot collectors pulled back, staring at Rose in consternation. Whispering started. "Rose Freemont . . . She had an argument with Zunia . . . I heard she's dangerous!"

Thunder rolled and crashed, the hotel convention room lighting up even through drawn curtains. Police had responded swiftly to the 911 call, and two deputies had first hustled them all to a sitting area at the far end of the hall, one staying with them to be sure no one talked about what they had seen. But soon after their arrival the Butterhill police detectives had herded them down the stairs, which was a slow process with the number of seniors in the group. In the convention meeting room the police had established an organized hub: a U shape of tables and a few chairs, extension cords snaking across the floor for laptops and a printer and a separate interview area that consisted of a long table with two chairs on one side, and four on the other. Everyone with a room on the second floor—and that meant all of the teapot collectors who were staying at the inn, except for Horace and Malcolm—was sitting with the others facing the police hub.

Josh stood alone, watching everything. He didn't appear alarmed, just interested. SuLinn was yawning and checking her watch. She had her phone with her, but the police had told her to refrain from using it. Rose and Laverne sat on hard wooden chairs along one wall holding hands, still in their nightgowns and housecoats, getting chilly from the air-conditioning that now seemed to be working perfectly, unlike the afternoon before. Any time they tried to talk an eagle-eyed deputy—she was young, but her pale blue eyes looked steely and humorless to Rose—moved closer and asked them to please not discuss what they had witnessed.

But the girl couldn't stop Rose from thinking. As Penelope had pointed out, it was Rose's teapot beside Zunia's lifeless body, and it had, if she was not mistaken, a smear of blood on it. How was that possible? When did she last see the teapot? She knew she'd have to explain all that to the police, so she frowned down at her hand joined with her best friend's and thought it over. Laverne squeezed her hand every once in a while and they exchanged looks. Rose knew she was thinking, too.

The teapot—before she went down to dinner she had stuffed it in one of her bags, the blue tapestry one with the soft sides. It was a reminder of an unpleasant encounter that she still wasn't sure she had handled correctly. On the one hand, in her life she had learned not to be a pushover. But on the other, she knew that bold-faced contradiction often served the opposite side in a confrontation. It had made her look angry and insulting, which was far from her real personality.

And now Zunia was dead, presumably killed with Rose's teapot. How did the antique get out of her bag and become the murder weapon used against Zunia Pettigrew? Try as she might she could think of no possibilities. It was in her bag, then it was by Zunia's bludgeoned head.

She felt some tension radiating from Laverne, but she couldn't ask her why. Suddenly she felt a surge of excitement from her friend, who squeezed her hand harder. A young man in a tan summer-weight suit strode into the room. He was tall and handsome, dark-skinned with a high bridged nose and close-cropped natural hair. In other words he was a younger, taller male version of Laverne.

He briefly surveyed the room but his gaze stopped and settled on them. He looked conflicted, but then came over and crouched down in front of them. "Auntie Laverne, how did you get involved in this?"

Auntie Laverne? Rose turned to her friend in astonishment.

"First things first, nephew. Rose, this is Detective Elihu Hodge, of the Butterhill Police Department."

"Eli, Auntie Lala," he corrected, with a dazzling smile, pronouncing "auntie" to rhyme with "on tea." He met Rose's gaze and asked, "How do you do, ma'am?"

"I'm all right, considering the circumstances," Rose replied.

He nodded, acknowledging the situation, then turned back to Laverne. "I was going to take you and Granddad to lunch today, but that doesn't seem likely now. He just called me and told me what happened. How are you mixed up in it?"

She was about to answer, but he shook his head and put up one finger. "No, that's all right. Save it for the detective. This isn't my investigation and I won't interfere with a colleague's work. But I *will* get them to let you and your friend go upstairs. I'll make sure my buddy O'Hoolihan takes your statements right away and lets you get some rest." He stood, stretching out his long body to its full height.

Rose looked up at him. "I don't think our statement will be over that quickly," she said.

"Why is that?" His tone was indulgent, as young people's tones often are toward the elderly or differently abled.

They didn't mean to be patronizing, Rose knew, it was just that youth and health invigorate the young with a sense of invulnerability; those approaching the end of life, or those mired in disability, must be pitied. It was a credit to their empathy, but the fact remained, they had it backward. In her experience poor health and age sometimes—though not always—enlightened the mind, rather than inhibiting it, though that tidbit would be pooh-poohed most severely by those invincible young.

So she didn't fault him for his condescension and calmly said, gazing up into his unusual gray-blue eyes, "Unfortunately the teapot that bashed in Zunia Pettigrew's head was mine, and it's the same one we argued over earlier in the day."

Thelma sat alone and fretted, darting glances over at Rose and Laverne, who were talking to a tall dark fellow, one of the police, from the looks of it. That little girl police officer, the one who kept shooting suspicious gazes at Thelma, had turned her back and let him be, so he *had* to be police. He walked away and chatted with one of the other plainclothes cops, the older redheaded fellow who wore the rumpled suit and grumpy expression.

Others who were staying at the inn, ITCS members from the Niagara, Monroe and Genesee Valley groups, clustered together and watched the Gracious Grove Silver Spouts as if they were going to make a break for it, or stand up and confess all. Bunch of gossips! Every one of them had been *more* than happy to hang on Thelma's every word at the tea the previous afternoon, even though she had just been hoaxing about Rose's sordid reputation. Couldn't anyone tell a joke from the truth anymore?

Rose sure wouldn't if she found out. She and her best friend would find some way of blaming this all on Thelma. That Laverne was too sharp-eyed and sharp-tongued, and they had noticed the buzz in the tearoom the previous afternoon. It had made her squirmy when they questioned her, but she was darn sure she was not going to confess what she'd done. Looked like maybe she should have, 'cause now they'd find out in the worst possible way.

But how was Thelma to know the danged woman would go and get herself knocked off, and with the same stinking teapot she and Rose had argued over? She sniffled and pawed in her housecoat pocket for a tissue, into which she honked. The sound echoed in the convention room. Faces turned toward her. She glared at a couple of the women, and they hastily turned away.

The detectives were now interviewing folks, starting with the Genesee Valley Tea Totalers, who were briefly questioned and escorted away. They headed out of the room, not meeting anyone else's gaze. The tall young man who had been chatting with Laverne and Rose was still talking, but the detective was shaking his head vigorously and waving his hand toward the crowd.

They appeared to part on bad terms and then the others were called up, one by one, starting with Penelope Daley, the plain-faced gal who had been mooning over the sweaty pastor at the meeting the previous afternoon. She was talking shrilly, practically hysterical; Thelma could hear every word she said. She had heard the alarm and dashed out of her room, holding on to her purse, and found Zunia dead. She was the first one there and had screamed loud.

The detective regarded her calmly and then started her going back over her story, from the beginning. If he was going to do that with everyone, this could take forever.

Just then there was a commotion at the door and a deputy came rushing in after a middle-aged woman who raced into the convention room and looked around wildly. When she saw that boy, the young fellow who belonged to the Silver Spouts, she cried out and rushed to him where he stood watching everything with an avid stare. "Joshy! My poor boy!" She grasped him to her, pushing his head against her shoulder. She glared at the police detective seated nearby and said, "I hope not one of you has questioned him without me present!"

He pulled away, rolling his eyes. "Mom, I'm sixteen, not ten. They can ask me anything they want, and I can answer."

R ose had been watching Laverne's nephew as he appeared to have a disagreement with the other male detective. He then strode back to them and crouched beside their chairs.

"I'm sorry, Auntie, Mrs. Freemont, but given what you told me and what I passed on to O'Hoolihan, he wants to interview the others first and then you both."

"That's okay, Eli. You did the best you could," Rose said. "I expected this would take a while. Are they going to let us have a drink? I need to take my pills. Oh! I don't have them with me," she finished, patting her housecoat pocket.

"Are they important, ma'am?"

"One is; I need to take my heart pill in the morning. My pill container is in my purse."

His handsome face firmed and he stood. "I'll do my best to get your medicine for you, ma'am."

As he strode away, Rose said, "He's a nice boy. Now, which one of your brothers is his father?"

"My oldest brother, Abraham. Elihu is his youngest from his second marriage."

"I lose track of your big family," Rose said, wistfully. They didn't mention Rose's son who died in Vietnam, nor her other son, Jack, who had taken off for California years before and hadn't been heard of in ages. She had spent years trying to track him down, but to no avail. "I envy it, actually."

Also unspoken between them was Laverne's disappointment in love. She had been engaged once, but the man married another and left Gracious Grove. That was decades ago now, their separate heartbreaks.

"I love all my nieces and nephews. *And* my goddaughter," she said, speaking of Sophie and putting her arm around her friend's shoulders.

"She's the light of my life," Rose said. "Oh, I adore her brothers, too, but those boys . . . I know they love me, but Sophie *loves* me!"

Laverne nodded, noting the distinction. She was silent for a moment, as the low buzz of voices hummed through the convention room. But then a frown etched lines on her handsome face. She whispered, "What do you make of this, Rose? Zunia was not well liked, as far as I can tell, but *murder*! That's beyond just being unpleasant to folks."

Rose nodded, examining the others in the convention room, who were mostly pretending to ignore Rose and

Laverne while covertly watching them. All except for Thelma, who sat in grumpy solitude staring down at the floor. The female deputy gave Rose a fishy-eyed stare, so she remained silent until the young woman turned away to talk to one of the guests, then murmured, "Do you think it had anything to do with Orlando and Frank's set-to last night? I don't suppose so. Zunia didn't even poke her head out during that fracas."

"That's odd, don't you think?" Laverne folded her hands in her floral housedress–covered lap. "It sounded like it was *about* her, after all."

"That's so, isn't it?" Rose said. "And she's not the kind to be silent."

The deputy turned back to them, so they hushed once more. One by one the tea convention folks were being interviewed and dismissed, as well as the few hotel staff. Bertie Handler sat with one of the detectives right then, and he seemed extremely upset, as well he might be with such a nasty event happening in his hotel. He was red-faced and waved his hands around, the occasional word drifting back to them. Judging from those words he spoke about the argument the night before, the storm, the alarm, the basement and his office. The detectives then interviewed Pastor Frank, who had a bit of a shiner and a split lip. Orlando was nowhere to be seen. Perhaps they were holding him separately, or questioning him somewhere else.

As the convention folks left the room every single one of them averted his or her gaze from Rose and Laverne. Rose shivered again, and this time it was not just the air-conditioning. An ominous sense of dread was building up in her; she kept visualizing Zunia's dead eyes staring straight up at the ceiling, blood streaked across her forehead.

She frowned. There was something not right there, some-thing that tugged at her, but what? Ah . . . the blood should not have been streaked across her forehead unless she had been knocked down by the blow, and landed on her side, with the wound upward. Then the blood would have dripped down across her forehead in that way. She shuddered. But the perfectly logical explanation was that Penelope Daley had turned her over when she found the poor woman.

Thelma was called up just as Eli came back in and strode over to the detective who was free, a young women in a suit and open white shirt. He gestured toward Rose and Laverne, but she shook her head and said something more, waving toward the other male detective.

Eli came back and sat down next to Rose, his gray-blue eyes narrowed, flashing as if lit by an inner light. "Detective Messier said they are almost to you, and then you'll be able to get your pills. They wouldn't let me get your purse because they aren't done with your room quite yet, but I *could* get your medication for you, if it's important. I'll threaten them if I have to."

They had given permission for the police to search their room, of course, in light of the teapot having come from there. It seemed to be taking a while, but then there was a lot for them to do.

Rose eyed the young man. "If it's only going to be another half hour or so, I'll be okay. What aren't you telling us, Eli?" she asked.

He looked over his shoulder. "I shouldn't say this, but one of your group has caused some concern with things she said yesterday."

Laverne and Rose met each other's gaze and said, together, "Thelma!"

Eli regarded them levelly, his expression impassive. "You know who I mean?" he asked.

"Thelma Mae Earnshaw. Who else?" Laverne said, and explained who she was in relation to Rose. "You tell your colleagues not to pay any attention to that woman. They're interviewing her right this minute," she said, jabbing one finger in their direction. "She is the devil's handmaiden when it comes to causing trouble for Rose, of whom she has been jealous her whole natural-born life."

"What exactly did she say?" Rose asked, eyes narrowed.

His lips twitched as he eyed Rose. "She apparently considers you a dangerous sort, and referenced someone who had died in your tearoom in Gracious Grove. Are you a dangerous sort, ma'am?"

"I just may be when it comes to Thelma Mae Earnshaw!" Rose fumed, knowing they would be able to straighten out that particular misunderstanding in a moment with one call to the Gracious Grove police department. But still, why did the woman have to complicate everything? "She had better watch herself. And no, of course I am not serious, but this foolishness has *got* to stop!"

The young female deputy came over to them and spoke to Laverne. "Ma'am? Detective Messier would like to speak to you now."

Laverne stood, towering over the young deputy, and straightened her back with a wince. "Eli, I would appreciate it very much if you would check on your grandfather," she said, turning to her nephew. "I normally would have made sure he took his medication and had breakfast—he eats real early—but since we've been tied up here and haven't been able to leave," she said, with a fierce glance at the uniformed officer, "I fear he will have forgotten his morning pills." She then marched over to the female detective's desk.

Eli chuckled and saluted. "Yes, ma'am," he said, under his breath. He turned to Rose. "Detective Dan O'Hoolihan will be interviewing you, Mrs. Freemont. Given Mrs. Earnshaw's statement and that your teapot was found by the body, he'll be taking you over events in Gracious Grove very carefully as well as your movements here, but please don't be alarmed. Apparently all the other old bid . . . uh, the other teapot collectors have mentioned your name when asked about anything suspicious, so we have to clear it up."

"Am I a suspect?" she asked, her voice quavering. She cleared her throat. This was just silly.

"I can't comment on that. I'm sorry, ma'am, but I just can't." He looked down at her with compassion and touched her arm. "Just be honest and we'll clear this up as quickly as possible."

"Of course I'll be honest," she said tartly. "Perhaps you will remind them to be sure Thelma is, as well!"

Chapter 6

Once she was sitting opposite him, Detective O'Hoolihan asked a lot of questions: her name, her address, how long she'd lived there and about her business in Gracious Grove. He asked why she was in Butterhill at the hotel. She told him about the convention and rambled on, giving a lot of details. He was calm and thorough . . . *very* thorough, jotting down notes and asking more and more questions. Rose began to feel every year of her age, and as the questions kept coming, she got a little confused. "May I have a drink of water?" she asked, her voice croaky and dry. "And I really will need my pills soon."

"We're almost done," the detective said, examining his copious notes.

"Not really," she tartly rejoined. "We haven't even gotten to Zunia Pettigrew yet, and the incident at the convention talk yesterday. So far we've mostly talked about Gracious Grove and Thelma Mae Earnshaw." She noticed Laverne was done with the young female detective and was about to sit down to wait for her. She waved her out and mouthed, *See you soon.* Laverne would be worrying about her father, and so she should. Malcolm was in good shape for a ninety-something-year-old, but that still required some time and trouble to keep him that way. Laverne was devoted to his care and should go to him, though she would bet that Eli would have made sure he was all right. He seemed like a very nice boy; she wondered if he was single, and if he was, who she could fix him up with.

"Mrs. Freemont!" Detective O'Hoolihan said, passing one hand over his eyes.

Rose had a feeling it was not the first time he had said her name. She needed to buckle down and listen; maybe the shock of seeing poor Zunia Pettigrew's body was fogging her brain, because none of it felt real. "I'm sorry, what did you say?"

He motioned to the young deputy and asked for a glass of water for Mrs. Freemont. Once Rose had quenched her thirst, he said, "Ma'am, I do want to move this along, but a woman has been killed, and I need to understand everything about it. If we continue, I can then let you go get your pills and breakfast. Take me through this confrontation between you and the victim. We have it from several sources, but none of them seem to match."

"I'll bet," she said. "Thelma Mae Earnshaw made the rounds yesterday afternoon and poisoned every mind there against me. I don't know what is wrong with that woman."

He referred to a note on the table in front of him. "Actually, ma'am, just now she told Detective Messier that she misspoke about the incident in Gracious Grove. It was just a little joke, she claims, and it got out of hand."

"*What* was a joke?"

"Her telling everyone that a woman died in your tearoom."

Rose calmed herself as she prepared to answer the young man across the table from her. "Thelma is an old friend, but she does have the worst sense of humor and even poorer timing." She explained about the woman who died in Thelma's tearoom. He nodded, and she had a feeling she was going over ground that he had already researched.

From there they went over the previous day, through the speeches at the convention, and up to her taking the teapot back up to her room.

"What did you do with it?" O'Hoolihan asked, watching her eyes.

"I put it in a blue tapestry bag that I was using to carry some books and other things." Rose paused and examined his blue eyes, shadowed by dark circles and with bags under them. He was relatively young to her but on the shady side of forty, she'd guess. This was a man who didn't sleep well, she thought. "To be completely honest," she said, impulsively, "I shoved it in the bag because I didn't want to see the darned thing again. I felt bad about my argument with Zunia Pettigrew. It wasn't my finest moment, and the teapot reminded me that I'd been impatient. She just got on my last nerve after I saw how she treated the others."

"The others?"

"Jemima Littlefield and Faye Alice Benson; she treated them very shabbily, and in front of the whole group. It was shameful. I'm sorry Zunia's gone, but you have to wonder how she treats folks in private if she's willing to humiliate them in public."

She could see his interest in the events of the previous

day and wished she'd kept her mouth shut. Of course nothing would do but to reiterate exactly what Zunia had said to each woman. She felt like a stool pigeon, but it never for a second occurred to her that he would suspect either of them for such a heinous crime. She said just that when she was done, but he didn't answer.

"Now, back to your teapot. What time would this have been, that you put it in the blue bag?" He jotted a note without even looking down at the paper.

"About five o'clock. The tea was about over, though there were still folks lingering to talk." She told him about leaving the dining room and running into the inn owner, Bertie Handler. "Then we went up to our room, Laverne and I. I stuffed the teapot away, then lay down—so did Laverne—and had a little nap. We both woke up, I'm not sure what time. Then we got changed and went down to the convention dinner."

"Who all was at it?" he asked, referring to a list in front of him.

Rose named everyone she remembered.

"You didn't mention Thelma Mae Earnshaw."

"No, she didn't come to the dinner. Not sure why. I think she either went out or had dinner in the coffee shop in the front of the hotel." She paused, frowning down at her hands resting in her lap, then plucked at a loose thread on her housecoat, wrapping it around the stem of a pearl button. "I wonder if she was even then regretting what she'd said to them all about me and didn't want to face folks? She's an odd duck."

"You also didn't mention . . . let's see . . . Emma Pettigrew, Nora Sommer and . . . Mr. Frank Barlow."

"I didn't see any one of them. I know for sure Orlando

Pettigrew was there, and so was Zunia. They were fighting, I think, about something."

His gaze sharpened. "She was having an argument with her husband? What were they saying?"

"Now, that was just an impression," Rose said, alarmed. What had she just said? She sure didn't want to get anyone in trouble, and yet she kept doing it! She was so tired, like she could sleep for a hundred years, and when she was tired she tended to ramble. But Eli had told her to be honest, so she was. "I didn't overhear a thing, Detective, so I don't know that for *sure*!"

"However, it was your impression that they were arguing?"

Rose thought back. She could picture them at a small table for two by the wall, and there was an intensity as they leaned across the table toward each other, but it was not the intensity of love. They were at war with each other. "That was my impression, yes," she confirmed.

"What happened then?"

"Nothing. I mean, they left the dining room before I did, and I didn't see them . . . or, rather, Zunia . . . again that evening. Laverne and I went upstairs, did our nightly rituals and chatted, and Thelma came in briefly to talk."

"Excuse me, ma'am, but did you notice the teapot in the bag at that point?"

She paused and pondered. Was the bag there? Yes. But was it still full, as it had been when she'd shoved the teapot into it? "I didn't have a reason to go into the bag," she said, with regret. "I can't remember if the bag looked like the teapot was still in there or not."

"Did you notice anything in your room disturbed?"

She shook her head. "No, not a thing."

"What happened then?"

She shrugged. "Nothing. We turned in."

He checked his notes. "Until everyone on the second floor was awoken by an argument."

"Loud voices. I didn't know it was an argument until I opened my door and saw Orlando Pettigrew and Pastor Frank struggling."

"Did you hear what they said?"

Rose told him everything she had overheard, and he had her name off every person she had seen, and those she hadn't. "Then I went back to bed. Next thing I knew that alarm was going off and I heard a woman scream. I guess that was Penelope Daley."

"When you went into the hall, did you notice who all was there?"

"Let's see . . . Josh Sinclair came to his door rubbing his eyes. A lot of the other teapot collectors came out of their rooms and followed the noise. I saw Jemima Littlefield. Thelma. Uh . . . SuLinn Miller, too; of course, she's one of our Silver Spouts." She named the others she saw.

"What about . . ." O'Hoolihan checked his notes. "What about Orlando Pettigrew?"

"I didn't see him."

"Emma Pettigrew?"

"I don't think she was there. Josh would have been more likely to notice her."

"The Sommers?"

"No." She looked down at her hands, rubbing an age spot on the back of one as she thought. "Now, that's odd. Their room was right there, close to the elevator on the other side from us."

"How do you know that?"

"I saw him when he looked out during the argument; he said then that Nora was sleeping and that they'd wake her up." She frowned. "But when there was all that commotion with Zunia being found . . . you'd think the fire alarm would have woken them up, if nothing else."

He went over his notes briefly, then looked up. "Okay, Mrs. Freemont. You're free to go up to your room, but please don't leave Butterhill for now."

Rose hesitated. Should she ask? "Detective, I suppose you've told the others the same? Not to leave Butterhill?"

"For the moment."

"Do you know if they intend to go on with the convention?"

He shrugged. "I have no idea, ma'am. We'll be done with this room in a few hours, and I suppose there's nothing barring it, other than the death of Ms. Pettigrew, who was the chapter president, as I understand it from Mr. Sommer. You'll have to ask him."

"Of course." She stood, but wavered for a moment.

Eli Hodge was approaching just then and he took her elbow to steady her. "Let me help you upstairs, ma'am. Auntie Laverne asked me to come get you. Your room has been cleared."

She looked up at the handsome young man. "Thank you, Eli. I appreciate your help. I'm just hungry and I think I need some coffee and my pills."

Laverne's nephew exchanged a charged look with Detective O'Hoolihan. "No problem, Mrs. Freemont. I'll escort you to your room. Let me just talk to my colleague here for a moment."

Rose moved away, but could hear them talking.

"Did you really have to keep her for so long before letting her have something? She's eighty, for God's sake."

O'Hoolihan stiffly muttered, "Eli, you've got no reason to be here. This is *my* case."

"I'm not stepping on your toes, Dan, really, but my aunt and granddad are here and I'm looking out for them. I'll stay out of the investigation, I promise."

"See that you do."

Eli didn't say another word, but his lips were pressed into a thin line. Rose, watching him as he approached, thought that there was much he would have liked to say. He took Rose's elbow and guided her from the room and toward the elevator. She caught a brief glimpse of Bertie Handler at the check-in desk; he had his head down on his arms. He had been so on edge, worried about the loss of the yearly convention and how that would affect his revenue stream. He didn't know then that murder would be a bigger threat. She was sympathetic toward him. Having run the tearoom for so many years she knew how much any service establishment relied on the customers you could count on and word of mouth, neither of which would be helped by all of this.

"Are we allowed to use the elevator?" she said, as they waited for the car. "Given that . . . well, that the body was there on the second floor?"

"We have the spot cordoned off, and they've dusted the elevator for prints," he said tersely.

They rode up in silence, Rose apprehensive about the sight she would see. But when the elevator doors opened seconds later she had to sidle around the area cordoned off and screened. Crime scene tape held up with lobby stanchions surrounded a plastic opaque screen, behind which Zunia's body still lay. Rose shivered, her memory returning to what she had witnessed. It made her think of her teapot, and she staggered slightly.

"Are you okay, Mrs. Freemont?" Eli asked, as he guided her down the hall.

"Yes, I'm fine," she said, pausing outside their room door to catch her breath. She was exhausted and needed more sleep, but she needed her heart meds and something to eat first. She grabbed his hand and looked up at him in the dim corridor light. "Eli, please tell me what happened. Do you know yet? Do you have a suspect? It scares me so much that she was killed right there, at the elevator not twenty feet from my room. And with *my* teapot! How is that possible?"

"I'm sorry, ma'am, but I can't say anything at this point," he said, his voice gentle as he looked down at her. "Please try not to worry about it. Murderers are resourceful. If it hadn't been your teapot the killer used, it would have been something else."

"But . . . *why* my teapot?" she said. "Was it because of the argument I had with her about it? And how did the killer get it?" That indicated forethought, a premeditated murder, then, not a sudden impulse crime.

"Try to get some rest, Mrs. Freemont. I'll have someone bring up some breakfast for you. Tell my aunt I'll talk to her in a while." He turned and strode away, then bolted through the door to the staircase, eschewing the elevator.

Saturday had been a calmer day at Auntie Rose's Victorian Tea House, one Sophie handled by herself except for the waitressing of one of Laverne's great-nieces, a sweet fourteen-year-old named Cindy, who the patrons seemed to adore given the amount of tips she collected. The girl was bright and asked a lot of questions about the cooking industry along the way. Gilda Bachman, next door at La Belle Époque, had handled the day mostly alone as well, with just a couple of hours of waitressing help from Cissy, Thelma's granddaughter and Sophie's friend. They hadn't been as busy as Auntie Rose's, but had still had a steady stream of customers.

Cindy headed home on her bicycle. Sophie closed up and cleaned, happy the week was done. Sunday was the one day a week they were closed. She looked forward to sleeping in, and then having time to fuss around in the kitchen with some new ideas she had for tearoom lunches. Autumn was just around the corner, so she was toying with some squash and pumpkin soup recipes. She had hoped Jason would call her to go out, but he hadn't so far. Maybe she'd call him tomorrow and invite him to come over and sample whatever she whipped up.

She was done setting the tearoom itself to rights, and started scrubbing the kitchen down, wiping out the oven, then using a bleach solution on the counters, making sure everything was as clean as her grandmother liked it. She was just restoring order to the fridge when she glanced out the kitchen window and spotted Gilda bolting across the lane.

The woman banged on the door. "Sophie, Sophie!" she cried.

"What is it, Gilda?" Sophie asked, throwing open the door. Since everything seemed to panic the woman, Sophie wasn't overly concerned. After the awful incident in the spring—the death of one of Gracious Grove's leading citizens in La Belle

Époque's tearoom—Thelma had eased up on some of her poor treatment of her sole employee. Gilda now lived at La Belle Époque in her own suite of rooms upstairs, which was easier on Thelma than trying to rent them out. The dirty-tricks campaign against Nana had stopped, a pleasing turn of events, as Thelma Mae Earnshaw and Rose Freemont made a kind of uneasy peace after a long-standing quarrel (on Thelma's part) over the theft of Harold Freemont at the Methodist Church picnic back in the middle of the last century.

But Gilda was worse than usual, out of breath, her frizzy hair wild around her head.

"Gilda, calm down, what's wrong?" Sophie asked, pushing the woman into a chair so she could catch her breath.

She looked up at Sophie and clutched at her hand. "There's been a murder at the hotel where Thelma and Mrs. Freemont are staying!"

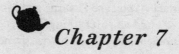

Chapter 7

"**W**hy didn't you call me?" Sophie cried into the phone to her grandmother, minutes later.

"Sweetheart, I was going to after the tearoom closed, but I didn't want to worry you in the middle of the day when you couldn't do anything."

Sophie calmed down; she sat on one of her grandmother's chairs petting Pearl as Gilda paced back and forth, fretting and pulling at her frizzy hair. "Is the convention going to go on? Why don't you and Laverne just come home?"

Her grandmother filled her in on Zunia Pettigrew's death and what she had learned that day between naps, news brought to her by Laverne, who ventured out to have lunch with her father and speak with the others, and Thelma, who was wide-eyed with wonder, loudly concerned about them all being "murdered in their beds." The Sommers felt that they did need to stay and go on with the convention because it was "what Zunia would want"—nonsense, Nana said, given the self-centered nature of the victim—and there still had to be a decision made in regards to the New York State division presidency.

"That doesn't mean you have to stay there, Nana. I'd feel a lot more comfortable if you and Laverne just came home."

"I can't. I haven't told you everything."

There was a moment's hesitation on her grandmother's end of the line and Sophie was breathless; what more could there possibly be?

"Sophie, it was *my* teapot, the one I took to show the group. It was *my* teapot that was used to bash her head in!"

Sophie was stunned and wordless for a long moment, then filled with questions that required a lot more explanation. "How did the murderer get it? Was it in your room? Why the teapot?"

"I don't know anything. I'm so afraid they think I did it, after the fight I had with Zunia in front of everyone."

"That's ridiculous," Sophie exclaimed. "No one could ever think *you* capable of murder."

"That's what Laverne says, but you haven't seen how all these folks looked at me as we were all being questioned. Or rather how they *weren't* looking at me! Some actually averted their gaze as they passed me on the way out of the convention room."

Sophie gave Pearl a last pat, and set her aside on the sofa. "I'll be there in an hour."

Her grandmother sighed. "Yes, please, sweetie; I would appreciate it."

She spent twenty minutes throwing some things in a bag, at the same time writing instructions for Gilda, who would look after Pearl. She adored the cat, so it would be a treat for her, in truth, to have a reason to pet and pamper Pearl. The best thing about moving into La Belle Époque for Gilda was that she had been able to adopt Sweet Pea, the chocolate-point Siamese left ownerless by the death of the woman who had been murdered in that tearoom in May. Sweet Pea treated Gilda as if she were his personal servant, and that seemed to suit them both just fine.

Poor Gilda was well intentioned but scattered. Sophie had had staff members like her in her own days in the restaurant industry; written instructions along with frequent contact and reassurance was the only way to be sure an employee like that would not panic and get flustered, so Sophie made the instructions very detailed indeed, even down to making sure Pearl had fresh water in her dish at all times. Leave nothing to chance, she figured. Maybe that was why she had been called a details-obsessed micromanager in the past. And a tight-ass.

She then called the head of the local chamber of commerce and asked if they would mind very much shifting their Monday meeting to La Belle Époque. She would be sure Gilda had treats and goodies enjoyed by chamber members in the past; she always kept some in the freezer for emergencies. It wasn't as good as freshly made, but it was better than nothing. She hated doing it, but she wasn't sure she'd be able to come back to Gracious Grove by Monday to open. The chamber of commerce director got back to her immediately and agreed.

In rapid succession Sophie made a sign for the window saying they'd be closed until Wednesday, when they would reopen for regular hours. She then posted a message on social media saying the same, all while Gilda followed her around gabbling at her, offering messages to give to Thelma, things to ask Thelma, a request to have Thelma call her back.

Sophie texted Dana, asking if she could check in on Gilda the next day, and Dana called her to say she would. She'd haul Thelma's granddaughter Cissy Peterson along, too, Dana said, if she could drag her away from Wally, her new boyfriend, who happened to be a police officer in Gracious Grove. Cissy or Dana could help Gilda with the tearoom on Monday, too, though Thelma might well be able to come back to town, even if Sophie's grandmother couldn't. She was on the road and almost to Butterhill, about fifty miles away, in little more than the hour she had quoted to her grandmother.

Butterhill was a medium-size town in Wayne County, somewhat north of Gracious Grove, closer to Lake Erie. The way there was through farm country and apple orchards, past silvery rivers and through wooded glades. It would have been a lovely drive if Sophie weren't fretting the whole way about her grandmother's predicament.

How could anyone think her Nana could commit murder? That astounded her. But she was quite ready to tear a strip off anyone who disrespected either her grandmother or her godmother, Laverne Hodge. She slowed as she entered Butterhill. The town was pretty enough, though it didn't have a patch on Gracious Grove, but she was too busy following her cell phone's map to the Stone and Scone Inn to pay much attention.

The inn was bigger than she had expected, a cobblestone building, two full stories and taking up the whole town block it was on, with a sign out front proclaiming its build date of 1837. She turned into a lane and followed it behind the building to the half-full parking lot, noting several police cruisers parked in a cluster along the tree-lined edge. She grabbed her duffel and handbag from the back of the SUV and locked it, then crossed the cracked and pothole-riddled pavement.

A blonde girl with two long braids lounged outside the service entrance, smoking a cigarette by an empty green-painted Dumpster, the lid propped open against the brick wall. Ribbons of crime scene tape fluttered from the handle of the service door and from a light overhead. That gave her a queasy feeling in her stomach; it appeared probable that they had taken away the Dumpster and that this was a new one. She didn't want to imagine why they had taken the Dumpster away.

"Hi," Sophie said, pausing. "Is the only entrance to the inn on the street out front?"

"Unless you want to come through the kitchen," she said, a stream of smoke erupting from her mouth. She dropped the cigarette, put it out with her tennis shoe and then deposited the squashed butt in a coffee can by the rust-brown service door.

"Actually I'd *rather* come through the kitchen," Sophie said, with a smile. "I'm a cook; that's my comfort zone."

"You going to be working here?" the girl asked holding the door open for Sophie.

"No, I'm visiting. My name is Sophie Taylor."

"Too bad," she said. "They could use a better cook than the one we have now. The last good one quit two weeks ago in a huff. You sure you want to come this way?"

"I'm always interested in kitchens."

She led Sophie down some dim stairs to the basement, then through a windowless, well-lit kitchen where a cook worked alone at a prep station by deep stainless steel sinks. He was gangly and tall, with a hairnet on his head and a beard net over his chin. He nodded to them, his gaze following Sophie with curiosity. There were two other cooks working at the gas grill and a steam table, both moving too slowly to be truly efficient. It didn't give Sophie a good feeling about their ability, but at least the place was clean.

"Do you work in the kitchen?" she asked the young woman she was following.

"Nope. I'm Melissa, the housekeeper. Chambermaid. Whatever you want to call it, I'm it! We're supposed to have someone come in for the inn itself in the evening—you know, vacuuming the dining room, dusting, the hallways, garbage, reception area—and I'm responsible for guest comfort."

"That's a lot of work."

"You're telling me. Even more right now. Brittany, the evening girl, often doesn't come in, never shows up on time and isn't great even when she's here. My hours are supposed to be eight to five, but a lot of days I actually work longer, like now, until seven or so, just to give guests a chance to get out of their rooms so I can clean 'em. Brittany didn't even come in the last two evenings, so I've been on my own this weekend of all weekends! We're *never* at full capacity except for this teapot convention thingie they're having. I haven't had a break in days."

They were following a narrow corridor that branched off into different locked rooms—storerooms, she supposed, as well as one area that was a walk-in freezer. There were dusty security cameras mounted near the ceiling in odd spots along the corridor and near the back door. Sophie took in a deep breath, the smells of a basement restaurant kitchen oddly familiar, and yet . . . there was a staleness to the air, a faint sourness.

"What's that door there?" Sophie asked, as they passed a windowed steel door on their way toward an open staircase.

"That's the stairs up to the dining room," she said, as a

waitress carrying a plate laden with a half-eaten steak pushed through it and passed them, going into the kitchen. Shouting voices erupted, as she told the cook the patron had sent the steak back and he yelled his displeasure.

"There's a coffee shop, too, at the front of the inn right on the street," Melissa continued, raising her voice to carry over the din coming from the kitchen. "But they only serve soup, hamburgers, sandwiches . . . that kind of stuff. They have a flattop and an oven and make their own stuff. Some folks will eat at the coffee shop because they say it's better than the S and S dining room."

"S and S . . . oh, Stone and Scone!" They passed another door. "What's that room?"

"We call it Bertie's panic room," she said, with a snicker.

"What does that mean?"

"Just a private joke," she said hastily.

They ascended some steps and emerged through a door into a short hallway with a door to the left and a divider to the right. Sophie blinked and looked around. "Where are we?"

"That's the door to the owner's suite," she said, pointing to a door right on the hallway. She then grabbed Sophie's sleeve and tugged her beyond the divider into an open area. "There's the check-in counter," she said, pointing to a wood-paneled chest-high divider, beyond which Sophie could see an office, with a plaque reading PRIVATE on the open door.

Just then the front door of the inn opened and Rhiannon Galway, of Galway Fine Teas, wandered in toward them.

"Rhiannon!" Sophie called, to get her friend's attention. She turned to the chambermaid. "Thank you so much for helping me find my way, Melissa. My grandmother's staying here, so I came in a hurry when I heard what had happened last night."

Her eyes widened. "I know . . . a *murder*! Nothing like that has happened in Butterhill, except for the occasional domestic situation, you know. Is your grandmother one of those teapot collectors? What a nutty bunch! A lot of them are staying here in the inn except for the Monroe group; they live close by, I guess, and just drive into town for the convention."

Sophie's grandmother had told her that, and that some others stayed with local members while in town, so not all convention attendees were staying at the Stone and Scone. Rhiannon saw her and waved as she headed for the check-in desk, where a balding man stood, head in his hands, staring down at a ledger.

Sophie waved back, but turned to Melissa. "Were you here when it happened?"

"Are you kidding? That was the middle of the night; I was long gone. But," she said, moving closer and looking both ways, "I hear that some awful woman named Zunia Pettigrew was killed. She badmouthed one of the old ladies, so the woman bashed her over the head with a silver teapot."

"That's not true at all!" Sophie said. No wonder her grandmother was concerned, if that's what people were saying. "Do you honestly think a little old lady is going to bash someone over the head? It's ridiculous."

"All rightie!" the girl said, giving her an uncertain look.

Maybe she had been a tad vehement, but it just riled Sophie to think of anyone suspecting her grandmother.

"I gotta go," Melissa said. She dashed behind the check-in desk, grabbed a patchwork slouch bag and hefted it over her shoulder. "I'm done for the day. I'd be gone already but the cops had the rooms tied up for most of the morning so I couldn't get to them until this afternoon. I've already done as much of the other stuff as I'm doing. See you tomorrow," she said, waving.

"Wait a sec," Sophie said, racing after her. "So did you clean the dead woman's room, too?"

"No way," Melissa said. "The cops still have that one sealed. They let the woman's husband retrieve some of his stuff, but then he had to move into a room with his daughter." She cocked her head to one side. "Why do you want to know?"

"No reason; idle curiosity. Bye, Melissa. Have a nice evening." She turned and walked over to Rhiannon, who was talking to someone in the little alcove on the other side of the divider near the front glass door, where there was a seating area with a few chairs and potted palms. "Hey, Rhi, how are you? You look tired."

The other woman shrugged. Rhiannon Galway was in her midtwenties, with dark auburn hair curling down her back, big green eyes and a pale face covered in freckles, not the kind just sprinkled over the nose but all over her cheeks and down her neck. "I'm fine. It's been a rough couple of weeks."

They hugged, and Sophie asked, "Why? What's up?"

Her gaze slid away from Sophie as she shrugged again. "Oh, you know, just . . . preparing for the convention, that's all, as well as a few personal things. I had to make goodie bags and fight with Zunia about what to put in them. Working with *her* was a nightmare."

"At least you weren't staying in the inn last night when all the commotion happened," Sophie said. "I'm here to help Nana through it. It's awful, isn't it?"

"I can't believe it! I was just saying that to Frank," she

said, indicating the man she had been speaking to. "Pastor Frank Barlow, this is Sophie Taylor."

He stood and gave a curt kind of bow, not taking her hand. He was a gentleman in his fifties, probably, with a swoop of graying hair over a balding forehead and a potbelly that stretched his plaid short-sleeved shirt. He wore wire-framed glasses. His pale blue eyes watered behind the smudged lenses, as if he had been crying. He had his finger in a book that proved, on closer examination, to be the Bible. "Terrible . . . simply terrible. Poor Zunia. I know she was a little strong-minded, but she was a wonderful woman. *Whoso findeth a wife findeth a good thing*."

Rhiannon stared at him, eyebrows raised. The scripture quote seemed oddly out of context.

"Are you here for the teapot-collecting convention, then, Pastor?" Sophie asked.

"Frank is a member of the same group that Zunia was in," Rhiannon said.

"I'm *so* sorry for your loss," Sophie said sincerely. She saw the genuine sadness on his face, and on an impulse said, "I'm going to be joining my grandmother and godmother for dinner here and I'd love to hear more about Zunia. Would you and Rhi join us?"

He blinked. "Your grandmother?"

"Mrs. Rose Freemont, of the Gracious Grove Silver Spouts."

He blanched and shook his head. "Oh, no, I don't think—"

"Frank Barlow, you don't honestly for one moment believe that crap about her doing Zunia in, do you?" Rhiannon scoffed. "Rose is five foot nothing and eighty years old."

Sophie didn't say that her grandmother still hauled

thirty-pound garbage cans out to the street if Sophie forgot, or that she worked from dawn until evening with more vigor than many thirty-year-olds.

"If you say so, my dear Rhiannon. All right, I will."

The reverend had a curiously old-fashioned air about him for a man just in his fifties. She supposed there were worse attributes than being old fashioned. Sophie nodded. "Where is the dining room? Do I need to make a reservation?"

"It's to the right when you're facing the check-in desk, just before the door into the coffee shop, but don't worry. They're only serving dinner for another two hours. I'll talk to the hostess and take care of it," Rhiannon said, giving her a brief hug. "I was here to . . . to see about their tea supply, so I had to speak with her anyway. Go on up to your grandmother."

Sophie headed to the desk first, though. She introduced herself, and the fellow told her he was Bertie Handler, owner and manager of the Stone and Scone Inn. Bertie . . . as in Bertie's panic room? She examined the middle-aged man, his ashen face marred by scars from long-ago acne and graying stubble lining his soft jowl. What had Melissa meant by a panic room? She was familiar with the phrase, but the housekeeper had said it was a joke. "I was hoping you had an extra room I could book?"

He shook his head, shuffled papers together on the counter then disarranged them again. "I don't have a thing. I'm sorry, but with the police here, and one room off-limits and no end in sight and . . ." Tears welled in his eyes. "I don't have that many rooms to begin with and they're all taken." One tear welled over his lower lid and trailed down his cheek.

She had dealt with these kinds of emotional fellows before. Male cooks were, in her experience, more mercurial than their female counterparts. There was only one way to handle them, matter-of-fact and cool with a dash of bracing good sense. "Well, I'm staying overnight, so I'll need a trundle bed in my grandmother's room until we get this mess all sorted out."

"Sorted out?"

"Until we all find out who did this awful thing. It wasn't my grandmother, obviously, but someone tried to make it look like she did it, and I want to know why."

He looked doubtful and shook his head. "I don't know what to do. Those police won't let anyone leave," he said, sending a dirty look at a uniformed police officer who strolled through the lobby. "I've got guests coming in tomorrow night. Not a lot, but a few. I just—"

"Mr. Handler, the faster this is resolved, the faster your inn will be out of the limelight for all the wrong reasons."

"That's true."

"Sure it is! This will all be over with and you can go on with your business," she said in her most bracing tone. "So please don't forget: I need a trundle bed for my grandmother's room, and I'll pay the extra occupancy fee. We're going to have dinner in the dining room. It's nice to meet you, Mr. Handler," Sophie said, thrusting her hand over the check-in desk. "My grandmother thinks a lot of you," she made up on the spot. She had no idea how her grandmother felt about Bertie Handler, but it never hurt to build people up.

He shook her hand, brightening considerably. "I'll get a cot for your grandmother's room right away—room nineteen. And I hope you enjoy your dinner. Do try the chicken. It's very good!"

She looked around, decided not to wait for the elevator, which in older inns was invariably slow and clunky, and took the stairs instead on the other side of the little hallway out of which Melissa had guided her. At the top of the stairs she emerged into the corridor, letting the door swing shut behind her.

At the elevator was a cordoned-off area screened from view by dividers and crime scene tape. It made her queasy to think about the life lost just past that divider. Someone was there working; she could hear a small vacuum. She surmised that the body had been taken away. There was one room that was sealed with police tape. *That must be the Pettigrews' room*, she thought.

The hall wasn't really very well lit, but she found room nineteen and rapped on her grandmother's door.

Laverne called, "Come on in!"

She pushed the door open and breezed in. "Let you two troublemakers out of my sight for one day and look what happens!" she joked.

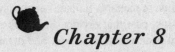

Chapter 8

"**M**y Sophie, I'm so happy you're here!" her grandmother cried, as Sophie crossed the floor for a hug.

Her grandmother and godmother, both dressed in their leisure outfits, similar velour tracksuits, were sitting at a little table by one of the tall narrow windows overlooking the street below. Sophie hugged Laverne, too, and sat cross-legged on the end of the bed, telling them who she had talked to, what had been said and her plan to have dinner with the Silver Spouts, Rhi Galway and Pastor Barlow. It was damage control, something she was good at from her past experience in the restaurant industry.

She let them in on the arrangements she had made in Gracious Grove for the two establishments, theirs and Thelma's, and how she had left Gilda in charge. Then she got the whole story out of her grandmother and godmother. It had rattled them both but they seemed to have taken it in stride and bounced back.

"We've spent most of the day cooped up in here," her grandmother said, after the tale was told. "First, we both slept because we were woken up in the middle of the night. I didn't think I could, after seeing . . . you know . . . but I did. Then we visited with Malcolm and Horace in their room for a while, but those two old foxes went out walking in the village and I didn't feel like doing that."

"I sure hope my daddy didn't cause any commotion. He's been known to fake heart trouble when he sees a pretty woman," Laverne said, shaking her head.

"Horace will keep him on the straight and narrow," Nana said.

"Has anyone had dinner yet?" Sophie asked.

"With the day so jumbled, we all ate a late lunch," Laverne said. "So no, we hadn't decided what to do about dinner yet. Your plan sounds fine."

"I'll get changed and let's go down!" Sophie said brightly. "I'll leave you two in charge of rallying the troops."

"All of them?" Nana said, exchanging a look with her friend. "Even Thelma?"

"*Especially* Thelma," Sophie said, with feeling. After the trouble she'd caused, they needed to keep a tight rein on the woman.

It was a while after seven by the time they rounded everyone up and entered the dining room. Rhi Galway stood and waved to Sophie, indicating the long table she had snagged. Altogether there were ten of them. The waitress, Joyce, was a pleasantly plump middle-aged woman. She brought them drinks, then rattled off the dinner specials.

Laverne was sitting next to Sophie and pointed out other ITCS members in the dining room, especially ITCS president Walter Sommer and his wife, Nora, sitting awkwardly at a round table for four with the grieving widower, Orlando Pettigrew, and his sulking daughter Emma. Josh, seated on the other side of Sophie, waved to Emma, who nodded, then went back to her phone, texting under the table.

"What's up with them?" Sophie asked Josh. "She's the dead woman's stepdaughter, right?"

"They didn't get along, Emma and her stepmom."

"You've talked to her?"

He shrugged. "Yeah, there weren't any conference things happening today, so we hung out while her dad talked to the police."

"I thought your mom came when she heard about what was going on?"

"She wanted me to come home but I said I wanted to stay here, since they're going to go on with the convention tomorrow. The talk I really want to hear on the history and development of the teapot was scheduled for tomorrow morning anyway. Mom had to go right back to GiGi to work, but she's coming back here tonight unless I can talk her out of it. I have to call her in half an hour."

"Why is Emma Pettigrew here at a teapot collectors conference?" Sophie glanced over at the girl, who was still texting, ignoring the adults at the table. "You're a collector, but I can't imagine she is."

"Her dad made her come. He likes to present a united front, she says." He frowned and looked over at her, blinking.

"What's she like?"

"She's okay, I guess; she hates her life. The breakup

between her parents happened really fast, and it's all still pretty new to her. She lives with her mom, but stays with her dad and stepmom every other weekend and at Christmas. She can't wait until she's eighteen and doesn't have to visit him anymore, but that's a couple of years away."

"You said it's recent. How long has this been going on?"

"Her dad married Mrs. Pettigrew just a year ago, I guess. Or less. Or more. She wasn't really clear."

"And she didn't like her stepmom."

"She says that Mrs. Pettigrew was a nightmare. I believe her, 'cause I saw that woman in action. I mean, it's not just like the wicked-stepmom trope from fairy tales, she really was mean."

Trope? Where did a kid like Josh get a vocabulary like that? But, of course . . . he was taking college courses already, some in English literature. At every Silver Spouts meeting he brought a literary reference to tea drinking, tea making or teapots to read out loud to the group.

"You should have been at the meeting yesterday!" he continued, his long-lashed eyes wide with amazement. He adjusted the collar of his golf shirt so it would stand up, as he glanced over at Emma. "I feel bad for her," he said, referring clearly to Emma. "Mrs. Pettigrew was mean to everyone, even your grandmother, and *no one* could not like your grandmother! She's way cool, for an . . . for a senior citizen."

Sophie flashed him a look, knowing he'd been on the verge of saying an old lady. But he was always respectful, so she couldn't fault him for what he *didn't* say. The boy was peculiarly grown-up and yet still a teenager, both sides coming out in odd ways at odd moments. He might collect teapots, but he also played PS4 and Xbox One. "Nana says that she heard Mr. Pettigrew and his wife fought all the time. Has Emma said anything like that?"

"Sure. She says her stepmom knocked her dad around once in a while—like, she was real physical. And Emma told one of the guys that works here that she cussed her stepmom out so bad once, she called the police on her. I mean, the stepmom called the police on Emma."

"Emma Pettigrew has a room on your floor, right? Was she in her room? Do you remember seeing her when her stepmom's body was found? Or . . . at least when you all came out of your rooms?"

He shook his head. "I didn't see her, but I'm pretty sure she wasn't in the inn. I saw her coming in later when we were downstairs talking to the cops, and I think she was wearing the same clothes that she had on the night before."

"That's odd, isn't it? Why would she be out in the middle of the night?"

He shrugged. "I don't know."

"What time was that?"

"Not sure . . . maybe four or five A.M.?"

"Can you find out where she was? Without things getting weird, I mean."

He looked thoughtful. Josh was a very bright fellow, beyond even book smarts, but he was pretty good with people, too. Collecting teapots was a passion because he believed in the historical importance of everyday objects. Sophie and he had talked a lot over the last couple of months and he already knew his path; he was going to be a writer, or a historian, or, mingling the two, a historical writer.

Nodding as he glanced over at Emma, he said, "I can talk to her. She trusts me, I think, and I know some of the staff she's been talking to, like the waiters and prep cooks. I can join in and hang out with them after dinner tonight." He looked a little put-upon, as he added, "As long as my mom doesn't end up coming back to stay." He glanced down at his cell phone. "It's almost time to call her. If I don't call on the dot she'll be on her way here."

"I'll talk to her if you want, okay? Tell her I'm here; maybe it'll help. And let me know what you find out about Emma Pettigrew." Sophie glanced over from behind her menu, examining the foursome. Orlando Pettigrew was not a small man and Zunia was apparently tiny. That didn't necessarily mean anything about who was the aggressor in any tiffs the two had, though. She had seen enough tiny women with hair-trigger tempers who acted out physically. She'd even employed a couple. However, could the stepdaughter's accounts be trusted? Emma didn't have a good relationship with the woman, clearly, but was she exaggerating or fabricating out of her own loathing?

Plenty of possibilities there for follow-up as to who killed Zunia Pettigrew. One thing was clear: Whoever did it was going out of their way to make it look like Nana committed the murder because of the confrontation at the convention seminar.

While Josh was ordering his dinner, Sophie turned to Laverne. "So that's the ITCS president and his wife, right?"

Laverne twisted to regard the couple sitting two tables over with the Pettigrews. "Sure is. Walter and Nora Sommer."

"What are they like?"

She frowned. "Well, I've only met them at the convention, and they kind of keep to themselves. When we joined a few years back he was on hiatus from being the overall ITCS president, and was just the division president of the New York City teapot collectors group, so he didn't attend our convention. He got the presidency back four years ago, now. He seems . . . I don't know . . . proper, how you imagine the dean at a ritzy private college would be, you know? Nora is like the ultimate club woman, the kind who joins lots of organizations and does charity work, but not for the charity, for the networking and notoriety." She smirked. "The kind who volunteers for everything then delegates the work." The waitress approached and Laverne set about ordering broiled sea bass.

Sophie examined the Sommers with interest. He was tall, with a thatch of white hair above a long, narrow face. He was probably in his sixties, and he wore wire-framed spectacles over green eyes. His face was gaunt. He looked like he worried a lot. Nora Sommer was small, dark and intense, her hair dyed an improbable shade of brown. She had her hand on Orlando's as the bereaved widower snuffled into a tissue. She was dressed dowdily but expensively in a navy skirt suit that appeared two sizes too big and was way too warm for an August day in upstate New York.

Walter looked like he'd rather be anywhere else but there, and in his perusal of the room, his gaze settled on Rhiannon. They exchanged a charged look, then Rhi looked away, biting her lip. Sophie frowned, wondering what was up between Rhi and the ITCS president. As his wife kept her focus on Pettigrew, Walter met Sophie's gaze, bowed his head in a stately manner, and went back to drinking his wine.

It was an interesting exchange. Sophie had worked her way through culinary school. Her father said he was fine with her following her own path but he wasn't paying for it, so a combination of grants, loans and hours of work in restaurants put her through a double-diploma program at ICE. Working as a waitress she had studied people to watch their habits as they ordered, ate, talked, drank and interacted with one another and their serving staff. She had, as a result, become very mindful of slight exchanges, glances, charged expressions.

Walter was aware that she was watching him. He stiffly ordered another bottle of wine, talked to his wife and ignored Orlando Pettigrew. He was either not comfortable with the mourning widower, or there was some personal reason for his uneasiness. It could have just been his awareness that Sophie was watching him, or was it something else? He leaned over, said a word to his wife, and she turned to stare at Sophie, then looked away.

Sophie turned to Laverne. "How did Walter Sommer feel about Zunia Pettigrew?" she asked, as there was a lull while they waited for their dinner.

The woman frowned into her teacup. "Well, now, it's funny you ask that," she said. "At the meeting I would have sworn Walter didn't approve of Zunia's handling of the meeting yesterday, but he never said a word. He was uncomfortable but he didn't reprimand her even when Rose begged him to get her under control, and he's *never* been afraid to act before. I don't know what was up with him."

Sophie turned her gaze back to the man who was staring off into space, sipping a glass of wine. What indeed?

Chapter 9

While waiting for her dessert after an all but inedible dinner consisting of overcooked and then microwaved fish with a too-salty and undercooked risotto, Sophie looked around for Rhiannon. She wanted to ask her friend a few questions, but the woman was not in her place at the table.

"Did you see Rhiannon leave the room?" she asked Laverne, who was sipping tea and waving the waitress over to take her plate.

"She darted out of here in a hurry. Maybe she went off to the washroom. This food would be enough to send anyone there."

"Was it always this bad?"

Laverne shook her head and frowned. "Last year it was real good—home-style, but well made, you know."

"Cutting costs, I'll bet, and maybe some personnel issues. What do you think of Rhiannon?"

"Poor girl. She just doesn't seem like a happy sort. I hadn't met her before this, so I barely know her. What is she like?"

Sophie folded her hands in her lap and looked off into the distance, considering. "She's nice. Smart. Her mother started Galway Fine Teas. Rhi tried to take it to New York City, but the shop there failed so she moved back here, to Butterhill."

She sighed and looked down at her hands. "Maybe that's why we became friends so easily; we both had our failures in NYC. Her mother got married and they decided to move to Arizona. She's started a Galway Fine Teas there, so she gave Rhiannon the shop here in Butterhill. I think after the disaster in New York City Rhi is deathly afraid of failing this time. She feels like she owes it to her mom to keep it going, but I'm afraid she just isn't a good enough businesswoman in some ways."

"What do you mean?"

Sophie rolled her eyes. "Listen to me, the failed restaurateur talking about how someone should do business. But she takes things too personally. I guess this Zunia person wanted to get Rhi out of the ITCS, didn't want her to be the supplier anymore. She's been complaining about it nonstop since I met her. I get the feeling it's important to GFT—you know, the contacts and prestige, and probably even the actual business— but I said there could be a million reasons the woman might feel that way. Rhi was convinced it was personal."

"I think she's right in this case," Laverne murmured, glancing around. Sophie's grandmother was holding court with Horace on one side of her and Malcolm on the other, charming both elderly gentlemen. Laverne leaned closer and said, "It started last year. There was something going on between Rhiannon and Walter, some of us thought. Zunia was miffed; she didn't think it was proper, whatever it was."

"Rhi and Walter?" Sophie said, eyes wide, remembering the look that passed between the two. "But he's married and older and . . . are you *sure*?"

She hunched one shoulder. "Not positive. But that was the rumor going round, apparently the dirt Zunia used to force Rhiannon to back out of running for the ITCS New York State division presidency."

"I had heard the woman started a rumor about bad finances or something like that, or at least that's what Rhi implied when she was complaining about her. This is *awful*! You mean Zunia threatened Rhiannon that she'd reveal the affair—or whatever—to . . . what, the world? Who would care? Unless it was the ITCS members? Or . . ." Sophie paused. "Mrs. Sommer?"

"I'd say Mrs. Sommer. Nora looks genteel and retiring, but the woman has claws of steel sheathed in velvet gloves. I don't imagine Rhiannon wanted to face that."

"If it's even true," Sophie said, not able to wrap her mind around vibrant Rhiannon Galway and white-haired Walter Sommer. "Is it possible that the rumor was started by Zunia herself as a way of sabotaging Rhi?"

"I suppose," Laverne said, doubt lacing her tone. "But then why wouldn't Rhiannon just tell her to back off?"

"Anyway, even if it was personal—the issue about dumping her as ITCS tea supplier, I mean—Rhiannon should be lobbying the other ITCS chapter members, not letting Zunia determine it for her. I guess the point is moot now, with Zunia gone."

Shadow of a Spout

The waitress brought their desserts and Sophie poked at hers, lava cake, the enduring fad among second-rate restaurants. Still, a well-made lava cake was *good*: warm and decadent, chocolaty and sweet with a depth of cocoa flavor that should make you hum a happy tune, not able to sing out loud because you were too busy filling your face. She was no food snob and enjoyed hot dogs, French fries and everything else if they were done well. One of the best meals she had ever had was poutine in Montreal from a street cart: real cheese curds and hot, delicious gravy over hand-cut fries . . . awesome!

But this lava cake was topped by a spiral of whipped topping from a can, and had a drizzle of what looked like commercial chocolate syrup over it. She cut into it, but there was no warm gush of chocolate, no sweet lusciousness, no rich scent wafting to her nose. She took a bite and chewed, then pushed it away. "Awful," she muttered.

Laverne chuckled. "Should have stayed with the store-bought rice pudding; at least they couldn't mess that up."

Sophie eyed the Sommers, who still sat listening as Orlando Pettigrew poured out his heart, it appeared. The widower took out a tissue from his jacket pocket and wiped his eyes, then blew his nose loudly. Emma muttered something to her father and bolted out of the dining room. Josh excused himself and went after her—to snoop, Sophie hoped. Walter Sommer steadily drank as his wife darted unhappy glances in his direction while chatting quietly to Orlando.

Then the ITCS president stood and began a slow ramble about the room, stopping to talk to the other ITCS members at their various tables, as well as other folks who appeared to be just diners from the town of Butterhill. Their waitress paused near Sophie and watched him with a frown.

"He doesn't seem too steady on his feet," Sophie said to her.

"I'm worried his waitress has over served him, but at least he doesn't have to drive anywhere."

"He's got a room on the second floor with all the other ITCS members, I suppose," she said.

"As much good as that does him."

"What do you mean?" Sophie asked.

The waitress looked around, then leaned over and said, "I've heard the man sees each convention as a hunting ground for new playdates, if you know what I mean. Don't know how his wife stands it!" She was just then hailed by another diner and sailed away to take an order.

Walter continued his progression around the room, stopping longer by the younger women's chairs. He seemed to be successfully charming them, because many giggled, and one actually blushed. Sophie glanced over at Nora Sommer. Could this whole thing be as simple as a woman scorned? Was Zunia involved with Walter herself, this year? And had she become the victim of a wife's wrath?

She shook her head. If Zunia had truly used some indiscretion between Rhi and Walter as fuel to get her to quietly withdraw from the division presidency race, it wasn't likely that she would then turn around and get caught in the same trap.

Pastor Frank, who had been sitting alone at a table, got up suddenly and headed over to Orlando Pettigrew. He stopped and said a few words, but the grieving widower did not seem to appreciate whatever he was saying. He bolted up and shouted, "Shut your face, Barlow! We were just fine and you're an idiot. Zunia was *not* going to leave me for you."

The pastor backed away and a hush fell over the room as a red-haired man in a rumpled suit entered and spied the confrontation. He paced over to the two men and took the pastor by the elbow, escorting him from the rom.

"What was that all about?" Sophie whispered to Laverne.

"That was one of the detectives, O'Hoolihan. Must want to ask the pastor a few questions. He *said* he'd be back."

"The guy's got timing," Sophie muttered. "I was afraid they were going to come to blows in another minute."

"On the other hand, it might have been interesting if he hadn't interfered."

Sophie nodded, acknowledging that she would have liked to have heard more. "Rhi introduced me to the pastor. What's his story?"

"I've always thought Frank was a lonely soul," Laverne said. "He's a pastor without a congregation; what could be lonelier than that?"

"But what did that mean, Pettigrew saying that Zunia was not going to leave him for the pastor? That implies the pastor thought she was, and just told the guy now!"

"It doesn't seem likely—Zunia and Frank?" Laverne shook her head, puzzlement in her dark eyes.

"I can't imagine it, from what I've heard about Zunia Pettigrew. Wouldn't that be trading down? She wasn't one to trade down, from the little I know of her. Too ambitious."

"Hard to say," Laverne replied.

Horace and Malcolm got up and headed back to their room, likely to play a few hands of gin rummy before they turned in, Laverne said. Walter at last approached their table and bowed, wavering a bit and smelling of wine.

"Miss Laverne," he said, with a slight slur. "Would you be so good as to introduce me to your *charming* companion?"

Laverne turned to Sophie. "Sophie Freemont Taylor, this

is Mr. Walter Sommer, esteemed president of the ITCS. Walter," she continued, turning to him, "this is Sophie Taylor, Rose's granddaughter and *my* goddaughter."

There was a hint of warning in her tone, but the gentleman didn't appear to hear. He took Sophie's hand and bowed over it. "What a beauty you are," he breathed, the scent of red wine on his breath.

Sophie was accustomed to handling drunken flattery; any woman who has ever been a waitress is. "Thank you. I think your wife would like to speak to you, sir." She pointedly looked over at Nora Sommer, who stared straight ahead while listening to Orlando, who was still talking.

"Nah, she's good, listening to poor old Orlando." He hiccupped and sat down in Josh's vacated seat. "Miss Sophie Taylor, may I ask you a question?"

Sophie sighed. Would the next words from him be the reasonably polite standard *Did it hurt when you fell from heaven? 'Cause you sure look like an angel*, or the more casually insulting and insinuating *What would you like for breakfast tomorrow morning?*

Instead, he said, "Do I look like a lady-killer to you?"

Chapter 10

"I beg your pardon?"

"Stupid detective kept asking me 'bout Zunia." He put his elbow on the table and cradled his chin. "Poor old Zunia."

She paused, then smiled encouragingly. "I'm sure you had an alibi for the time of the death. My grandmother said you weren't even out in the hall when the commotion happened and she was found."

He shrugged glumly, shoulders slumped, then he tried to sit up straight, wobbling a bit. His chin went up. "I was shlee . . . uh . . . sleeping. Cop doesn't believe me."

"How do you know he didn't believe you?"

"Kept ash . . . asking the same question in different ways, you know?"

"You didn't hear the alarm or the screaming?"

He shrugged, wavering back and forth. "Sleeping like a baby."

He said the words, but he just didn't seem convincing to Sophie; maybe that was because he was drunk, though. "What about *Mrs.* Sommer?"

"Nora? She was already *snoooring* her head off when I got back, 'bout ten. She's always like that, takes shlee . . . sleeping meds, conks out cold." He stuck his palm up, then flapped it down, like someone standing upright, then lying flat out. "She was out like a light 'til the police made me wake her up."

"Then neither of you has anything to worry about, correct?"

He nodded, but still looked worried, his addled gaze wavering, his gaunt face drawn in a frown, lips pursed. He shook his head. Why *was* he worried?

Nora Sommer, her arm through Orlando Pettigrew's, strolled over and grabbed her husband's jacket sleeve. "Come along, Walter. We're going with Orlando to see that officer and find out what he is doing to poor Frank. You *know* he mustn't be treated harshly, even if he is a little deluded. Poor man's a saint!"

Orlando was silent, his expression showing that though he might not agree with what Mrs. Sommer said, he wasn't going to contradict the wife of the group president.

Sophie stood and stuck out her hand. "Mrs. Sommer, I'm Sophie Taylor, Rose Freemont's granddaughter. I came as soon as I heard about this awful tragedy."

The woman looked at the outstretched hand but didn't move to shake. "I can't imagine why."

"It was Nana's teapot stolen from her room and used as a weapon. Didn't you know that?"

"I hadn't heard," she said coolly. "Come, Walter. *Now!*"

She tugged his jacket sleeve again and Walter stiffly stood

with the exaggerated care of a very drunk person who wishes not to appear drunk. He bowed, almost fell over, and said good-bye to the table at large, no longer singling Sophie out.

Laverne and Nana went upstairs, as it was getting late by early-to-bed standards. Sophie beckoned SuLinn, who slid into a seat next to her.

"I'm so glad you're here," SuLinn said, touching Sophie's bare arm delicately. "Not that . . . well, I know with that woman dead and your grandmother . . . Oh, I'm just happy to see you!"

They hugged. "If you're that relieved to see me, maybe this isn't the place for you?" Sophie joked, eyeing her friend. SuLinn had started out shy and for a while Sophie wasn't even sure the other girl liked her, but she was slowly emerging from her shell and now was much more open.

"I don't know. I guess the convention isn't what I thought it would be." She glanced around the room. "I should have known, but I like hanging out with your grandmother and Laverne and thought the others would be like them."

"I know what you mean." Sophie noticed that the wait-staff were clearing tables and gathering linens, a sure sign they were getting to the end of their shift. It was only eight thirty, which in her world would have meant that the dinner menu would be in full swing. In Fashion stayed open until almost midnight for theatergoers and others, but a dining room in a small-town inn would be done by nine.

She already knew that the local museum tour that had been planned for Saturday evening had been canceled out of deference to the loss of the chapter president, who was to lead the walk. Convention attendees had been left to their own devices, which meant an early bedtime for most. No one really knew yet how the convention was to proceed after Zunia's tragic passing. Nana had told Sophie that Nora Sommer had informed the conventioneers that she would have plans decided upon by the next morning, after she talked to the ITCS executive board, which consisted of her husband, herself and one other local member who acted as treasurer.

So . . . what to do? Shopping always filled in the gaps, and she had needs. "I forgot a couple of things," Sophie said, grabbing her handbag and pushing her chair back. The dining room was empty now; her and SuLinn were the last ones sitting. She smiled apologetically to their waitress, and stood. "Is there a drugstore in town that would be open this late?"

"Sure is. It's a nice night," SuLinn said, sweeping her dark straight hair back into a ponytail and tying it with an elastic as she, too, stood. "I'll walk with you and show you where I saw one on our way into town."

"Perfect. You'd think I'd know the town better. I've come here a few times to pick up tea, but Rhiannon's place is on the outskirts, so I never have a reason to actually venture down Main Street."

They headed out the front door past the café that was still open. Sophie sniffed the air from the café as someone exited, catching the aroma of freshly brewed coffee and a hint of spicy cinnamon. "That smells good," she said. "I'll bet the food is better in the café than in the dining room. Maybe I'll try something from here before bed."

"How do you eat so much and stay slim?" SuLinn asked.

Sophie glanced over at her with a quizzical look. "And *you* ask *me* this? I've seen you inhale your share of dessert platters, girl."

SuLinn chuckled, a laugh that was heard only by her closest friends. Sophie smiled at the heartwarming sound. Coming home to Gracious Grove had meant life opened up like a flower. In New York she had met a few nice people but they were all in the food industry and too busy to hang out together. In Gracious Grove she had reconnected with old friends like Cissy Peterson, Dana Saunders and even Jason.

She had made new friends, too, in particular SuLinn and Randy Miller. They all did things together: movie nights at Cissy's, barbecues at the Millers, and girlie outings with just SuLinn, Cissy and Dana. Rhiannon joined occasionally, but mostly stayed to herself. Sophie worried about the rumor that Rhiannon and Walter Sommer had been having an affair. Rhiannon's secretiveness could be attributed to that, she supposed.

SuLinn led the way down Main Street, past darkened shops, to Butterhill Drugs, a little pharmacy in an old store-front but updated with fluorescent lighting and mirrored cosmetics counters. Sophie grabbed a basket, picked up a notebook and some pens, then found some travel-size bottles of her favorite shampoo and body wash, and selected a deodorant stick.

"You forgot toiletries?" SuLinn asked, her dark eyes widening with surprise. "Those are the first things I pack. I have to have my moisturizer, makeup, toothpaste, contact solution, contacts, favorite brush, body lotion . . . The list goes on and on. When we go anywhere, Randy says we need a trailer just for my cosmetics."

"Y'know, when you find out that your grandmother's mixed up in a homicide investigation you forget a lot of things." As she scanned the shelf and nabbed a cheap comb and brush set, she noticed Emma Pettigrew standing near the soda cooler in intense conversation with a middle-aged woman. "Who is Emma Pettigrew talking to?" Sophie asked her friend.

SuLinn put down the industrial-size bottle of shampoo she was examining and followed Sophie's nod. "I don't know!"

"Introduce me to the girl?"

"I hardly know her myself." SuLinn demurred, folding her slim arms over her body. "I just met her yesterday for about two seconds."

"Just introduce me; I'll do the rest."

They approached the two and SuLinn made a stilted introduction, then melted away toward the snack-food section.

"My grandmother and her group the Silver Spouts are at the ITCS convention," Sophie explained, mostly to the older woman. "Nana was just saying how nice it was that Josh had someone to talk to other than all the old ladies and gentlemen at the convention!" She examined the older woman; she was probably in her fifties, slim but with wide hips and graying sandy hair, her mouth bracketed with lines and her hazel eyes underlined by dark circles. She was dressed casually, in tan capris and a sleeveless cotton blouse.

"Who is Josh?" the woman asked the teenager, her eyes narrowing.

"Just a kid," Emma said, eyeing Sophie with perturbation on her face.

It was easy to see that she looked like the woman, and equally easy to see that Sophie was interrupting a conversation of some sort, something heavier than what chips to buy, or whether Emma could dye her mousy hair. Sophie explained, "Josh Sinclair. He's just sixteen, the youngest member of the Silver Spouts. Probably the youngest member of the ITCS! You must be Emma's mother?"

"I'm Dahlia Pettigrew," she said with a nod.

"Are you here for the convention, too?" Sophie asked.

Dahlia stiffened and grasped the strap of her shoulder bag with a fierce grip. "I wouldn't be caught *dead* with that bunch of hypocrites!" Two red spots bloomed high on her cheeks and her eyes widened slightly, maybe as she realized what she had just said. But she went on: "*Worse* than hypocrites; they're a pack of wolves in sheep's clothing. I've done my time with them all, and look what happened: Zunia stole my husband then got herself killed. If Orly didn't make such a big deal out of it and threaten to withhold child support, I would never have let Emma within a hundred feet of those . . . those *jerks*!" Her voice sounded like tears were clogging it by the end of her statement.

Emma looked like she wanted to sink into the floor after her mother's rant. The woman had stopped as she caught her daughter's look, though it appeared that she was stifling more that she would have liked to say. She took in a deep, calming breath and let it out through pursed lips. "I shouldn't have said that, given what's happened, but it's been difficult. Zunia *made* it difficult. Excuse us; we have to run. We have a lot to talk about, number one among those things whether she should even be staying there with some murderer running around loose. You understand, I'm sure."

She took her daughter's arm and the two marched out of the store, leaving Sophie to watch them go. Where had Dahlia Pettigrew been the night before, and how much did she hate her ex-husband's new wife? Enough not to be sorry she was dead, it seemed from her comment.

Sophie bought her stuff. As she and SuLinn walked back to the inn, Sophie told her what had been said and what she was wondering. "Maybe Josh will have more info. I'll have to track the kid down. That woman was practically shaking and crying, she was still so angry about the way her marriage ended."

"You can't blame Dahlia Pettigrew for being bitter, though. I would be, if some woman stole my Randy."

Sophie didn't answer. Could a husband be stolen? He wasn't like a billfold left on a park bench. It was a nice August night, and they strolled back slowly. Sophie told SuLinn about her evening out with Jason and how she thought there was a kiss coming, before the storm washed it away. "I wish I knew what he was thinking, how he was feeling."

"Ask him," SuLinn said. "I could never do it, but I'm sure you could."

"I don't know about that," Sophie said. There were roses somewhere. She breathed in deeply; the fragrance was heavy on the warm evening air. It made her think of rose hip tea, something she was considering serving at Auntie Rose's. She let her mind go back to Jason, though, and her feeling that she just didn't know where she stood with him. "Jason and I are friends again, but there was a time when he wouldn't even talk to me, I hurt him that bad."

"Years ago, when you were kids!" she said. "He's an adult, Soph, and so are you. I'm sure he's let go of that."

"Maybe. Even if he has, though, he's moved on." They paused outside the inn and Sophie examined it in the floodlights that illuminated the front. It was an old building, a couple hundred years, probably, constructed of cobblestone. A pergola jutted off to one side. She checked her watch. "I don't want to go in yet. My nana has this weird nighttime ritual of bending and stretching you would not believe, and

I'd rather give her and Laverne space and privacy. Want to walk around there and see if there's a garden?" she asked, pointing to the pergola.

"Sure. I want to phone Randy," she said, naming her husband, an architect with a local firm. "He has a meeting this evening and will just be getting home. I'll give him a few minutes to get a drink and relax, but the garden would be a great place to phone from."

They strolled down the front sidewalk and climbed some crumbling concrete steps. Beyond the pergola there was an enclosed garden accessed by a wooden gate and lit by solar lights. Benches lined the fence, interspersed by gardens that created private little alcoves for chatting or relaxation. Sophie was interested because she had often thought the back of Nana's tearoom property could be developed in a similar manner, with private tables for intimate brunches or picnics.

She paused by a rosebush, breathing deeply the heady fragrance of an old, open type of rose that had thorns thickly strewn all the way up each stem. It was a divine scent, and she closed her eyes, close and distant sounds washing over her. Traffic, someone laughing somewhere, a dog barking, people arguing.

Arguing? The patio and garden appeared deserted, but the voices were close and sounded like they were raised in anger.

"Wonder what's going on," Sophie said to SuLinn, as she led the way along the winding paths through the garden, past a clump of tall ornamental grasses that swayed in a sudden breeze.

As they rounded a bend in the walkway, Bertie Handler, the inn owner, strode past them, his expression grim. Sophie turned and watched him storm off, then followed the path. Pastor Frank was sitting alone on a bench, his head in his hands. At the sound of their scuffling feet he looked up, tears on his cheeks.

SuLinn dashed toward him. "Mr. Barlow, are you all right?"

He looked up at her with a lost expression in his eyes. "I s'pose." He pulled off his steel-framed glasses and knuckled his eyes, sniffing miserably.

Sophie approached behind her friend, who had pulled a tissue from her handbag and gave it to him. "Pastor, were you and Bertie Handler arguing about something? Is everything all right?"

"He was mad because . . . because of that incident in the dining room, I guess," he said, his gaze shifting back and forth. He hung his head. "I feel so alone!"

Sophie sat down on a chair by the bench he sat on. Remembering the pastor's outburst in the dining room, she gently said, "You can talk to us, Mr. Barlow. You must be devastated by Zunia Pettigrew's death; you were so close, in the same group and all."

"We *were* close!" the pastor exclaimed, his eyes watering behind his glasses. He dabbed at his eyes with the tissue SuLinn had given him, shoving the glasses up on his forehead so he could dry his welling tears. "*So* close! No one understood her. She was magnificent, fiery, so passionate and full of life. But I shouldn't say another word. It's not my place." He eyed SuLinn, who stood nearby.

Sophie exchanged a look with SuLinn and faintly motioned with her head for SuLinn to leave them alone. She knew it was easier sometimes to confide in a stranger than someone you may actually see again.

"I want to call my husband," she said, "so I think I'll just go over to the picnic table there and do that." She took out her cell phone and retreated.

"Mr. Barlow, I'm so sorry," Sophie said, leaning over and patting him on the back. "It's much harder on you because you were close with Zunia, and maybe no one understands *how* close." She wasn't sure how to bring up what she had heard in the dining room.

"We were. I've only known her a year or two, but I'm the one who really understood her. Better than her own husband!"

"I didn't know the woman at all, but from what I've heard she didn't seem to have a lot of friends. Why is that?"

"People were jealous. After she won the presidency of the division last year all the infighting escalated. Rhiannon was the worst—so petty! Zunia was just trying to save her hurt feelings because the girl didn't have a chance, you know. Not against Zunia." He snuffled and his chin trembled, a low moan escaping him. He swept back a long hank of gray hair and sighed. "My poor darling Zunia!"

His anguish seemed so extreme that Sophie wondered, was it fake? It felt over-the-top, but she had known many people who indulged their emotions to an extent that it seemed they were putting on a show when they were being as genuine as they could ever be. The pastor might be one of those.

Or he could be lying through his teeth. But why would he lie about having an affair with her? That put him square in the police's sights as someone who had an intimate relationship with Zunia. "I'm truly sorry for your loss. You seem more heartbroken than even her husband."

The pastor nodded as he took his glasses off, wiping the lenses with the tail of his plaid shirt. "That's something we shared, Zunia and me; we both felt things deeply, you know, and so few people really do." He shoved his glasses back on, clenched his fist and hammered his chest, leaving his hand there. "We *both* had big hearts, full to overflowing. I don't think I'll ever get over this, and I want whoever did it to pay."

"The police will find the guilty party."

"I'm not so sure about that."

"Why do you say that?"

He shook his head, but stayed silent.

"Who do you think did it? Do you have any ideas?"

Crickets nearby chirped, as he looked off into the gloom. A rumble of thunder rolled across the heavens. "I don't want to point fingers."

So he *did* have an idea. "It won't go any further," Sophie said, softly. "I don't know any of these folks. I'm only here to support my grandmother, who I know for sure would never do anything like that. Who are you thinking?"

He looked to the right and left, and whispered, "I think that Orlando is in over his head, you know? He should *never* have married Zunia . . . not man enough for her. She was dissatisfied, and I know for a fact *he* was regretting it, too."

"But why would he try to place the blame on my grandmother? Whoever did it stole the teapot from my grandmother's room and used it to kill Zunia."

He choked on a sob. "I don't know. I just don't *know*!"

"Mr. Barlow, my godmother told me that there were rumors going around last year that Rhiannon Galway was having an affair with Mr. Sommer." She felt disloyal to her friend even saying such a thing. Her intent was not to paint Rhiannon as the villain, though; it was to get more information on the dynamics of this odd group. "What did you think of that?"

"Oh, that was *true*!" Barlow said. He pushed his glasses up onto his forehead again and used his wrist to stanch the flow of tears, which never seemed to stop. He took in a deep, shaky breath. "Zunia was appalled! I didn't want to say it earlier, but that is precisely why she tried to save the girl trouble. She very wisely convinced Rhiannon to withdraw from the division president election rather than let it get around. Better for everyone, you know." He settled his glasses back down on his nose and nodded. "Better for *everyone*."

Blackmail as a public service: That was a new one. But Sophie was not going to say what she really felt, that Zunia sounded like a poisonous witch with a *b*. "I felt sorry for you when the detective came up to you in the dining room and escorted you away in front of everyone. What on earth did he want?"

"He just had a few questions, that's all. I . . . I had better get going," he said, standing and brushing off his slacks.

He seemed nervous all of a sudden. "Mr. Barlow, why did Mr. Pettigrew say his wife was not going to leave him for you, in the dining room, just before the detective came in?" Sophie examined his face in the yellow glow of the one of the lamps that lined the pathway.

"That is private business," he said, his voice trembling. "Between me and Orlando."

"Unfortunately everyone must be talking about it because he made quite a big deal out of it in front of everyone. That's so awkward for you. Where were *you* last night when everything was happening?" Sophie asked, hoping to force an answer while he was flustered.

"I was, uh . . . tied up. Busy. Look, I've got to go. Excuse me." He backed away, then whirled and bustled down the path a ways. But he stopped and turned back to her. "I don't care what Orlando says; it's true: Zunia and I were planning on running away together. We were just going to get this conference out of the way, and she was going to tell him." His voice broke. "She was too good for him!" He whirled and strode off to the side door of the inn and disappeared.

SuLinn, slipping her phone in her shorts pocket, strolled toward Sophie. "What the heck was that all about?"

Sophie told her what they had talked of. "I wasn't sure about the rest, but that last bit sounded like the truth. She really was planning on running away with him."

"Or at least he *thought* she was," SuLinn said.

"Good point. And as long as he was convinced it was so, he would sound that sure." Would a woman as ambitious as Zunia Pettigrew really give up everything to run away with Pastor Frank Barlow? He just did not seem like the type to incite the kind of passion that would overwhelm a sensible woman's judgment, and she'd be trading down from Orlando Pettigrew, even though that guy didn't seem like much of a prize to Sophie. She considered Barlow's certainty, and remembered from a long-ago job at a restaurant in Little Italy a woman who had all the staff crazy for her. She played them off against one another and each fellow was sure of her affection for him until she finally ran away with the restaurant owner.

That guy gave up everything—his family, his business, his kids—just to be with her. But then they divorced within a year and he came slinking back to his wife, who remarried him. Was this a similar case? She shook her head. There didn't seem to be a thing to support that. Except . . . Her eyes widened as she considered the presence of Pettigrew's ex-wife in town. Where did she fit into the puzzle?

"You're not trying to figure out who did it, are you?" SuLinn asked, watching her.

"I can't leave it alone, not when Nana's teapot was used as a weapon. She's really upset about it, and I won't have her used like that." Sophie's heart thudded. She had been accused before of feeling like she needed to correct everything, wanting to make everything right for everyone. It had backfired innumerable times in her career, but she kept making the same mistakes. This time, though, there was no question it was right to want to help her grandmother.

"SuLinn, someone with murder on their mind snuck into my grandmother's room when she wasn't there, stole that teapot, then killed Zunia Pettigrew with it. They went out of their *way* to make it look like she did it." She nodded sharply. "So yes, I'm going to do my *darnedest* to figure out who did it and make sure they go to jail."

As they walked back into the inn one thing bothered Sophie about the conversation she had just had. If Pastor Frank had nothing to do with Zunia's murder, then why didn't he answer her innocent question about where he was? Granted he didn't owe her an explanation, and she had no real right to ask, but still . . . why not just tell her where he was instead of evading the question?

Chapter 11

Thelma Mae Earnshaw didn't like feeling bad about her behavior. Sometime in the last few months she had grown a conscience, and that was an uncomfortable thing to own, like having a parrot on your shoulder that only ever squawked when you did something wrong. Now she felt bad for talking trash at the convention, spreading that stupid stuff about Rose Freemont being a dangerous sort. But who would have thought that bunch of ninnies would believe that sweet little grandmotherly Rose Freemont would be a killer? And how was Thelma to know Zunia Pettigrew would up and get herself murdered straight away? *With* Rose's banged-up ugly old teapot?

It was like the good Lord was testing Thelma, and she did not appreciate it. After a lifetime of hardship, she and He were already on uneasy terms, and it didn't appear that it was going to get any better. He needed to start cooperating or it would be no wonder that she kept choo-choo-chugging off the rails.

There was only one way to feel good again and that was to figure out who did it, then march right up to that O'Hooligan, or whatever his name was, and tell him. So Thelma was skulking, trying to find clues. She had skulked in the coffee shop to no avail, lingering behind booths and listening in on a few of the teapot convention folks' conversations until an exasperated waitress asked her if she was ill. Now she was skulking behind a bamboo bush in the lobby. Everyone knew the husband was always the first suspect, and right now Zunia Pettigrew's husband . . . What the heck *was* his name? She couldn't remember, except that it was a city. No one ought to be named after a city. That would be like calling her Nimrod Earnshaw, after the town in Oregon where a niece of hers lived, or Elephant Butte Earnshaw, after the park in New Mexico where her cousin three times removed got stuck in a crevasse.

Whatever-His-Name-Was Pettigrew was on his cell phone, which, by the way, was the devil's own invention. If God had meant man to be able to talk to others wherever they were, he would have made them telepathetic!

Orlando—*that* was Pettigrew's name. Orlando, as in Florida. Thelma skulked closer, and the fellow's voice was clear as a bell. Why a bell? she wondered, distracted once again. Was a bell clearer than a foghorn or a bassoon? No one said "as clear as a foghorn," but you sure could hear one a ways away.

Anyhoo, Pettigrew was talking, kind of sobbing. "I'm going crazy with grief! What am I going to do without my Zunia?"

Thelma clasped her hands to her bosom and snuck closer. Poor fella! A waitress passed by going from the dining room toward the door and gave her an odd look, but Thelma put one finger to her lips. The woman smiled and continued on her way.

"I don't know *what* the cops are doing. They keep asking me the same questions, over and over: Where was I? What was I doing? Why was Zunia out of the room? Didn't I know where my own wife was?"

Thelma crept closer and the bush rustled a bit, but she stilled and the noise stopped.

"No, I told them about that. I *knew* she was involved with someone else, but it was going to blow over. You had to understand Zunia; she got caught up in this other guy's fantasy and went along for the ride, but that was finished."

Thelma almost fell off her orthopedic loafers. So the woman was having an affair and the husband knew about it? Seemed like a good motive for murder.

"No, she wasn't about to leave me. She told me that herself." He paused. "Yes, I'm sure. We talked about it, and she was going to put an end to it. She was beginning to be concerned about the guy. He scared her." He paused. "Why? You mean why was she scared? She said he was far too serious."

Thelma tried to get closer but bumped into one of the chairs by the fake palm and stumbled sideways. Pettigrew bolted up out of his chair and whirled around.

"Are you okay, ma'am?" he said, grabbing her arm with his free hand and guiding her to the chair.

"Just a little light-headed, you know." She stared up at him. "I should be asking if *you're* okay, having just lost your wife and all."

He looked awful, with bags under his bloodshot eyes,

clothes rumpled, chin stubbled with a day's growth of whiskers and some bruising underneath it from the confrontation the night before with the weird pastor. "It's like a nightmare I can't wake up from. I keep thinking, what if we hadn't come to the conference? What if I had been awake when she left the room? What if . . ." He shook his head and passed one hand over his face. "I'm sorry, ma'am, but I've got to get back to my call," he said, raising the cell phone to his ear.

"Who you talking to?" she asked.

He looked taken aback and put one hand over the phone. "Uh . . . a friend back home. I have to tell folks, you know."

She nodded. "I guess we'll need a new president, right? Not to be indelicate."

He looked mortified, gray eyes wide, grimace on his lips. "This is *certainly* not the time to be talking about this." He moved away, speaking rapidly in a mutter to his friend on the phone, then he touched the screen and put the phone in his pocket as he headed for the elevator.

Well, that got her a big fat nothing, except she knew that the dead woman was afraid of her boyfriend. Could be something there. But who was her boyfriend? That babbling pastor? No one would be afraid of that guy.

S ophie had returned to the inn room. Nana was sitting up in bed reading a mystery. She looked tired, but worse than that, she looked pensive and worried, her round face lined and weary under her tousled head of fluffy white curls. Sophie sat cross-legged on the end of the bed and shared a look of concern with Laverne, who was rubbing lotion into her elbows. "How are you, Nana?"

"I'm just fine, my Sophie girl. Now don't you go getting that mother-hen look with me. I'm old enough to be your grandmother," she joked.

"She won't tell you how worried she is about all this," Laverne said, pausing and eyeing her old friend. "Will you, Rose?"

"Now, Laverne, you hush. I'm just fine, and I'm plenty old enough to look after myself." She examined her granddaughter's expression. "Talk to me," she commanded Sophie.

"I don't know if you really want to talk about this awful business or not."

Sophie almost thought Nana hid a smile, but she simply said, "I want to see that whoever did this using my poor teapot is caught. We might not still hang murderers, but he or she can spend the rest of their life in jail. I sometimes think that's worse than a quick death at the end of a rope."

"Whoever strikes a man—or woman—so that he dies shall be put to death," Laverne said.

"Vengeance is mine, says the Lord," Nana said, smiling over at her friend.

Laverne chuckled. "Just testing your knowledge of the good book."

It was an oft-repeated conversation, since Laverne was an active churchwoman and Nana preferred to do her praying at home, as she said each time the subject came up. Sophie could see that Laverne was purposely keeping the atmosphere light.

"Tell us what you've learned," Nana said, sticking a Stone and Scone Inn pamphlet in the book, a large-print Agatha Christie from the Gracious Grove library, and closing it.

Sophie went over the two encounters she had, with Dahlia and Emma Pettigrew, and with Pastor Frank Barlow.

"That doesn't really explain what Orlando Pettigrew said to him in the dining room," Nana commented.

"No, but isn't the husband always the last to know when a wife is leaving? I've had a few male friends blindsided by divorce," Sophie said. "One said he never saw it coming until the day his wife served him with papers and moved out. Maybe Frank is right; maybe she *was* going to leave Orlando for him."

"Maybe," Nana said, but didn't sound convinced.

"What do you think about Emma's mother being in the area?" Sophie asked them both.

"She may have just come today in response to this happening," Laverne said, putting the last dollop of body lotion on her elbows and capping the tube. "Like Josh's mom."

"I hadn't thought of that, but it's possible, isn't it?"

There was a tentative tap at the door. Sophie jumped up and crossed the floor. Josh stood in the doorway, looking a little embarrassed. She invited him in but he shook his head, and she didn't want to mortify him further. She stepped out into the dim hallway. "What's up? Is your mom coming back to stay tonight?"

"No, luckily. I love my mom, but she worries so much! I did what you said, told her you were here, and she seemed better about it. Anyway, I hung out with some of the staff here and they said Emma was always bumming smokes off them and talking about how awful her stepmom was . . . before the convention started, I mean. I guess the Pettigrews came the night before, like, Thursday, so that Mrs. Pettigrew could set up the meeting room for the seminar and stuff. I saw Emma for a bit but then she took off, said she was meeting her mom."

Sophie told him how she had bumped into the mother and daughter at the drugstore. "But the mom was in a hurry. I wonder if Emma called her to come to Butterhill."

Josh's eyes widened. "No, that's not how it happened. Mrs. Pettigrew was already in the area. Guess what for?"

Sophie shrugged. "I can't guess. Tell me."

"She's checking out Cruickshank College for Emma. She came down the *same day* as they did, and I think she's staying at the college!"

Sophie was stunned. From being at the bottom, Dahlia Pettigrew was making the ascent up the list of possible suspects. "Do people stay at the college while they're checking it out?"

He nodded. "Sure. They use the dorm rooms, sometimes. I went to visit an out-of-state college with my mom and dad and we stayed overnight."

Sophie pondered that. "So Emma's mom *could* have been here at the inn last night when all the excitement happened."

"But she wouldn't *kill* Emma's stepmom, would she?"

Sophie didn't want to enlighten him on the complicated world of adult relationships. She had never felt the urge to murder, but one of her more unstable acquaintances had trashed her ex's car, shredded his clothing and destroyed his prized old movie collection. Sophie had backed away from that friendship, not sure how to deal with someone like that. The ex–Mrs. Pettigrew sure seemed to still be upset about the divorce. "Who knows what she'd do? Probably not, but it's one more person to add to the list. I wonder how we can find out if she's involved somehow."

"Maybe you could call Mr. Murphy," Josh offered hesitantly.

"He could help you figure out if she was there at the college that night."

It was a good idea, but how would she ask him for information like that? Would he even know? "I'll think about it," she said. "Thanks for the info. Good night, Josh."

He headed down the hall to his room and she stood watching, wondering what he made of the adults he had encountered at this, his first collectors' conference. Just then Thelma Mae Earnshaw trudged down the hall from the elevator, looking as if she bore the weight of the world on her shoulders.

Nana and Thelma may have mended fences and come to uneasy terms over an invitation to join the Silver Spouts teapot collectors society, but Thelma was still Thelma. Nana had told Sophie all about what she suspected and knew for certain that Thelma had whispered among the other convention attendees, but it mystified Sophie that she would say such things.

Thelma saw her as she reached her own room and came to a halt. "Thought you ought to know, I saw that fella, that Pettigrew fella. He didn't see me, though. He was talking on the phone and he told somebody that he knew his wife was cheating on him, but he didn't care because she was done with the other guy and was even scared of him."

Sophie stuttered, "Uh, thanks for the information, Mrs. Earnshaw."

"Then he saw me and he told me he was real tore up. Got huffy when I just mentioned that we'd be needing a new president for the group, though. Don't know why." She sagged against the door frame as she rustled around in her huge bag for the room key.

"Are you okay?"

"I never complain," she grumbled. "Nobody ever asks about my health, and I don't complain."

"Are you not feeling well?" Sophie asked, coming over to her. "Would you like me to call Cissy, see if she can come to visit you?"

"No, that's okay." She reached out, her eyes watering, and touched Sophie's wrist. "You're a nice girl, Sophie Taylor. Never did like your brothers, but you're a nice girl and a credit to your grandma. Just like my Cissy." She fumbled with the key, opened the door and entered, slamming the door behind her.

Sophie returned to make up her little cot by the window. She had moved the table and chairs to the center of the room so they could still be used. Nana was reading again, while Laverne had the TV on, watching CNN. There was a political scandal somewhere, a financial crisis loomed, and one analyst was saying the current government was the worst they had ever had and was going to be the death of democracy and end civilization as they knew it. Or something like that. It wasn't that Sophie was cynical, but she was young and yet had lived long enough to hear the same guff over and over since she was a child.

When she was done making up her cot she sat on it cross-legged and told the two older women what Josh had reported and what Thelma had said. She watched her grandmother's face, the wrinkles that outlined her mouth emphasized by the pool of light from the bedside lamp. "What are you thinking, Nana?"

"I'm just wondering who Orlando Pettigrew would be talking to that he would tell so much, and how it could be precisely the information we would want to know?"

"What are you saying?" Laverne asked.

She shook her head. "I don't know. Don't mind me; I'm just tired, I guess."

But as Sophie showered and changed into pj's, she pondered what her grandmother had said. She wished she had been there to see exactly how it happened that Thelma overheard such a pivotal conversation. The woman was not stealthy and she was most definitely not quiet, though she seemed to think she was, so the man *must* have known she was there. Therefore he must have known she would hear him declare his wife a cheat.

Was it posthumous damage control? Was he trying to make it seem like he had no reason to kill her because there was no rift between them? Maybe. One thing was for sure, she needed to find out much more about what was going on in the ITCS, because there sure seemed to be a lot of skulduggery and extreme emotions.

Chapter 12

It was early, so Rose left Laverne and Sophie sleeping and went down to the café that fronted the Stone and Scone Inn for a cup of tea. Laverne rarely got to sleep in, especially on a Sunday, when church beckoned. Sophie had never been an early riser. Years of working in restaurants meant that she was accustomed to being up until three in the morning, and asleep until ten a.m. or so. But for Rose the early morning was the best time of the day, when it was shiny and new, fresh and green.

During the dark period after her husband and son died every morning just brought a fresh wave of misery, if she had even managed to sleep at all, but now she was content. Her grandchildren had been the saving grace in her life. Rosalind had her faults, and she didn't spend much time with her mother in Gracious Grove, but Rose would always be grateful to her daughter for bringing three children into the world and making sure they spent lots of time with their nana.

The coffee shop was comforting like a hundred others, with bright lights, the clink of china, and the faint sound of the radio tuned to an oldies station. There was a diner counter for folks to sip coffee at, red upholstered booths lined the walls and the windowed front, and a bank of booths with high dividers filled the center. There was a local paper on the counter near the cash register, the *Butterhill Bugle*; Rose picked up a copy and found a booth that had just been vacated near the front window. A waitress cleared the table while Rose ordered tea. She leafed through the paper while she waited.

The murder of Zunia Pettigrew had made the front page, but the article didn't have any information that was new to Rose. She soon laid the paper down and looked around with interest. Cheery waitresses dressed in gold polyester uniforms bustled from booth to booth, teasing regulars, refilling cups and clearing tables. Rose appreciated the scent of fresh coffee, and the smells were making her hungry, as were the sounds, especially the sizzle of bacon on the flattop, where a short-order cook whipped up breakfast for hungry Butterhill folk. She thought she'd stick to toast, though, her usual morning meal.

They overlooked the main street, which was just beginning to get busy with early churchgoers. The booths in the coffee shop were now packed. Folks still had to work and many stopped for a coffee or breakfast at the Stone and Scone coffee shop; there was a police officer, a couple of young women in scrubs—maybe employees at a local nursing home or hospice, since there was no hospital in the town—and as usual, the local gathering of farmers in dirty overalls, sitting together and laughing at old jokes while trading new gossip.

Rose had been coming to Butterhill every other year for several years. With only a couple of days spent each time she couldn't say she knew every corner of the town. But she did know some of the inn staff, and waved and smiled when she saw a familiar face. Bertie Handler, the inn owner, had slumped into a booth on the wall near the servery and was glumly stirring spoons of sugar into black coffee. He looked dreadful, like he hadn't slept for ages. She was about to go over to ask him if he was all right when Nora Sommer, sat down opposite him with a stack of paperwork under her arm.

The waitress brought Rose's tea and buttered toast, so she decided to eat before intruding. She wanted to speak with them both, curious if the convention was going on in the face of the awful events of early Saturday morning. Conversation rose to a lively chatter, with many folks arguing over the *Bugle* article, it seemed, from the number of times she heard Zunia's unusual name spoken.

Sophie had told them what she had gleaned the night before about the Pettigrews, and Rose put it together with what she knew. Zunia and Orlando had met as members of the Niagara Teapot Collectors Group, centered in Wheatfield, New York, near Niagara. Orlando, a real estate agent and antiques aficionado, had first joined with his wife, Dahlia, who was really the teapot collector of the two, if Rose remembered right from the first time they met. In fact, it seemed to her that Dahlia was a long-time member, maybe even one of those who had started the ITCS, though her husband was a more recent member. Dahlia was a nice woman but mousy and kind of sad-looking. She had little spunk and tended to melt into the background.

Her husband was not an overly attractive man, but he was vigorous and cheerful with his first wife in tow. Both the vigor and good humor appeared to have been sapped, truncated by the whirlwind that was Zunia, the new Mrs. Pettigrew. Orlando's divorce from Dahlia had happened offstage, so to speak, and Rose had not learned about the new Mrs. Pettigrew until Laverne reported back after last year's conference. It was a done deal, and Zunia had quashed her husband's stated intention from the previous year to run for the division head, taking center stage and declaring herself the front-runner.

Rhiannon Galway had tried to put her name forth as a candidate, Laverne told Rose, but Zunia had made sure that Rhiannon backed away. No one was *quite* sure what Zunia held over Rhiannon's head, other than vague rumors made worse by her quitting the race, but whatever it was did the trick. Zunia ran unopposed with her fawning husband's obvious approval. According to Thelma's report from her encounter with him, Pettigrew claimed to be crushed by his wife's murder. Something about the relationships among that group at the conference bothered Rose. She thought back to Friday, closing her eyes and picturing the conference room and the various interactions she had witnessed.

They had been seated in rows, but from her angle she could see Orlando as he watched his wife. Ah, yes, there it was, just a moment, but a pivotal one. *That* was the reason she didn't feel convinced of Pettigrew's grief! There was one brief flash, a look of intense distaste and dislike as Zunia critiqued the first two presenting their teapots. The scales had dropped from Orlando Pettigrew's eyes, and what he saw when he looked at his wife was anyone's guess, but it didn't look like love to Rose. She opened her eyes, wondering what to do with her thoughts. How could you tell the police that you just didn't think the victim's husband was really sad to see her gone? Maybe Laverne's nephew would be able to help.

Bertie Handler was just getting up from his meeting with Nora Sommer, so it didn't look like she'd be able to corner him alone, as she had intended. He retreated back into the inn through the glass door that opened onto the lobby. Rose, finished with her tea and toast, left money for the bill plus a handsome tip and approached Nora.

"How are you, dear?" she asked, sitting down opposite her in the seat Bertie had vacated.

"Pardon?" she said, looking up. "Oh, hello, Rose. I'm not bad. How are you this morning?"

"I'm fine. Just a little tired after yesterday."

Nora sighed. "I know. How dreadful! It's not good publicity for the ITCS. Walter is most concerned."

Funny that Zunia's death struck Nora first as a blow to the ITCS, but that was her main focus, Rose supposed. She noticed the schedule of events that Nora had marked up with a black pen. "Are we going ahead with the convention, then? We've only got today."

"We're going ahead and we'll cram as much as we can into one day," Nora said, not looking up from her work. "It's the highlight of the year for so many! We can't let all these folks down. Since many of us are staying until tomorrow anyway, I plan to canvass the other members and see if we can finish it up with an evening seminar, if folks don't mind cramming three presentations into one day. I've already talked to the speakers, and they're all on board."

"And we'll have to figure out what to do about the divisional presidency." Rose watched the other woman, wondering how to get onto the subject she really wanted to talk about.

"*Walter* will have to figure out what to do about that," Nora corrected, looking up.

"I suppose," Rose said.

"There's no 'suppose' about it. There would not normally be an election this year, as the president is elected for two years. Since this is midterm, though, Walter has the right to appoint someone to serve out the term."

For the first time Rose wondered if the real smarts in running the ITCS was the woman sitting opposite her. Was Walter nothing more than a figurehead? But why wouldn't Nora take over the society herself? Even a woman as traditional as she would certainly not think running a teapot collectors society was unbecoming of her womanhood. "I heard something about the convention not being held here in Butterhill after this year. Bertie seemed quite concerned."

"I just told him not to worry about it. We'll be back here next year as always. That was some wild speculation on Zunia's part."

"But I thought she and Bertie were special friends?" Laverne had said that the previous year Zunia and the inn owner were "thick as thieves."

Nora's carefully darkened eyebrows lifted. "A woman like Zunia . . . You have to know her affections were fickle in the extreme."

"She did seem mercurial, at the very least." Rose paused, but then plunged ahead with what she wanted to say. "You *do* know I didn't do it, Nora . . . murder poor Zunia, I mean. I could never . . ." She shook her head. Maybe it was ridiculous to think anyone would suspect an eighty-something-year-old woman, but the fact that it was her teapot had rattled her.

"My dear, of *course* I know you didn't do it!" Nora said, reaching across and patting Rose's hand, her diamond rings, adorning most fingers, glittering in the pendant light over the booth. "Set your mind to rest on that point." Her tone was warm and her smile genuine.

"Thank you, Nora. I appreciate that. Maybe it seems silly, but I couldn't bear it if anyone thought I did it."

"No one who knows you would think you would do something so awful, even to someone as *poisonous* as Zunia." Her expression was placid, but a snapping anger flared in her dark eyes.

Rose nodded, but her mind was on that look, even as Nora went back to her schedule. That was another thing she had seen at the convention: When Walter reached out to calm Zunia down, Nora had a look of outrage on her face. It was just momentary but unmistakable. And she remembered something one of the women had said, when chafed about running for division president, that she wouldn't want to work with "that letch," Walter.

There was one circumstance that would fit with Nora's fury and Orlando's disillusionment. Walter Sommer could have been having an affair with Zunia Pettigrew, but even if that was so, it didn't mean Nora had murdered Zunia. Why would she? Zunia was married and Walter appeared to be known for his flings. Or *rumored* flings, Rose corrected herself, not willing to make that assumption. That indicated a wandering interest that would never light on one woman for long. "I'm so sorry, Nora," she said simply, watching her.

"Sorry?" The woman stared across the table, arrested in the middle of making notes in the margin of the schedule.

Rose paused, trying to find the right words. "I'm so sorry for what you've had to put up with. I know it hasn't always been easy."

"What do you mean?"

"There have been rumors. Aren't there always?"

"Those women! What gossips," she said. "It was that Faye Alice Benson, wasn't it? She's got a big mouth."

Rose's breath caught in her throat; she didn't want to get anyone in trouble. "Actually, no, it wasn't her," she said. *Or not* just *her*, she thought, trying to justify the fib. "You must have known Zunia would talk."

Nora smiled, her demeanor calm after the momentary blaze of anger. "Whatever the rumor mill would have you believe, he was *not* going to leave me for her. He saw what was happening to Orlando and how poor Dahlia was suffering. Zunia was toxic, and Walter is not an idiot. He knows what side his bread is buttered on."

"Wiser men than he have been taken in by a certain kind of woman." Rose was just sending out feelers, probing in a quest to get at the truth. "I'll confess I didn't see what attracted them—not being a fan of Zunia's—but she certainly had some men wrapped around her little finger."

Nora shook her head, adamant in her conviction. "You may think my husband is a fool, but he's not *that* much of a fool." She hesitated, but then continued, leaning slightly across the table, "I'll tell you something in confidence, Rose: All of our money is mine. We married many years ago, but my father made sure my money was tied up right and tight.

I cried, begged and pleaded, because Walter was a little miffed when my father insisted on a kind of a prenuptial agreement, but Daddy said that if he loved me it wouldn't matter, and if he didn't, then I'd be protected. Walter knows where we stand, and he's happy with it."

"So you knew about everything?" Rose asked. She didn't need to be explicit.

"Of course. I've known about every one of Walter's little *adventures*. He *tells* me." She appeared amused. "I told him a long time ago, do whatever you want, just don't expect a divorce unless you plan on being broke. I promised 'til death do us part." She gathered up the paperwork and stood. "And now, if you'll excuse me, I have to go. I have calls to make and the rest of the day to plan. You *will* be coming to the talk on hallmarks, won't you? We're having it first thing this morning. I'm going off to tell everyone now." She whirled and swept out of the coffee shop.

Laverne, just entering the coffee shop, passed Nora and watched her stride off, then joined Rose at the table.

As Laverne had her coffee and cinnamon roll, Rose filled her in on what she had just learned. "It made me wonder . . . if Zunia demanded that Walter leave Nora, would that be reason enough for him to kill her?"

"Try this; it's so good." Laverne cut a quarter of her cinnamon roll and put it on a napkin in front of Rose. "I don't know; what do you think? You're the one who just talked to her."

"Maybe Nora got sick and tired of his flings." Rose thought about it, but it just didn't seem likely. "No, that just doesn't fit. She sounded resigned and tolerant. Amused, even. And what would be the point? Killing Zunia wouldn't stop him. If he's a serial cheater, he'll just move on to the next one. Now, if *he* had died, I might think she was the guilty party. She did say 'til death do they part."

"Still, I think we ought to find out where those two were at the anointed hour."

Rose gazed at her and smiled. "Maybe your sweet nephew could help out two old biddies in search of a murderer?"

Laverne chuckled. "Well, there's no harm in asking, though I doubt it. Eli takes his position in the police department very seriously. He's coming by later to take his grand-dad and auntie to lunch. I'll tackle him then."

I t was still early, just a little after nine. Sophie sat on the foldaway bed, staring out the window to the street below. Sunday traffic was sparse, but Butterhill, like Gracious Grove, was a town where folks walked for fun and exercise, so there were lots of people coming to the coffee shop at the inn while on their Sunday-morning stroll. Her grandmother and godmother had come back to the room after breakfast with coffee and a muffin for her, then they had gone back downstairs to the morning's rescheduled lecture, which was on silver hallmarks.

Sophie was into teapots but didn't think a whole lecture on hallmarks would be bearable, and she wasn't an official ITCS member anyway. She was free to snoop, but where to start? Josh's suggestion that she ask Jason if he could find out if Dahlia Pettigrew was at the college overnight was still rolling around in her brain. She had replayed the conversation a hundred ways, and every time it ended with her asking him if he was at all interested in rekindling their abruptly shortened romance from a dozen years before. Until she could be sure she wouldn't embarrass herself, she didn't want to call him.

Her cell phone buzzed and she picked it up. Josh sent her a text with a selfie of him cross-eyed—he was at the lecture, but like most kids, could do several things at once—briefly telling her that he had talked to Emma again that morning, and her mother was indeed staying at Cruickshank. He had not been able to establish where the mom was that night and, even stranger, where Emma had been. He had expected her to say that she was in bed, asleep, or explain where she was, but she shrugged off his roundabout question about seeing her come in early in the morning. She also, according to Josh in his next text, had not seemed overly upset that her stepmother was murdered. When asked who could have done it she pretty much said any one of a number of people, given how her stepmother couldn't talk without offending someone.

Sophie was able to glean all of that from Josh's cryptically abbreviated texts.

The suspect list was growing, and no one had yet been knocked off it. Her phone chimed again, but this time the text was from Cissy. She and Dana were on their way to Butterhill in response to a confusing phone call from Cissy's grandmother, who claimed that everyone in the Silver Spouts hated her and they all thought she had killed Zunia Pettigrew out of spite.

"Oh, for heaven's sake!" Sophie exclaimed. Who knew there were octogenarian drama queens? She swiftly texted back that everything was actually fine and no one suspected Thelma, but Cissy messaged back that they were on the road anyway, so they'd come to at least check in with Cissy's grandmother, and stay for brunch. Sophie texted SuLinn to tell her if she wasn't interested in the hallmarks lecture and wanted to sneak out, they could all join up and have brunch and discuss what was going on.

Before they arrived Sophie decided she'd better get herself organized. Someone had targeted her beloved nana, trying to pin the blame on her by using her teapot to kill the ITCS chapter president. There seemed to be enough folks who disliked Zunia Pettigrew that finding the actual culprit would be daunting but not impossible. If it wasn't for her fear that the police would actually believe her grandmother did it, she'd probably just leave it alone.

But *no* one messed with Nana and got away with it. She got out the notebook she had bought with the rest of the stuff at the drugstore the previous evening and scribbled a list of suspects and her own thoughts.

Orlando Pettigrew—the husband is always the first suspect, right? And according to what Nana discovered from Mrs. Sommer, Zunia was cheating on her hubby with Walter. They've only been married a year or so!

And on that note . . . Walter Sommer—the boyfriend is always the next suspect, at least on all the true crime shows I've watched. He could have been tired of Zunia. According to Mrs. Earnshaw's overheard phone conversation, Orlando Pettigrew had supposedly claimed that his wandering wife was afraid of her love interest, and not serious about him, but there was no independent verification of that.

*Emma Pettigrew—given how foul Zunia Pettigrew
seemed to have been, Emma may have gotten sick
and tired of her stepmom. But would a teenager be
devious enough to steal Nana's teapot and use it?
Get Josh's opinion. He knows her better than I do.*
*Dahlia Pettigrew—the ex-wife. There was certainly
hatred there, and what a coincidence that she just
happened to be in the area.*

Sophie thought for a few seconds, then jotted a note to
try to find out if Dahlia Pettigrew's trip to Cruickshank was
long planned or spur-of-the-moment.

And she hated to even think it, but she had to consider
something she didn't want to.

Rhiannon Galway, she wrote, then sat tapping the note-
pad with her pen.

Poor Rhi. Sophie refused to believe it, but the cops would
certainly be looking at her, given what had apparently happened last year. Zunia had destroyed her chances of running
for the presidency of their division of the ITCS, and Rhi had
suffered, in more ways than one. Had there been any other
fallout, Sophie wondered? Had she lost business or standing
in the community from gossip? Maybe it was time to have
a serious talk with her and find out where she was at the
important time. In all the true crime shows, which Sophie
had been watching obsessively on sleepless summer nights
over the last two months, finding out where the suspect was
at the time of the murder was the first line of inquiry.

Was Rhiannon at the morning lecture or not? Sophie
texted Josh and he responded immediately; she was not at the
lecture. Sophie texted Rhiannon to ask if she was at the shop.

Shadow of a Spout

One way or another, Rhi was going to have to talk. *Please don't let it be Rhiannon*, Sophie thought. She looked around the room. Missing was the blue tapestry bag her grandmother carried her knitting and books in. The police had confiscated it when they were searching the room. "And please don't let the police think Nana did it," she said out loud, looking up to the ceiling. As ridiculous as it seemed to her, the police couldn't rule out Nana just because she was an octogenarian. Weird things had happened, like the grandmother who had hired her grandson to kill her husband, or the silver-haired Oklahoma granny who was the local drug kingpin.

She *really* had to stop watching true crime shows.

Chapter 13

Thelma sat behind the other Silver Spouts as the hallmark woman yammered on and on and on. Who cared that silver hallmarking in Britain dated back to the year 1300, and was intended to protect the public against fraud? Or that it was a symbol 'cause no one could read back then? So they were a bunch of ignoramuses . . . so what?

Bertie Handler bustled into the lecture room and went right up to Nora Sommer and whispered in her ear. There! Proof of what she was saying; the woman was *clearly* carrying on with the inn owner, but no one would listen to her! Now, if Rose said it, everyone would be all agog and crowding around her asking her questions.

Brooding, she glared at Rose Freemont's back and curly silver hair. Why did everyone love the woman so much?

She supposed, if she had to admit it, Rose was usually smiling and greeted everyone with a sincere question about their day, their health or what their week had been like. And she always seemed to be doing something for someone else. Rose donated extra baked goods to the food pantry at Laverne's church. Gilda made sure Thelma heard all about it.

The woman was just too . . . Something was buzzing. *What the heck was that?* She peered around and spied SuLinn looking at her infernal cell phone again. Her roomie quietly got up and sidled out of the row of chairs, then left the room. May as well have that thing glued to her ear, her and Josh both. *And* Sophie. *And* Cissy. Whole lot of them, a lost generation that could only communicate by some device, rather than face-to-face. The art of communication was gonna be lost forever.

Though it sure would be handy to have one of those thing-amajigs for times when you got yourself in a spot of trouble, Thelma thought, screwing up her mouth and staring up at the ceiling. Like the time Thelma got locked in the storeroom at La Belle Époque after Gilda had gone home for the day and had to bust the door handle with a can of tomatoes. Or the time she got wedged into a parking space at the MediMart in Ithaca and had to wait until a skinny fellow came along to help her out.

Maybe she'd have to get her one of those blasted things after all. Then she'd be able to call Cissy whenever she wanted! She nodded. That's what she was going to do, and then she'd be one step up on Rose Freemont, a senior pioneer in a brave new world!

S ophie was just adding another name to her notes because it had occurred to her that the pastor's weird obsession with Zunia, combined with his apparent lack of success with her despite his delusion that she was about to run away with him, made him a prime candidate for murderer as a spurned lover. Just as Pastor Frank took his place on her suspect list, there was a tap at the door. Sophie got up, flung the door open and Cissy threw herself into Sophie's arms.

"Soph, oh, Soph, is Grandma okay? Are you *sure* she's not a suspect? I'd feel just awful if she had done something stupid."

Sophie held up under the assault and exchanged a wry look with Dana Saunders, who entered behind Cissy and shrugged.

"I've been trying to tell her on the whole drive here that it is just her grandmother dramatizing herself again, but Cissy is convinced the woman is in trouble. I never knew that 'drama queenism' was a gene mutation."

"What does *that* mean?" Cissy asked, looking over her shoulder at her friend and employee.

"Nothing! Nothing at all." Dana rolled her eyes.

"First, no, Cissy, your grandmother is not a suspect. Nana kinda is, kinda isn't, which is why it's important they get the right person." Sophie hugged Cissy, then released her. "I'm so glad to see you guys. Have I got a lot to tell you!"

Just then SuLinn poked her head in the open door. "Is this a private party, or can anyone join?" she said, with a shy smile, her straight black hair swinging down over her shoulders.

"SuLinn! So you *did* sneak out of the lecture."

The young woman sighed, dramatically. "Oh my word, boooring! The woman knows her stuff, but I swear she could tell me the most interesting piece of gossip and I'd still fall sleep. I don't care about silver hallmarks anyway." Her tone changed subtly, as did her expression. She eyed Sophie and murmured, "Can I talk to you for a minute?"

"We know when we're not wanted," Dana said, tossing her streaked dark hair and widening her eyes. "We came prepared to stay overnight, but the inn owner says he's got no rooms, so Cissy and I will drop our bags in your room, SuLinn. Then we'll go get into some trouble downstairs. Meet us down there and we'll find a place to eat."

"Not here," Sophie said. "The dining room dinner was awful last night."

"Someplace else, then," Dana agreed. "Meet us in the lobby, you two. After brunch I have something to show you."

When the other two had gone, Sophie drew SuLinn over to her folding bed and sat down cross-legged opposite her. "So is rooming with Mrs. Earnshaw as much of a drag as I'm afraid it would be?" she asked as they settled.

SuLinn shrugged. "She's okay, I guess, but she kind of scares me. She's like my grandmother, always watching to see what I'm doing, trying to find something else she can criticize."

"But that's not what you wanted to talk to me about," Sophie guessed.

"No. It frightens me, the murder happening so close. It was right outside our rooms." She wrapped her arms around herself, like a big hug.

"And?"

SuLinn looked down for a moment, then released herself from the hug and looked into Sophie's eyes. "I can't keep this to myself. I thought I could, but I have to tell someone. Rhiannon Galway and Zunia Pettigrew had a nasty fight the evening before Zunia died, and Rhiannon said that the other woman had ruined her life and she wished she was dead."

"*What?*" Sophie goggled at the news, stunned.

"I hate this so much!" SuLinn said, hugging herself again, her voice trembling. "Telling on her, I mean. She's a nice person, but . . ." She sighed and shook her head. "When I saw her yesterday for just a moment I asked her about where she was that evening, and managed to work in the time I know I saw her. She told me she was home, but she *wasn't*. She was here in the inn, fighting with Zunia."

"Did you confront her?"

SuLinn's eyes widened. "No, of course not! I'd *never* do that."

"Maybe she mistook the time."

But SuLinn was already shaking her head. "I was pretty specific about the time because I had just checked my watch before I saw her. And anyway, how could she mistake where she was in the evening, when there was no reason for her to be at the inn? I came down to the lobby to call Randy. There was no way I was going to call my husband with Mrs. Earnshaw in the room." She blushed, a beautiful rosy tinge on her tan cheeks. "She listens to everything!"

Sophie was silent, trying to digest the news. She could think of a hundred reasons why Rhiannon might be at the inn in the evening, but not why she would lie about it.

Anxiously, SuLinn said, "I wouldn't have told you about Rhi lying about where she was, and about the argument, but if they're accusing Rose . . . we can't have that. And I wanted to tell *someone* the truth."

"You didn't tell the police?"

Her dark eyes wide, she lifted one shoulder. "They never asked me about Rhiannon. It probably doesn't mean anything, right? She was just mad."

Sophie reached out and touched SuLinn's arm, patting it. "I appreciate you telling me. I was going to go talk to Rhi anyway, but now I know what to ask."

"You won't tell her what I told you, will you?"

"If I do I won't say it was you who told me, okay? Anyone could have overheard them or seen them arguing."

She nodded, a relieved look on her face. "I'm so glad you're here, Sophie! It's good to have friends." She hesitated, but then with an earnest look on her oval face, she said, "It's weird, but in the year that I've lived in Gracious Grove I feel like I've lost my identity. You wouldn't have recognized me in New York. I was the assistant manager for advertising at a food and lifestyle magazine. I was so decisive, so take-charge, with staff answering to me."

"Are you looking for a job in GiGi? Someone with your skills could probably find something good."

"Randy and I have been trying to start a family, but it's not happening yet. I think I am going to look for a job. He didn't want me to start something just to have to quit if I got pregnant, but there's no sense in waiting."

"It'll happen," Sophie said, hoping it was true.

"Right this minute I'm glad you and Dana and Cissy are here. You all make me feel happier to be in GiGi," she said, calling their town what all locals called it.

"Let's go down and meet them."

Once they gathered in the lobby, where Dana was looking at the postcards, they decided to give the coffee shop a chance and Sophie was pleasantly surprised. The French toast she ordered was thick, properly soaked in the egg mixture with a hint of cinnamon, and seared on the flattop to a golden brown crust with a creamy interior. It was served with real butter and blueberry coulis. As they enthusiastically ate, they discussed what had happened. Sophie told them her theories.

"We've decided we're staying until tomorrow morning," Dana said, stirring sweetener into her coffee. There was mischief in her eyes. "I want to be in on the case again. I'm starting to think I missed my calling in life. I should have been a detective."

"Speaking of which, I saw the one my grandmother was interviewed by," Sophie said. "He was talking to the inn owner and the poor guy looked like he was going to have a heart attack!"

"That's Bertie Handler," SuLinn told the other two. "He's a real sweetheart, but kind of nervous. *Terrified* of storms. There was an awful one that evening right into the night. I was sitting in the lobby trying to call Randy, and I heard him telling one of the waitresses that he was going to hide out in the cellar if it got bad."

"That's where the kitchen is, in the cellar," Sophie said. "Su, was that before or after the . . . the other thing?" she asked, obliquely referring to the argument between Rhiannon and Zunia. "Not that it matters."

"Uh, just after."

"Okay."

Dana raised her brows but didn't ask about the exchange.

"About the cellar," Sophie said, returning to the topic. "I came through there from the parking lot when I arrived, guided by one of the staff. There's a lot more than just the kitchen down there."

Cissy roused herself out of her abstraction and said, "I

stayed here once in high school when we came to Butterhill for a swim meet. A bunch of us were doing a scavenger hunt and I was looking for . . . I can't remember what. I went downstairs and got lost, ended up in this little tiny room, no windows at all. I got locked in and it took *hours* before anyone found me!" She shot a side glance at Sophie. "We didn't all have cell phones back then. That was just for rich kids."

Like me, Sophie thought. She'd had a cool red Nokia phone the summer she was sixteen that had been the envy of them all, but she only ever used it to call her mom, because no one else she wanted to talk to had a cell phone.

"Enough about murder, as fascinating as I find the topic. I have someplace to show you girls, but you have to promise not to tell a soul," Dana said, standing and stretching.

She was gorgeously attired in an off-the-shoulder top with a peacock feather design and white walking shorts, her feet clad in gold Roman sandals. Her long dark hair was now streaked with gold and it lay in perfect loose curls caressing her neck. Peacock feather earrings dangled from her perfect lobes. She was flawless, as usual, Sophie thought, watching her.

"What is it you want to show us?" SuLinn asked as Cissy grabbed her taupe bucket purse off the bench seat.

"Shopping! It's a consignment shop with to-*die*-for fashions. I called and made sure they're open on Sundays, and they are!"

"You buy your clothes there?" Sophie asked. "I'm in!"

They all laughed together and headed out to the lobby, but were arrested by the sight of a tall, dark, good-looking man in a chocolate-brown suit jacket and tan slacks. He was at the check-in desk, his profile showing close-cropped hair, a clean-shaven sharp jawline and full lips. Bertie Handler bustled out of his office up to the desk and the man asked in a rich, carrying voice, "Could you tell me when the teapot society meeting is going to end?"

"Hubba hubba," Dana murmured, eyes wide.

Sophie approached and said, "My grandmother is a society member. Can I help you with something?"

His gaze moved from Sophie to the cluster of young women and settled on Dana, who eyed him back. *Definite sparks*, Sophie thought, her gaze flicking between the two.

"I'm Detective Elihu Hodge," he said, putting out his hand. "My aunt, Laverne Hodge, is also a member. And you are . . . ?"

"Sophie Freemont Taylor," she said, taking his hand. It was warm but not damp, and his clasp was firm. "I'm Rose Freemont's granddaughter."

He nodded. "Okay, sure . . . the chef who moved back to Gracious Grove. And your friends?"

She introduced them, Dana last, and *their* hand clasp lingered just a little longer. Dana actually blushed. Sophie hadn't *ever* seen her blush. Detective Hodge was a very good-looking man, the Seneca and African-American heritage showing even stronger in him than in Laverne. He had blue-gray eyes, *crazy* cool and hypnotic, set under a dark fringe of lashes and thick brows.

He tore his gaze away from Dana and spoke to Sophie. "I was going to take my aunt and granddad to lunch, but the chief asked me to help my colleagues investigate the murder that happened here. I'm going to have to cancel my lunch date, though I will be around the inn for most of the day."

Sophie was on her guard immediately. She was going to go speak to Rhiannon, but she was certainly not going to divulge to the police what SuLinn had overheard—not yet, anyway. There was no way Rhiannon had anything to do with the murder of Zunia, but Sophie felt it was important that the tea purveyor 'fess up to why she was in the hotel that night. Then they could decide if she needed to tell the police.

Just then the meeting room doors opened and the ITCS members—or what was left of them, since a few had gone home—spilled out in chattering groups. The detective caught his grandfather and aunt's attention as they emerged and took them aside to explain. He held his grandfather's elbow in a solicitous manner and both older folks listened to him intently, looking up at him with affection. Dana watched closely, her focus purposeful.

"What do you think?" Sophie said, sidling up to her.

"If he's single, I'm going to marry that man."

Sophie smothered a chuckle. "Come on, Dana, you don't even know him. He could be impossible!"

"Look at how he holds his grandfather's arm and how he talks to them! He's handsome, well mannered and dedicated to his relatives. He's employed. He's ambitious, or he wouldn't already be a detective." She glanced over at Sophie, eyebrows raised. "What's not to like?"

"Well, all right. I don't suppose *he* has anything to say in the matter."

"Oh, it'll *all* be up to him," Dana said, tossing her hair back over her shoulder. "Or at least he'll *think* it's all his idea."

Thelma trudged out of the convention room, looking grumpily around until Cissy waved. Her eyes lit up and her expression changed in a moment, from irritable to eager. Sophie thought that was adorable. She had decided to look at Thelma Mae Earnshaw as a special snowflake, an Oscar the Grouch in a world of happy Muppets. They all had to just accept her as she was, because she wasn't truly going to change. That she and Nana had reached a truce—or at least a cessation of hostilities, which was not quite the same thing—was a miracle, one to be protected and coddled at all costs, especially since they were next-door neighbors and in the same business.

Cissy reunited with her grandmother as Sophie took SuLinn aside. "I'm going to check in on Rhi and see what I can find out. Can you take care of the girls and give the message to Nana? Just say I have an errand to run. I want to do this on the sly, no questions asked."

SuLinn nodded.

Sophie slung her bag over her shoulder, slipped out the front door onto the sidewalk and oriented herself. She had to go south a couple of blocks, she thought. She got out her cell phone and checked her GPS app. She was right, and started walking. The day had turned hot and muggy, with a lowering sky that held in the humidity and foretold a storm in the evening. It was fortunate that she was wearing shorts and a tee and had her dark hair in an updo, because it was sweltering, the steamy air feeling like a warm breath on her skin.

Butterhill wasn't a big town and Rhiannon's tea shop was not that far away, seven blocks, maybe. It was an older building right on the sidewalk in an older part of town. The picture window with GALWAY FINE TEAS in gold lettering was shuttered and the lights off; a sign on the door said SEE YOU TUESDAY!

Sophie had expected that; Rhiannon was closed on Sundays and Mondays. But she lived behind the shop, so Sophie went down the sidewalk to the little blue door with the number 735 on it. Rhi's Ford was parked in the lane, so she was probably home. Sophie tapped on the door.

It took a couple of more taps, but finally the lock clicked and Rhiannon opened the door, blinking sleepily. "Soph! What are you doing here? Was I supposed to meet you? What day is today? What time is it?"

"Hey, Rhi. I'm here to see *you*, and no, you weren't supposed to meet me, and today is Sunday, and it's about eleven. You ran out of the dinner last night before I had a chance to talk to you."

The girl yawned and stretched, then pulled her tee down over the top of her thin cotton bed shorts. "Do you want coffee? Or tea? I've got English breakfast, Irish breakfast, rooibos, maté, chai, oolong . . . you name it."

"Nothing hot," Sophie groaned. "It's sweltering out here! Are you going to invite me in or what?"

"Sure, of course . . . Come on in." She turned and headed back into the dark apartment. "Make yourself at home," she said over her shoulder. "I'm going to get some clothes on."

Sophie entered the living room, closing the door behind her and looking around curiously. It was cool, with a slightly stale odor that hinted at poor dusting habits. A stained beige sofa and scratched coffee table were lined up in front of an old-style clunky TV, with a side table sporting an ugly lamp and a stack of magazines on a chair by the window that overlooked the lane. A vase with dead flowers was on the windowsill, alongside a fern that was brown and crispy.

On the wall by a bookcase there was a collage photo frame surrounded by other pictures. She scanned them as she tried to figure out how she was going to ask Rhi the difficult questions, like . . . Why did she lie to SuLinn about being at the inn that evening? What had her relationship with Walter Sommer truly been? Was it an affair, as the rumormongers would have it? And did she kill Zunia Pettigrew? There was no delicate way to tiptoe around a question like that, but she had to try. Though she didn't believe it possible that Rhi was a killer, it sure would be good to hear about her innocence from Rhiannon herself.

Sophie absently looked over the photos of Rhi when she was a kid, in her mother's shop, at the lake, as well as at various ITCS conventions through the years, first with an older dark-haired woman who must be her mother and then more recently alone, with the Sommers and various other members. It was an important part of her life, it appeared, and had been for many years.

How much had Zunia's threats cost Rhi, emotionally? Zunia was a fairly recent member of the society while Rhi had been a member for years, so it must have been a bitter pill to swallow, feeling compelled to withdraw from the presidency election as she had. It was telling that no one had apparently even told Rhi about the new schedule of events, starting this morning. Was she being ostracized for some reason, sidelined to avoid embarrassing the ITCS president and his wife?

The room was tidy enough, if drab and boring, so there was little else to look at. She read the titles of the books piled haphazardly on the shelves. Some were paperbacks, a whole lot of Stephen Kings sprinkled with some Dean Koontz, Clive Barker and Peter Straub. Sophie shivered. Nothing she'd read! Especially at night with the lights out and alone. The only time horror novels or movies were good, Sophie reflected, with more than a little gloom, was if you had a boyfriend you could cuddle up to. In other words, never, in her case.

Shadow of a Spout

There was a pretty little box with stone inlay on the bookshelf, and she picked it up to admire it, but as she turned it over, a piece of paper fell out. She opened it slightly, enough to see "*For my darling sweet Rhiannon . . .*" in a familiar hand, when she heard Rhiannon coming. She folded it back up, stuck it in the box and put it on the shelf. She recognized the handwriting from notes her grandmother had received in the last few weeks concerning the ITCS convention. That was the sloping cursive of Walter Sommer, a man who prided himself on sending handwritten invitations to each teapot-collecting society.

She hadn't wanted to believe the pastor when he said Rhi and Walter were having a fling, but how else did one explain his note? He wrote "*For my darling sweet Rhiannon.*"

Chapter 14

Rhiannon, now dressed in jean shorts and a tank top, returned to the living room, sweeping her auburn hair up into a ponytail and fastening it with a thick purple elastic. "What brings you here?"

"I was just wanting to get an insider's view of some of these teapot society members. I can't believe it, but folks are actually gossiping that Nana killed that woman with her teapot!"

"I *heard* that it was done with your grandmother's teapot. Weird." She went into the little kitchenette that was off the living room. "I've got some iced tea I made with fruit zinger tea and some lemon balm from a neighbor's garden," she said, sticking her head out of the tiny room. "Want to try it?"

Sophie said, "Sure."

"Sit. I'll bring it into the living room."

Rhiannon seemed so nonchalant about all that had

happened at the inn. Was that innocence, or an attempt to *feign* innocence? Sophie couldn't believe where her mind was going, that she was even considering the notion that Rhiannon had anything to do with the murder, but SuLinn's information about Rhiannon lying about being at the inn had thrown her for a loop. Sophie slipped off her sandals and sat cross-legged on the sofa. A moment later Rhiannon came into the living room with two tall glasses, condensation frosting the outside. "Here, give it a go. My mom e-mailed me the recipe."

Sophie sipped and then took a long drink. "That's good. I might try something like this in the tearoom. We've got iced tea, but I'd like something a little different—a signature drink, you know?"

"I'll write this down, and you can play with it. You're the chef!"

"Maybe I could use a chai blend, or something like that." Sophie examined Rhiannon. "I was noticing the photos on the wall. You've been going to the ITCS convention for a long time."

"Long as I can remember. My mom was one of the founding members before I was born. She lived in New York City at one point, and then moved here when she got pregnant with me."

They had talked enough over the summer that Sophie knew Rhiannon's mom was a single mother who left the big city for the good of her unborn child. She used some inherited money to start a tea shop in Butterhill, trading on her Irish heritage to import the very best of English and Irish blends, at first, before getting into professional blending herself.

"But it seems lately that there has been some infighting," Sophie said, eyeing her friend. She was going to sugarcoat it, but what was the point? She had always been straightforward, and it generally served her well. "You got caught in the cross fire last year, I understand."

"Cross fire?" Rhiannon asked, her voice cool.

After looking at the photos, Sophie could see that Rhi resembled her mother except for having thin lips and a strong set to her chin. "You must know what I mean." Sophie's mind was jumbled with too many things she wanted to ask about; the note had confused her and put her off balance. She wondered whether there was any connection between that and Rhi's conflict with Zunia. "I heard that Zunia Pettigrew black-mailed you into dropping out of the division presidency run last year."

Rhiannon took a long drink of her iced tea. In the dimness of the apartment, with the shades still drawn against the heat of the day, her pale skin glowed, the freckles dotting her face standing out. She flipped her ponytail with one hand and put the cold glass against her neck. The silence stretched out, but she finally said, "My mother would say I shouldn't speak ill of the dead."

"Nana says the same thing. But then she says she supposes it's better than speaking ill of the living."

She flashed a quirky grin, only one side of her mouth lifting. "I love your grandmother. She's awesome."

"So what I'm saying is, why shouldn't we speak ill of Zunia Pettigrew? It doesn't seem that anyone other than Pastor Frank liked her much."

"Poor Frank," Rhiannon said softly. "I'll never understand why Zunia was leading him on like she was."

"You think she led him on?"

Rhi took another long sip of her iced tea. "She had the poor guy tied up in knots. You didn't know her, but she was like . . ." She made a noise in her throat and shook her head, her thick ponytail swinging. "My mother says that her Irish grandmother talked all the time about imps and sprites, and one in particular. She'd tell Mom that if she wasn't a good little girl, the goblin would get her. I guess a goblin is an evil, crabby, nasty creature. Ever since I met Zunia Pettigrew, she's who I picture when I think of goblins."

"Wow, I know I said we should feel free to speak ill of her, but . . . that's harsh!"

"But it's true! She *was* evil. Five foot nothing, squat and mean-looking. How she got a husband I'll never know."

"She must have had something going for her. She got Orlando Pettigrew to leave his wife and Pastor Frank was crazy for her." Not to mention Walter Sommer, apparently. Who could throw beautiful Rhiannon over for Zunia Pettigrew? *If* that's what happened to Rhiannon and Walter's relationship. The woman must have had a bizarre kind of sex appeal.

"I guess she had that confidence thing," Rhiannon mused, staring down into her glass. "I've never been able to master it, but men seem to fall for it. You know, that *I know you want me* kind of thing. Zunia was like that."

"But she couldn't have been nasty *all* the time, right? Otherwise *no one* would like her."

Rhiannon glanced up, a brooding look on her pretty face. "The first time I met her, I guess I thought she was pretty terrific. She had this passionate character and it was riveting, in a way. She just seemed to care so *much* about everything, like she was going to suck life dry. You felt . . . How can I explain it?" She sighed and shifted. "It was like her world was intense color and everyone else was gray."

"I guess that would attract people."

"You should know," Rhiannon said, darting a glance at her. "You kinda have that, you know—the passion thing. When you get talking about stuff you care for, it's like no one else can get a word in edgewise."

Sophie shrugged off the uneasy feeling that it wasn't meant as a compliment. Her enthusiasm for life and her chosen profession was sometimes an asset, sometimes a liability, depending on how it struck those with whom she was dealing. Maybe Rhiannon was one of those who found it off-putting. "But why the teapot society, do you think?" Sophie watched her friend, her emotions tangled with all she feared and wondered about, the fight Rhi had had with Zunia, lying about it, the note Sophie had found from Walter Sommer.

"Why did she belong to it, you mean? Instead of some bigger, glitzier society, like the New York Classical Music Society, or the Italian Art Society? I have a feeling she met Orlando Pettigrew in some other capacity and joined the society to get closer to him. Poor Dahlia; she never saw Zunia coming."

"I've met Dahlia. I guess she's pretty bitter."

"Wouldn't *you* be?" Rhiannon said, a flush tinting her skin with pink. "I mean, you'd think you'd be safe going with your husband to teapot collectors' meetings, right? But no, some skank comes along and steals your husband right out from under your nose. It stinks."

"You seem to feel strongly about married men not doing that kind of thing, cheating on their wives," Sophie said, tiptoeing toward asking about Walter.

"I sure do!" she said. "Women shouldn't poach other women's husbands; that's all there is to it." Her expression changed, becoming pensive. "And if . . . if something happens, if you get caught up in something, then you pull up your big-girl panties, back off and leave him alone. You try to forget him. You just . . . You go away."

Sophie heart constricted. She felt so bad for Rhiannon, who must have been caught up in much the same thing with Walter: an older man wooing her, her attempts to resist, loneliness and a moment of poor judgment making her weaken to his charms. She didn't get it, especially not with Walter, but it must be difficult to live with yourself after. "Some men just have to have any woman they see," she said obliquely, hoping that wasn't offensive.

"No kidding! Anyway . . ." She tossed back the rest of her drink. "What was it you were here for? I don't think you've said yet."

"I guess I just wanted your take on what happened. You know them all a lot better than I do. Who do you think killed Zunia? And who would be cold-blooded enough to set Nana up for it by stealing her teapot and using it as a weapon?"

"Geez, that's a lot to ask."

"Okay, let's start easy. You were at the first meeting that Friday afternoon, right?"

"Sure."

"It seems like Zunia went out of her way to anger several people. I mean, she was really dismissive about a couple of the ladies who took their teapots up to her for evaluation, and then she pretty much told Nana her teapot was worthless. Did you notice anyone getting upset?"

"Other than your grandmother, who tore a strip off Zunia?"

"I would have loved to see that. What are the chances? Nana's so mild-mannered usually, and the one time she puts someone down, the woman gets murdered. The real problem is that during the tea after the meeting Mrs. Earnshaw went around and jokingly told everyone Nana was a real firecracker and that folks in GiGi were afraid of her. She even said someone died in Nana's tearoom, which is *totally* not true. I can't believe people fell for it."

"Why would the woman do that?"

"You have to know Mrs. Earnshaw. She had every kid in the neighborhood afraid of her when I was young. And over the years she played a bunch of dirty tricks on Nana before they declared a truce a couple of months ago." Sophie then went through what she knew about everyone's movements that night. "What were *you* up to Friday evening?"

Rhiannon colored faintly. "I just watched some TV and went to bed and read a book. Normal Friday night. What else?"

Sophie shrugged. "Someone said they saw you at the inn, that's all."

Rhiannon stiffened and narrowed her eyes. "What's this all about?"

Watching her friend, Sophie said, "I just thought if you *were* there you may have seen something, or someone, out of the ordinary, you know?"

"I may have stopped in there for a second. Poor Bertie is having trouble with the inn, and I said I'd try to find him another cook."

"So that explains why the food was so awful if he's having trouble with his chef." Sophie still watched Rhiannon, and asked, "What time *was* that?"

She shrugged. "I don't remember. It was just for a moment, no big deal. What is this all about, Sophie, really? Don't you believe me? What are you suggesting?"

"I'm not suggesting anything, Rhi. You know me better than that."

"Do I?" Rhiannon stood and took Sophie's empty glass. "I have to get moving. I have stuff to do today. We talked a week or so ago, and I think I remember your grandmother saying she wants an order of Auntie Rose's Tea-riffic Tea Blend, so I'm going to print the labels this morning and put together a box for her."

Sophie stood, too, and touched Rhiannon's bare arm. "Rhi, listen to me: I'm sorry, and I don't mean to imply anything, but someone did see you at the inn, and . . . and they saw you arguing with Zunia. I know darn well you wouldn't have done anything to her, but people are bound to talk, you know?" Her words hung in the air, practically visible, the tension between them like a wire. What she wanted Rhiannon, her new friend, to say was, yes, she had been there, yes, she had argued with Zunia because . . . of something silly, like she bumped into her in the lobby, or insulted her dress.

Instead Rhiannon's chin went up, and she said, her tone sharp as a needle, "You want the scoop on Zunia Pettigrew? She was a hateful, miserable, manipulative, needy little husband stealer. Now, I have a busy day ahead of me, Sophie, so I'm sure you'll understand if I ask you to leave."

A few seconds later Sophie was on the other side of the door staring at the brass numbers. What was there to do but turn and walk away, knowing that Rhiannon was watching and waiting for her to go, peeking out of the door curtains. Maybe she hadn't spent enough time with her new friend to notice that she was moody and changeable. Of course, confronting her about being seen arguing with a murder victim probably wasn't the best test of a new friendship.

The sultry humidity made the air feel like she was swimming through a vat of thick pea soup, the kind Sophie made only for cold, blustery New York afternoons at In Fashion. She turned her mind away from the conversation with Rhiannon and thought about soup. Food always soothed her nerves. Fall was coming, even though the August heat made it seem that the cool winds of autumn would never arrive. She had to consider what kinds of soups she would add to the menu, and when. Focusing on her plans for the tearoom helped her get through the walk back to the inn in the sweltering air.

But the sight of three Butterhill police cruisers in the parking lot didn't do her mood any good. The police detective had asked Nana to stay in Butterhill for the time being, her grandmother had said, but that was silly! She was only an hour away, for heaven's sake. Sophie walked into the lobby and let her eyes adjust to the dimness, while the cool air from the air-conditioning evaporated the film of perspiration on her neck and arms. It was just about noon, and she wondered where everyone was. The coffee shop was full as usual and the dining room appeared to have folks in it, but no one from her party of friends. She texted Dana, saying, *"Where R U?"*

Maybe they all headed off to Dana's secret consignment shop, and maybe her grandmother and the other Silver Spouts were at another convention event. The convention room doors were shut tight, and there was a MEETING IN PROGRESS sign on the door, so that was a good guess.

Sophie couldn't think of anything but getting Nana off the hook. What was bothering her most was, how did someone get into Laverne and Nana's room to steal the teapot? They had both agreed that they locked the door behind them before going down to dinner.

She shouldn't interfere because the police would be asking these same questions, but no one else was as motivated as she was. Bertie Handler would be able to tell her about security, how the keys were handled, how the cleaning staff was selected, how the master keys were guarded, that kind of thing. Would someone random be able to just lift a key from the maid? Was there a way to jimmy the locks? She went over to the check-in desk and leaned on it, trying to see into the office through the open door. She dinged the little bell on the counter. "Hello! Mr. Handler? Yoo hoo!"

No one came out of the office. Maybe he was in there and just hadn't heard her. She went around the counter and ducked her head in, then, eyes wide, walked right in. It was as if a whirlwind had gone through the office, lifting every shred of paperwork and tossing it haphazardly around. It was a small room, wood-paneled and with a bank of file cabinets, tables, office chairs, stacked chairs and various pieces of office equipment squeezed in, lining every wall. But the wild flurry of paperwork distracted from other thoughts. It literally covered every surface, even the upturned stack of old dining room chairs, where a heap of file folders spilled sideways, saved from toppling off only by the rungs of the chair.

This was no way to run an inn. But as her gaze drifted she began to see a kind of organization and found the desk among it all, the desktop computer on, photographs of local scenes drifting lazily across the screen like ducks on a pond. How could anyone work in this chaos? She pushed some of the piles of papers on the desk into neater stacks, but one piece was longer than the others so she pulled it out. It was labeled COMPLAINT with a law firm heading. She scanned it and her eyes widened even farther.

Summarizing the jumble of legal jargon, it stated that Zunia Pettigrew was suing Bertie Handler, owner of the Stone and Scone Inn, for defamation of character. It claimed that Bertram Julius Handler did with malice use electronic mail to inform Mrs. Nora Sommer of a purported affair between the complainant and Mr. Walter Sommer. It was dated the day before Zunia's death. Sophie dropped the paper as if it were on fire, but then swiftly tucked it back into the pile, sending the stack askew as it had been. It stuck out of the stack but she didn't have time to correct it, as she heard footsteps.

"What are you doing in my office?" a voice behind her said.

She whirled to find Bertie Handler standing in the door and staring at her in an accusatory manner, his expression dark and very unlike the meek demeanor she had noted the night before. "I came looking for you, Mr. Handler."

His face reddened as he noted where her hand rested, on the pile of papers. "If that's the case, then why are you snooping through my papers? You should get out."

Chapter 15

He may have intended to sound menacing, but just came off as peevish.

"I wasn't snooping. I came in here looking for you, but I saw how the place looked, like . . . like someone had rifled through all your stuff. Have you had a break-in?" she asked, assuming an air of innocence.

"No, this is how it always looks. I'm not big on organization," he admitted, bustling over and pulling the lawsuit paper out of the stack. He glanced at it and threw it down with a sniff.

"What's that?" she said, looking down at it as if for the first time.

"Something that isn't your business and doesn't matter now anyway." He took a deep breath, and his expression changed more to the one she recognized, conciliatory and mild. "I'm sorry, I'm just so . . ." He shook his head. "It's been an awful couple of days. I'm so uptight, and the police are crawling all over my inn." His gray eyes watered and he slumped down in the chair by the computer and put his head in his hands. "I just don't know how I'm going to go on."

She perched gingerly on the edge of the desk and said, "I know it seems like it's going to do you in, but just tough it out, Mr. Handler."

"What do you know about toughing it out?" he said miserably.

"I know, trust me."

"You're so young. You know nothing!" He stared at the lawsuit paper. "At least I don't have to worry about *that* anymore," he said, pushing the legal page aside.

"A lawsuit," she commented, reading it. The law firm name was Green and LaPacho, attorneys-at-law. She frowned; something wasn't right. The letterhead looked odd, not very professional, and the firm name . . . "How was this delivered to you?"

"It was left in an envelope on the check-in desk. Why?"

Sophie didn't answer. As far as she knew, notice of a legal complaint had to be delivered by a process server. And it all seemed to have happened suspiciously quickly. Legal matters took a while. "Why would Zunia Pettigrew sue you?" Sophie asked.

"For lies! She made things up and then had the *nerve* to sue me."

He seemed on edge, and she already knew he was worried about losing the ITCS convention. "I thought you two were friends?"

"We were. I never had any trouble with Zunia, but suddenly . . ." He paused, then said, "I guess it doesn't matter anymore. Suddenly she accuses me of e-mailing Mrs. Sommer to snitch on her and Walter's affair! As if I'd do that. Why would I?"

Why indeed. "She was mistaken, I suppose. How did it come out? Was Mrs. Sommer actually told by e-mail? *Was* there an affair?" She already knew that was the case from what Nora Sommer had told Nana, but she was interested in what he'd say.

Bertie looked over at her with a sly smile. "Oh, sure, there was an affair. With Walter there was *always* an affair; I've known him long enough to know that." His smile died. "But I told Zunia, I didn't say—or send—a *word* to Nora. Why would I stir up *that* hornet's nest? The only person worse to deal with than Zunia is Nora, though at least she's always fair. In the end, Zunia believed me and was going to withdraw the lawsuit. She told me so that . . . that night."

"But you *still* had an argument with her, before you came to terms," Sophie said, hazarding a guess.

His gray eyes narrowed. "How did you know that?"

She didn't until that moment, and stayed silent.

"Did someone . . . ?" He took a deep breath and shook his head. "Zunia started it, not me."

"Was it a *bad* argument?"

"Not in the scope of Zunia Pettigrew arguments."

"Mr. Handler, everyone agrees that she was an unpleasant woman. Why did so many folks go along with whatever she wanted?"

"You had to know Zunia," he said, on a sigh. "Every single time I have tried to be reasonable with her when she's asking something impossible she turns it around and becomes the injured party. I don't know how she does it, but it happens *every* time. She could be sweet as pie, but that was when she was most dangerous, so you just learned to go along with what she wanted."

"To avoid a quarrel," she said, nodding in sympathy. "I had a cook like that at my restaurant once. He always made every disagreement a personal vendetta, like people were out to get him." She vividly remembered Paolo, who hated that she was female, younger than him, and had her own restaurant. For a time she had wallowed in guilt on that score because she knew she had gotten her own restaurant at such a young age in part because of her father's business connections and her mother's social ones. But then she had steeled her nerve and decided that didn't matter. The food mattered. But back to Paolo . . . "He was a nightmare. It got so that the other cooks were circumventing my orders just to placate him."

"What did you do?"

"Fired him," she said. It had taken every ounce of guts she had, but she did it through the howling maelstrom of his invective. He wasn't willing to go and actually had a knife in his hand—not that he was threatening her; he was threatening to cut himself—so she had the police remove him from the premises. She didn't have so much trouble being taken seriously in her own restaurant after that.

"You can't fire a customer," Bertie said.

"True, but was it worth continuous aggravation?"

"I only had to deal with her once a year," he said, with a shrug, and turned to his computer, rapidly typing, then turned to sort through a stack of papers to the left of his desk.

Perhaps that was true, Sophie thought, but Zunia was threatening his livelihood by recommending that the ITCS move the convention. This was getting ridiculous. When she added up those she knew of who had a reason to kill Zunia, there were far too many: Bertie Handler, who was afraid Zunia would take the convention away from the inn; Nora, the spurned wife of Zunia's lover; Walter's ex-lover Rhiannon, who had been replaced, presumably, in Walter's affections by the dead woman. Who else? A whole nest of Pettigrews: the soon-to-be-deserted husband, Orlando; the miserable stepdaughter, Emma; the abandoned wife, Dahlia.

How was she ever going to cross anyone off the list of suspects? Taking a deep breath, she reminded herself it wasn't her job. This was a homicide and the police were dealing with it. She trusted that they were dedicated and would get the right result in the end, especially now that Laverne's nephew was on the job.

However . . . in the meantime, Nana was suffering. She would never let anyone know but Sophie could tell this was wearing on her, and no one—aside from Laverne—would care about her well-being the way Sophie did. Poor Nana was worrying that because of Thelma Mae Earnshaw's unfortunate jest, the killer had taken the opportunity to point the finger of blame directly at Rose Freemont and use her teapot . . .

Use her teapot!

Sophie leaned against the office doorjamb and pondered. It all started at the tea after the convention meeting. Whoever killed Zunia had to have been at the tea after the meeting, and so privy to the discussion about Nana being dangerous. She supposed an outsider could have heard about it, but how likely was that? Sophie had known all along that the culprit must be among the ITCS convention goers, but that kind of proved it.

Bertie Handler hadn't been in the room, as far as Sophie knew. He may have heard about the conflict between Zunia and Nana later, but it was far-fetched to think that he would have based a murder method on a secondhand story about a lethally dangerous elderly woman.

Her eye caught on the "legal" paper. In fact it was almost as far-fetched as Zunia Pettigrew's lawsuit. There was no lawsuit and no such law firm, Sophie was sure of that now. It was too much of a coincidence that the names "Green" and "LaPacha" had one thing in common: They were both types of tea. For some reason of her own Zunia wanted Bertie—and maybe others—to think she was suing him.

Why would you do that rather than actually file a lawsuit? She could think of several reasons, the most important being there was really no grounds to file it, and another was to placate someone else in her life, like her husband or her lover. She must have needed to assume the mantle of righteous indignation against the "rumor" that she and Walter were having an affair.

And another thing . . . Surely Bertie wouldn't steal a guest's item to kill someone with it since the police would know that of all people in the inn, he had access to every room. She eyed the innkeeper, who was staring at a split screen image on the computer. It looked like video from security cameras, and she could see the cooks moving around in the kitchen downstairs, as well as the back door propped open in another quarter of the screen and someone exiting the coffee shop into the lobby. Bertie seemed a million miles away, though, not watching it so much as staring blankly at it. "Mr. Handler, where were you that evening, anyway, the evening of Zunia's death?"

His cheeks flushed, and his watery eyes widened. "There was a terrible thunderstorm. I d-don't like thunder and lightning. I went down to the basement to wait it out."

"All evening?"

"Well, no, but until after the b-body was discovered. I was downstairs when the alarm went off." He sounded nervous now and fidgeted with his chair, using the lever to lower it, then rising to get it to come up again.

"Do you keep the office locked?"

"Of course!" He sat and pulled up to the computer again. "I lock it right and tight at the end of the day—usually by eight or so—and all calls coming in to the check-in desk are patched through to my suite of rooms, on the other side of the stairway," he said, flapping his hand in the direction of the little hallway where the door to the basement was. "It's exhausting. I'm never really off duty."

Except when he was hiding downstairs from storms. Was that the truth, or a handy alibi for being incommunicado at the relevant time?

"Do you keep your cell phone on you when you're downstairs?"

"When I remember. Look, I have to get back to work and figure out what to do about some guests that are supposed to be coming in this evening. This awful m-murder has thrown everything out of whack. It'll be the death of me yet!"

"Sorry to keep you," she said, pushing away from the desk. If he was telling the truth and he wasn't the murderer, then the killer must have gotten the teapot out of Nana's room using a master key. In that case it had to have been sometime while the office was unlocked and the key available. The housekeeper finished by dinner, at which time she presumably handed the key back to Bertie. "Talk to you later," she said.

He gave kind of a tired wave, and put his head in his hands, covering his eyes.

She hesitated, but then said, "Mr. Handler, one more thing."

He looked up.

"I've been trying to figure out how whoever killed Mrs. Pettigrew got the teapot out of my grandmother's room. How do *you* think that happened?"

He looked uncomfortable. "How am I supposed to know? The police asked me the same question, but those kinds of people are ingenious, right? I mean, if someone is going to kill someone . . ." He let it trail off.

As he spoke she eyed the pegboard with sets of keys hanging from the pegs. "Are those all the inn keys?"

He followed her gaze and shifted in his chair. "Sure."

"Are they all accounted for?"

"Of *course*!" He straightened and narrowed his eyes. "What are you suggesting, young lady? Are you saying I have been remiss? I assure you—"

Someone rang the bell at the desk and he jumped up and trotted past her. She waited a moment, but he appeared to be busy from the steady hum of voices she heard outside the door. She nipped over to the board on the wall and examined the keys for a moment.

The inn was old and old-fashioned, so even apart from the room keys a number of other keys were used, all different types, probably for locks that had been replaced over the years. At least the keys were labeled: boiler room; storage—main floor; storage—second floor; storage—basement; kitchen-basement; dining room; convention room . . . and voilà. Housekeeping master key. On an impulse she slipped it off the peg and shoved it into her shorts pocket then left the office, sliding past Bertie at the check-in desk.

A tall, slim older woman, one of the ladies from the ITCS

convention, was renewing her room for the night. "I only need it one more night, but given the trouble, I think I ought to get it free."

"Ma'am, I'm sorry, but it's not really my fault your convention is running on another day, and—"

"It most certainly *is* your fault, or the fault of the inn. You clearly have no standards and let the *worst* people in. For a good customer, given your slapdash ways and the housekeeper's terrible sloppy job with my room yesterday, you ought, at the very least, to give me a discount."

Housekeeper! Why wasn't Melissa there right that moment using the key? Sophie wondered. Maybe she was late. *Really* late! It was noon. Or maybe her schedule was not as set in stone as she had implied. Interesting thought.

"As far as our guests, the only people with rooms here right now are ITCS attendees," he said, his tone snippy. "Melissa does the best she can with the rooms, but she's only here until about dinner and then another girl is supposed to come in for the evening, but half the time she doesn't show up. I can't help what goes wrong after that."

"Doesn't matter," the combative woman shot back. "I wanted fresh towels the first night, and there was no one to get them! I even rang the desk."

"I'm so sorry, but that must have been during the storm, and you know it's dangerous to answer the phone with a lightning storm going on. I was . . . I was indisposed."

"Do you mean you were not even at the desk?"

His gaze flitted to Sophie, and he just shrugged. "I'm so sorry for your inconvenience. I'll give you a ten percent discount on the entire bill as compensation. Now let's get you set up for one more night."

Sophie, who was pretending to leaf through the postcards on a rack at the far end of the check-in desk, felt for him. As a restaurateur, she occasionally had diners requesting items be taken off their bill when they had eaten the whole thing or most of it, claiming it wasn't what they were expecting or wasn't up to snuff. She had learned to keep her cool and in most cases obliged; it wasn't worth the bad rap they would give the restaurant otherwise, especially with social media being as prevalent a way of communicating as it was today. It hadn't been easy at first, but she had become philosophical about it. *Most* people were good patrons and didn't rip her off.

Melissa, the housekeeper, breezed through the door from the basement, chattering to a young fellow who was following her. "I'll show you the routine and Bertie can sign you up as relief."

The woman toddled away from the desk, happy with her discount. Melissa waved to Sophie then said to her boss, "Bertie, this is Domenico Dominguez," she said, hitching her thumb over her shoulder at the small, nervous-looking dark-haired fellow, who was dressed in jeans and a clean T-shirt. "He comes highly recommended, so I said he could try out for the evening housekeeper job. He's going to shadow me today."

"What happened to Brittany?" he asked, looking the fellow over with skepticism. "Wasn't she supposed to be working today? Isn't today your day off? What's going on?" His tone teetered on the verge of hysteria.

"She never shows up when I ask her to. Do you see her here today? No. Did you see her yesterday? Last evening? No again. Night before last? Same thing," she snapped. "Left me doing *everything*, including vacuuming the halls and dusting, and I'm tired of it. I finally phoned her house this morning and her mom told me she's taken off, gone to California, or something. That's why I'm here. Didn't you wonder who was coming in?"

"Oh, Lord, why am I being tested?" Bertie wailed.

"It's okay, Bertie," Melissa said, her voice confident and the snappish tone gone. "Dom, here, is a great guy. He has two jobs and he's never late to either of them. You know Pete at the Pizza Stop . . . Dom does night cleaning for him, and he can fit this in before it. You can call Pete for a reference, if you want, but I've already spoken to him."

"Okay, but I need to get his particulars and we have to fill out an employee information form and a W-four," Bertie fussed.

They all went into the office and Sophie's stomach tightened. Would Bertie notice that the key was gone? Well, of *course* he would, because Melissa would go to get the key and ask where it was. She'd have to confess what she'd done or this was going to get ugly. She heard them talking and a file drawer slam.

She retreated to the alcove, where some chairs and a big palm hid her from view, but there was no roar of anger, no exclamation of puzzlement. The threesome came back out chatting, though she couldn't make out their voices. Melissa had a clipboard with some paperwork on it, and Bertie followed the two toward the coffee shop. Sophie seized the moment. She looked around, but there was no one else in sight, so she skipped across the lobby, slipped into the office, hung the key back up and hopped back out toward the stairs.

"Okay, when you're done we'll go through it all," Bertie was saying. "Can you bring me a coffee when you and Dom are finished with your lunch and you've explained the routine to him? I hope he works out better than Brittany."

Sophie raced up a few steps to the turn in the staircase and rested back against the wall, catching her breath. She had a weird feeling that this was exactly what the murderer did and how he or she felt. That little exercise had proved one thing: Bertie was not the most vigilant person in the world and there was ample opportunity for someone with good nerves to filch the key, run up to Nana's room, steal the teapot and replace the key with no one the wiser. Whether that was possible that evening was the question.

So now she knew how the killer had possibly gotten the key, but that didn't eliminate a single person from the list. It was time to call—or text—Jason to ask about Dahlia Pettigrew.

The lecture had been enlightening, Rose thought, but it was hard to concentrate when you knew that the police detective still felt there was a possibility you had killed someone. O'Hoolihan hadn't come right out and said it, but it was in the air every time he tracked her down to confirm or clarify some detail of her day or night. The last time, Rose had made sure he had an earful about what she thought of Orlando and Zunia Pettigrew's relationship. She told him about the conversation Thelma had overheard as Pettigrew talked on the phone to someone, and every other detail she could think of. There was no room for worries about being a snitch anymore when the murder was weighing this heavily on her mind.

Walter Sommer took the podium as the second guest speaker of the day sat down. A hush came over the group. He gathered them with his expert glance and cleared his throat. "As you all know, Friday night or early Saturday morning we lost one of our own to a horrible crime. Zunia Pettigrew will be missed by us all—"

There were a few mutterings in the crowd at that.

"—and her dedication to the ITCS and her own home chapter, the Niagara Teapot Collectors Society, still ably represented by Orlando Pettigrew, Pastor Frank Barlow and the others, is unquestioned. Pastor Frank, I believe you wanted to say a few words?"

"This oughta be interesting," Laverne murmured.

Rose glanced over at Orlando Pettigrew, who sat alone, his face frozen in distaste as the pastor shambled to the podium. The other members of the Niagara group, two sisters and Penelope Daley, glanced between the pastor and the widower uneasily.

"I'd like to lead you all in a prayer." He opened a leather-bound volume and haltingly led the group, they said amen in chorus, then he closed the book with a slap and looked around the group. "And now I'd like to speak about Zunia Pettigrew."

Some started chatting quietly among their own groups as he talked on and on, lauding the woman's greatness and purity of heart.

"How can he say all of this with a straight face?" Rose said to Laverne.

Penelope Daley had begun weeping like a hired mourner at a funeral, her soft sobs becoming louder the longer Frank spoke.

"You know, there are some men who time after time pick the naggingest, most difficult women to fall in love with," Laverne whispered. "There was a man in our church . . .

Everyone felt sorry for him for years because his wife made his life a living hell. Nothing he did was *ever* good enough. When she died every sweet widow and lonely heart wanted to console him. Thought he'd respond to good cooking, nice treatment, compliments . . . every kind of TLC. Well, didn't he up and marry Azalea Crowther, the meanest woman on the planet! Some men just don't know how to go along unless a woman is telling them which shoe to put on first and how they're not even good at that."

Rose glanced over at Orlando Pettigrew. Was that the case with him, careening from one mean-tempered woman to the next? Rose remembered Dahlia Pettigrew from past conventions, and she was a mousy, sweet-natured enough woman, so now, in his case he had jumped from one extreme to the other. He and Zunia had been married a year or so. Had he just had enough and decided to get out of the marriage in a permanent and quick way?

She looked over at Walter and Nora, who sat together in matrimonial solidarity. Nora had claimed Walter was never going to leave her to marry Zunia, but was Orlando sure about that? Did he kill his wife to keep her from leaving, as weird as that sounded? Wouldn't be the first time in a sorry world of hurt that a man killed a woman in a fit of *If I can't have her, no one can.*

When the pastor was finally done eulogizing Saint Zunia, as Laverne tartly named her in a whispered aside, Walter Sommer took the podium and said, "We'll break for lunch, and then meet back here at one thirty to discuss our plans for the division presidency for the New York State ITCS."

There was the usual bustle of chairs moving, people

murmuring, shoes shuffling. Josh, with a worried frown on his young face, joined them. "Mrs. Freemont, that Detective O'Hoolihan talked to me again. He asked me if I thought you were strong enough to hit someone with a teapot!"

"That's just ridiculous," Laverne said sharply. "As if she would. Who do they think she is, Buffy the Vampire Slayer? Xena, Warrior Princess?"

Even through her worry Rose smiled at her friend, who liked her female TV characters strong and feisty. "Rose, Warrior Teapot Collector," she said.

Laverne chuckled. "What did you say, Josh?"

"I said no way. I may have . . . uh . . . made you sound kinda weak and helpless. I hope you're not offended."

"Don't let it worry you, honey," she said, patting Josh's back. "Everything is going to be fine. The police are just exploring every possibility." She spied Thelma edging closer. "If certain people hadn't thought it would be funny to make me out to be the wicked witch of Gracious Grove, this wouldn't have happened." She was sorry the moment she said it, especially when she saw the stricken expression on Thelma's wrinkled face. Darn it, that was too harsh.

Thelma turned and shuffled away, out of the convention room.

"I shouldn't have said that," she fretted.

"Rose, don't concern yourself," Laverne said. "It wouldn't do her any harm to know she made a mistake and own up to it for once in her life."

"I suppose. I just hope this doesn't send her off to do anything even more foolish. I know Thelma, and she has no off switch for her brain."

Chapter 16

This was when she needed one of those cellular thingamabobs, Thelma thought, as she chugged into the lobby like a slow-moving train. Cissy had gone off with Dana Saunders to shop just when she needed her granddaughter's help! That Dana was a bad influence, getting Cissy to do stuff like shop and have fun.

She *needed* someone nimble and young to help her clear up this mess. And by "mess," she meant the awful bashing of Zunia Pettigrew, even if that woman was just a murder waiting to happen. She frowned as she pondered that thought.

A murder waiting to happen.

Seemed to her you could look at this like a sale. There were two different kind of sales; there was the planned sale, advertised and thought out ahead, but then there was the sudden pop-up kinda sale, one of those rare opportunities when you got to the store and found out they had a surplus of squash so they had slashed the price.

Pain shot through her left foot. She sure hoped her gout wasn't flaring up, because nothing in the world hurt like gout. One time her big toe knuckle had swollen up and gotten so red and hot, felt like it was on fire. All she could wear on her foot was an old carpet slipper of her late husband's with the toe cut out. She shuffled over to the alcove and sat down behind the palm tree, slipping off her orthopedic Rockport shoes. She'd worn them too long and they'd broken down until they were falling apart, but they were darned expensive and money didn't grow on shrubberies!

Anyhoo . . . was this murder like the advertised-in-advance kind of sale, or the pop-up sale of opportunity? Had someone close to Zunia, like that weaseling husband or nasty stepchild, planned this out, deciding ahead of time the how and the where and the when? Or had someone seen an opportunity, someone like that Galway girl, who always looked like she was sucking a sour lemon when she looked at Zunia, or that bossy Sommer woman, who couldn't keep her husband corralled in his own pen?

Either way the teapot was likely just a chance addition to a planned crime. It wasn't like someone had heard her say Rose was nasty and decided then and there to kill Zunia. Woulda happened anyway.

She nodded sharply. That was the truth! Invigorated, she got up and headed to the coffee shop. A cup of tea and a scone, and then she was going to investigate! She'd practically solved the last murder all on her own and she'd do the same this time. She would be Miss Marple, only the Margaret Rutherford portrayal of Miss Marple, not the namby-pamby one Dame Agatha had written down.

While waiting for her friends to return, Sophie decided to familiarize herself with the whole hotel in her effort to figure out how the perpetrator had met up with Zunia, so she retrieved her notebook to sketch a plan. She had taken a course in restaurant layout and design, and quickly realized that a buffet event needed a much different flow from a formal restaurant with designated seating, which in turn required a different layout from a casual-dining outlet. She had worked hard, honing her sketching skills during hours spent drawing up mock seating and floor arrangements for events, weddings, conventions and parties of all sorts, all in an effort to improve the flow of bus and waitstaff.

The ground floor of the inn was easy and took her only a few moments. She then ascended the stairs and turned toward the elevator. It had been cleared, nothing left but a big patch of gluey cement where the police had cut the carpet away. The sight left her feeling a little queasy, since she understood immediately why the carpet had been cut away.

She turned her mind away from the bloody carpet and began to draw up a plan with room numbers and spaces left to write in who was in what room. Really, though, the exercise was meant to give her a better understanding of the scene and force her to think about the sequence of events.

The whole thing seemed to have happened in a tight time frame. Nana said Penelope Daley, the first person on scene, told the other conventioneers she had tried to roll Zunia over, thinking she was just drunk. The body was still warm to the touch. Someone had to have killed her and then gotten away, or run back to their room.

If that's where she was killed, as it appeared to be, why would Zunia be at the elevator at that time of night, still in her day clothes? And where was her husband all this time? She had to be meeting someone, but who? Her lover, Walter Sommer? According to him, he was asleep in his room alongside his wife, Nora. They alibied each other, but they could both be lying, or Walter could have snuck out.

The other possibility was she was coming back with someone, perhaps even her murderer, however, why would she do that? Most of them were doubled up two by two in their rooms, and her husband was presumably in their room, so where would she be going? Maybe she was on her way out and was accosted and killed before getting on the elevator. Did that rule out whomever she was going out to meet? Sophie shook her head, not sure of the answer. The police would have Zunia's cell phone—unless it was missing—and would know if she was corresponding with someone, but Sophie had to work from a place of ignorance.

She stood in the dim hallway and imagined it as Nana had described it, the ring of anxious and horrified faces, the body on the floor, the alarm clanging . . . the teapot lying beside her bloodied head.

The teapot. Sophie had handled it and done some research on it for Nana, enough to suspect that it was Tibetan, not Chinese, and perhaps not even a teapot, but rather a holy water vessel, though she hadn't been able to confirm it. Zunia had apparently written it off as not old and not valuable, which showed how ignorant she was of antiquities. It was weighty, but certainly not heavy enough to be a logical weapon, not one you'd go out of your way to obtain, anyway. There were a thousand readily available murder weapons, and a Tibetan artifact was not what most would think to use. Not having seen the wound, Sophie couldn't evaluate if it was so, but she suspected that the teapot could not produce enough damage to actually kill someone. And if that was true, then another weapon had been used and the teapot was planted to point to Nana.

Anger burned in her gut that someone would listen to Thelma Mae Earnshaw and concoct a heinous plot to ensnare an innocent octogenarian. Nana was suffering, but so was poor Thelma; without the quirky lady's lies the murder would have happened anyway, but at least it would have been with some other instrument.

The elevator mechanism started humming and she could hear a mechanical groan, then the doors whooshed open, and Detective Eli Hodge stepped out.

"Miss Taylor," he said, his tone calm and measured. "I'm glad I caught you. I want to speak to your grandmother but she's with the convention folks right now. Maybe you can give me a sense of what happened that night. I'd just like to confirm my colleague's notes."

"I wasn't here for the convention. I didn't come until last night after I found out what had happened."

"I guess I misunderstood." He glanced down at her sketchbook. "What do you have there?" he asked, reaching out for it.

Too late, she wondered if the police would take her to task for involving herself. She handed it over. "Just a sketch of the layout of the hotel."

He fixed his gaze on her with a speculative gleam, then looked down at the notebook. "Yours is better than the one O'Hoolihan did, I'll tell you that. May I borrow it?"

"You're going to trust mine?"

He gave a half smile. "Oh, I'll confirm that it's correct." He held on to the notebook as he looked around. "This is right where the body was found, and that is the staircase there," he said, indicating the door.

Sophie examined him as he paced over, opened the door and peered down the stairs. She followed his thoughts: How did the murderer get away, by elevator or stairs? Or did the culprit—or culprits, because who was to say there was not more than one murderer?—just nip into their own room, change into pajamas and go to bed?

It would take a particularly cold-blooded person to do that. But then, what normal person would commit the murder anyway?

"I was thinking," she said, but then paused.

"Yes? You were thinking?" He met her gaze and raised his brows.

"I know the teapot in question," she said. "I handled it a lot as I was doing research on it. It was weighty for a teapot but not the easiest thing to use as a weapon, I wouldn't think. I know you can't confirm or deny this, but it seems to me that it can't have been the actual weapon used to kill Zunia Pettigrew."

His gaze was neutral. "Go on, I'm listening."

"In that case, there was a real murder weapon and then she was whacked with the teapot to make it look like it was the weapon while the real thing was carried away, concealed or disposed of."

He didn't reply, but at least he didn't dismiss her.

Talking to herself, she said, "So then the killer had to go somewhere to dispose of the weapon, maybe downstairs.

That changes what I was just thinking, that they killed her, then ran back into their room. They had to get rid of the real murder weapon first, and they sure wouldn't want it in their room." She shrugged and added, "There's not really anything more yet. I figure whoever did it must have been at the tea after the meeting. They heard Mrs. Earnshaw talk about how dangerous my grandmother is, and then decided to use that to point the finger of blame at her. It has to be someone who doesn't know her well."

"Why do you say that?"

"Because it's *ridiculous*! Anyone who knows my grandmother would know she could never kill anyone. Which, by the way, I hope you make clear to the other detective."

His expression turned from amusement to cool regard, his blue-gray eyes holding a chilly blankness. "We don't work that way, Sophie. We don't decide ahead of time who couldn't have done it and then work from there. You'd be surprised at the people I've arrested for murder or assault after being told there was no possible way they could be responsible."

Grudgingly, she nodded. "I see your point, but *I* know she didn't do it. I'm going to keep pointing out every other person who could be guilty."

"That is your right," he said. "And does that include your friend Rhiannon Galway?"

Her stomach clenched. "Why her?"

"Interesting that you didn't leap to *her* defense. I suppose I can tell you this, since we know you two are friends and you've visited her today. You may have even talked about it already. She doesn't really have an alibi for that night and beyond that I'm saying no more, except that O'Hoolihan has a feeling she's holding out on him and he doesn't know why. It's making her look bad."

"Making her look bad," Sophie echoed anxiously. They knew she had visited Rhiannon? Were they watching her or Rhi? Probably Rhi.

"It would really be in her best interest to tell us what she was up to that night rather than saying she was home when we know she was not."

Sophie snatched her notebook back. "She would never kill anyone, no matter what you think. Someone could have a million reasons for not wanting to tell the police where they were that night."

"Exactly my point. That's why she needs to tell us, no matter how embarrassing it is."

"Why would it be embarrassing?" Sophie said.

He sighed and looked off into the distance. His expression was detached, almost blank. When he met her eyes again, though, she could see that he had made some kind of decision.

"I'm going to tell you more than I should and only because it would be good for us if we could start eliminating people off the list of suspects. These folks are all going to want to go home, if not tonight, by tomorrow morning, and we have no cause to hold them here. That means we'll need to travel to wherever they are next time we want to ask questions, and it would be simpler if we can eliminate some of them."

"I get that. I watch *Cops*. And *The First 48*. And *City Confidential*."

"You do know those are edited to be entertainment, right?" He sighed and shook his head. "Never mind. We know that Rhiannon Galway was not home because a nosy neighbor saw her car leave and not come back until morning. She won't tell us where she was, so we're expending a whole lot of energy on tracking down anyone who saw her. We have a tentative sighting, but she needs to tell us the truth, and fast."

The elevator doors opened just then and Dana and Cissy started toward them, stopped in surprise, but then hastened to get off as the elevator doors started to close again.

"Hi there, Detective," Dana said, her cheeks getting pink, and not just from the heat outside, Sophie surmised. "You two look cozy," she said, eyeing Sophie. "What's this little tête-à-tête about?"

Both she and Cissy had a multitude of bags over their arms. Cissy ducked around them and murmured that she was putting the stuff in her grandmother's room.

Under normal circumstances when there was romantic tension between a couple Sophie would have felt like the third wheel, but the detective was polite and yet noncommittal, simply nodding in acknowledgment of Dana's greeting. "We were speaking of the murder. Sophie had some interesting insights."

"*Did* she, now?" Dana said, an edge to her voice.

Sophie shook her head. Dana had always been competitive with other girls, and Sophie had never understood why. In any group of women she would always stand out as the one the guys would drool over. In the past Sophie would have tried to be conciliatory, but she and Dana were friends, and friends shouldn't need to do that kind of crap.

She turned back to Eli. "Detective, if you have Zunia's cell phone, then you know if she was going out to meet someone, or if someone was coming to meet her here, right?"

His expression didn't change. "That would be correct."

She heard a subtle emphasis on the word "would." "But you don't have it," she concluded.

"I am not at liberty to confirm or deny the existence or whereabouts of Ms. Pettigrew's cell phone," he said, an edge in his tone. "And if you have in mind to be an amateur sleuth, I would seriously discourage you from that. *Someone* targeted Zunia Pettigrew and took the time and effort to point the finger of blame at your grandmother."

He leaned over slightly from the waist and looked directly into her eyes with a gaze intended not to intimidate, but to hammer home his point. "Look, I *get* that you're concerned about your grandmother. This affects me, too. Auntie Lala is my favorite aunt, and I can see how worried she is about Mrs. Freemont. That's why I made sure I was given the job of helping the lead detective on this case, even though he doesn't want me here. But O'Hoolihan *is* still the lead detective and I'm not out to usurp him." He took a deep breath, straightened, then finished by saying, "Don't interfere unless you're trying to make our job harder."

Well, she had certainly been told, hadn't she?

"Now, if I could borrow your booklet for a moment?"

She handed it over without comment. He propped it on a ledge near the elevator, whipped out his cell phone, took a photo of her sketch and handed it back to her. He had the grace to look sheepish as he said, "Like I said, yours is a lot better than the detective's and it'll save me time."

Dana bit her lip and tried not to laugh as she hoisted her bags further up on her wrist. "Now, that was unnecessary, Detective Hodge," Dana said. "I'm sure Sophie would have been happy to photocopy her sketch for you if you'd asked *nicely*."

Sophie snickered.

"If you ladies will excuse me," he said stiffly, "I'll go back to my job, which was to have a look at the layout of the inn."

Dana looked crestfallen, but Sophie thought if the guy couldn't take a little teasing then he was too serious for someone as vivacious as Dana. Sophie tucked the notebook under her arm, and said, "Come on, Dana, let's go to Nana's room and you can show me what you bought. Whatever it is, I'll bet you look gorgeous in it."

In reality Sophie's cell phone was buzzing in her pocket and she desperately wanted to know how Jason had replied, so she was relieved when Dana said, with a side glance at the detective, who was writing notes on a small pad, "I have to go to Cissy's grandmother's room. SuLinn is going to meet us here in a few minutes. She wanted to stay downstairs and call Randy to tell him she wouldn't be back to GiGi until tomorrow."

They all parted ways but Sophie noticed that the detective watched Dana sashay into Mrs. Earnshaw's room with a regretful expression.

This time the tea after the meeting was kind of a late luncheon, hastily put together by the Stone and Scone staff. The dining room was only used at lunch and dinnertime, so at this point in the early afternoon it was only the ITCS group that was eating. The food was better than the dinner they had suffered through the previous evening—just sandwiches, but fresh and full of flavor. Pickle trays, salads, rolls with butter, scones, biscuits and fresh fruit rounded out the meal. Rose surmised that the coffee shop cook had been pressed into service, and that was why the food was better.

She made a mental note to ask Sophie why Bertie would put up with such substandard fare from his inn cooking staff.

But her main focus today was on Walter Sommer, whom she eyed with curiosity. Nora was off in a corner talking to the two Niagara members, the sisters whom no one could tell apart or remember their names.

"I've seen that look in your eye before," Laverne said, her tone worried. "What are you up to?"

"It occurred to me that all these years we've belonged to the ITCS, we never really knew what the Sommers do—I mean, aside from this. Walter isn't old enough to be retired, is he? So what does he do for a job?"

"We know Nora's family has money."

"But is he dependent on her to live? Would he ever leave her? She said no, but no wife thinks her husband is going to leave before he does. I think I'll just talk to him a bit. Run interference for me if Nora looks like she's coming back to her husband."

"Run interference? Listen to you with your football terminology," Laverne said. "Should I tackle her?"

"No, but a sucker punch would ring her bells, wouldn't it?" Rose said, with a wink. "See, I can even mix sports metaphors!" She strolled over to Walter, who sat gloomily alone with his cell phone and a tablet device, frowning as if he was working so very hard. When she snuck a look she could see that he was playing some kind of brightly colored game on the tablet.

He warily looked up, closing the little booklet the tablet was in and setting the stylus aside. "Mrs. Freemont. What can I do for you?"

"Nora was talking about the ITCS division presidency.

Who do you think will run?" She paused, then slyly asked, "Will you consider Rhiannon Galway if she decides to run again like she did last year?"

He colored, his gaunt cheeks darkening. She could see the spider trails of broken capillaries over them and across his nose. "As much as I think she is a fine young lady and like her very much, I don't think Miss Galway will be standing this year even if we decided to have another election," he said, firmly.

"Why not?"

He huffed and moved things around on the table in front of him, then finally said, "She just won't. I'm very fond of her, but she and Nora do *not* see eye to eye."

I'll just bet they don't, Rose thought. "Then who? Laverne would be a perfect state president," she said. "I could probably talk her into standing."

"Nora says . . . uh . . . We believe the most expeditious manner to handle this is to simply appoint Pastor Frank Barlow to finish Zunia's term, which goes until next summer. He has served as his chapter president in past, and knows the work from his close friendship with Zunia."

"You're going to *appoint* someone? That's unfortunate." Rose leaned toward Walter. "Walter, I feel sorry for Frank, but he and Orlando came to blows that awful night, before the murder. How is that going to work with Frank as president? Orlando may believe that as the widower he should be asked to step in, don't you think?" She paused, watching his eyes; he didn't appear to quite know how to answer. "What was that fight about? Do you know?"

He sighed and shook his head, thrusting one hand through his thinning white hair, making it stick straight up.

"Look, Rose, I don't think I should be talking about Frank and Orlando's problems with you."

"You're right, Walter," she said, sitting down opposite him. "It's just . . ." She paused, patting the table surface with both palms as she chose her words carefully. "I know how important the ITCS is to you and Nora. You've been at this awhile."

"Founding members," he said. "Me, Dahlia Pettigrew and Lacey Galway."

"Rhiannon's mother? I did not know that."

He nodded. "That was, oh, more than twenty-five years ago now. We all lived in New York City."

Distracted, Rose cocked her head to one side and regarded him closely, truly seeing the man for the first time in a while. "Walter, I don't think I've ever asked you this before. How did you get interested in collecting teapots?"

She saw a spark alight in his cold eyes and was surprised by the warmth she felt toward him in that moment.

"It was my grandmother. My mother, father, brother and I lived with her in an apartment in the Village, you know?" It was clear that to him there was only one village, Greenwich Village. "She was very *Hochdeutsch* . . . high German," he explained. "That's a linguistic designation, but pretty much cultural, too. I was much smarter than my brother, who only wanted to play in the streets, so that is why my grandmother preferred me. Young Josh over there," he said, motioning with one elegant hand to the teenager. "He reminds me so much of myself! So comfortable in the company of adults."

Rose watched Josh, who had joined the group of Nora and the two sisters, both of them intently quizzing him on something or other. "Interesting," Rose said, more to keep the conversation going than anything.

"My grandmother would have all her friends over for tea and I would serve them, then have my cup, too, and listen to them talk." His eyes were misty with remembrance, his thin lips stretched into a smile. "They were not just old ladies to me; they were fascinating, worldly and wise. One was an opera singer from Vienna. Another had been married several times, once to a famous Spanish artist who died tragically when he leaped from a bridge. It was all so vivid, the tales they told and the lives they had lived. Now I wonder how much was true and how much was fantasy, but that never mattered. What tied it all in together was tea; the brewing of it was as detailed as a tea ceremony ever can be and had to be just so."

He fumbled with the tablet and for a moment she thought he was going back to his game, but instead he rapidly shifted to a folder and brought up an old black-and-white photo. "That's me," he said, pointing to a towheaded boy in a sports jacket, standing by an autocratic-looking elderly woman. Beside them was a round antique table with a cloth over it, an elaborate silver tea service exactly in the center. "That is Großmutter Sommer."

"I thought 'grandmother' in German was 'oma'?" she said, examining the photo, which was posed in a very stiff and formal parlor, with the woman in question seated, straight and proud, hands on the head of a cane, young Walter standing at her shoulder.

He smiled. "Oh, no, you *never* called her Oma. That was low German, you see, to her. She was Großmutter or ma'am, nothing else." His smile died as he traced her visage on the tablet, but his finger on the surface made it shuffle and vanish, like a reflection in a pond.

Rose was trying to figure out how to bring the topic around to what she wanted to know, but in light of his opening up, she decided to do the same. "Walter, I'm scared."

He frowned, gazing at her. "What?"

She clasped her hands in front of her. "I'm frightened. One of us is a murderer and tried to point the finger of blame at me. Do you have any clue who killed Zunia Pettigrew?"

He swallowed hard and cast his glance about the room. "Look, you didn't hear it from me, but Frank was pretty steamed up that night," he said in a low tone, still looking around the room.

"I know that; we witnessed the argument with Orlando."

"He insists Zunia told him she was running away with him."

"But that's not true!" Rose said.

"I know that. Zunia herself told me he was imagining it. I didn't think anything of it, but now I wonder . . . How would he react if it finally hit him that she was not leaving Orlando?" His eyes widened as he looked over Rose's shoulder.

Rose turned. Pastor Frank Barlow was sitting in a corner with Penelope Daley, who was talking earnestly to him, clutching at his arm. But he was watching them, his expression one of loathing toward Walter, of all people. A chill raced down Rose's back, and it was not her sciatica acting up. Was Walter right? Where was Frank Barlow that night after the confrontation with Orlando, and why had she not taken him seriously as a suspect until now? "So the argument was over Zunia, and whether she was running away with Frank," Rose summarized.

"Apparently. Nonsense, of course. Zunia was *not* going to run away with Frank."

Certainly not if she was having an affair with Walter, which would explain the expression on Frank's face when he looked at the ITCS president. "What did Bertie do with Frank after the quarrel?"

"I understand he hauled him away and locked him in some room somewhere to simmer down. I don't know where."

"There aren't any vacant rooms, we know that," Rose mused. How long had Frank been locked away? There were two people who knew that information: Frank and Bertie. One of them would tell her, but which one?

She eyed Frank, who was sullenly staring at the wall now, alone, as Penelope had left him to go talk to Nora Sommer. Rose didn't think she'd ask Frank, but who knew if the opportunity would arise? She sighed as a wave of weariness washed over her. What was her world coming to that she was considering asking a pastor about the violent murder of his illicit love interest not fifteen feet from her hotel room?

Chapter 17

Sophie sat cross-legged on her rollaway bed and called Jason. He had texted her simply to call him at home. He answered right away, and they went through the niceties before getting down to business.

His take on it was clear from the beginning. "Sophie, I hope you're not thinking just because you got lucky with the solution to that thing in May that now you're some TV-style detective."

Stung, she replied swiftly, "Of course not. It's just that the cops keep questioning Nana, and it *was* her teapot that was found with blood on it by Zunia's bashed-in head. Surely you get why I don't want to just leave her here and come home?"

"Yeah, I get it, I do!" he replied with a conciliatory tone, perhaps sensing her irritation. "I'm sorry, I'm just worried about you *and* your grandmother. What an awful thing to happen. So, your question was?"

She asked him about parents and college visits, and he affirmed what Josh had said: that parents could visit the college with or without their kids and often stayed overnight, especially in summer when most of the other students were gone. "We use the dorms for a lot of things, like conventions and symposiums, as well as parental visits."

"Is there any way to tell when someone comes back to the dorm?"

"There's no check-in policy or anything." He was silent for a moment, and she let him think. "The best way to tell when someone comes and goes might be the parking lot. If she is staying here overnight and has her car—she *must* have a car, since we're off the beaten path, unless someone dropped her off and picked her up—then she would have been issued a temporary parking pass that would trigger the lift bar in the parking building."

"Is it on a clock?"

"It is, and there's a security camera, too."

She hesitated, but then plunged ahead. "Jason, I hate to ask, but could you do me one teeny, tiny favor?"

He groaned. "You're going to ask me to find out if she was here, aren't you?"

"Her name is Dahlia Pettigrew. I don't know what she drives, but it should be easy enough to figure out."

"Why don't you just tell the police what you suspect?"

"I will, but they won't tell *me* anything in return, I guarantee it, and I need to know. Besides, Josh has kind of made friends with Emma. If I can clear her and her mom, I think he'd be relieved. Can you just check on Dahlia Pettigrew, please?"

"I have to go to Cruickshank anyway to prep for summer

class exams, so I'll see what I can find out. For your Nana and for Josh!"

"Thank you, Jason," she said.

"So, when are you coming back to Gracious Grove?"

"Tomorrow, as long as they'll let Nana go."

"They don't seriously suspect that sweet little old lady of murder, do they?"

"I don't know. One of the detectives said they can't rule anyone out just because they're not the *type* to commit murder, and I know what he means. But that's why I can't leave her here alone and why I need to make sure they clear this up. You understand, right?" She was anxious to make sure she got her point across.

"I do," he said, his voice warm. "I didn't mean to make light of your efforts, Sophie; I'd do the same thing in your shoes. I'll talk to you later once I find out what you need to know."

They signed off just as Sophie got a text from Josh saying to come see him in the dining room. He was very mysterious, but she would bet he had things to tell her. She exited her grandmother's room and knocked on Thelma and SuLinn's door.

"Hey, you guys there?"

"We're coming!" Dana sang out. She flung open the door and said, "Ta-da!"

SuLinn stood in the middle of the room, her dark straight hair up off her neck. She wore a red Chloé mandarin-collar dress.

"Wow!" Sophie exclaimed. "You look beautiful!"

"I know," she said, her voice gurgling with laughter. "Isn't it gorgeous?" She whirled. "It was all Dana's doing."

Cissy was busy with her bag, but she didn't look happy. "Can we get going?" she asked, complaint in her voice. "I don't know where Grandma is. Who knows what mischief she's gotten herself into."

Sophie and Dana exchanged a look, and Dana shrugged. Cissy sometimes got her nose bent out of shape if the drama in her own life didn't take top priority. She was a sweet girl most of the time, and Sophie loved her old friend, but she could be moody.

"Okay, let's move," Sophie agreed. "I need to hook up with Josh, who I think has some news for me. He's in the dining room, apparently. Let's enter the lion's den."

Thelma Mae Earnshaw plunked down on the prison cot, weak with exhaustion. The place was dusty and her voice was hoarse from shouting. Dang it, you'd think that punk kid in the kitchen off the hall would hear her, but he had those whatchamacallits, those earbuddies in his ears, the things her grandson Phil swore were headphones. Didn't look like headphones; looked like earplugs, and given that Phil always had them in his ears when she wanted him to listen to her, maybe they were just the same.

She had shouted herself hoarse, and was ready to expire. How had she gotten into this mess? It was all Rose Freemont's fault. If Rose hadn't brought the dumb teapot to the convention to be looked at and admired and marveled over as if it were something special, then Zunia Pettigrew wouldn't have torn a strip off Rose, and if she hadn't done that then maybe Mrs. Highfalutin Rose Freemont wouldn't have torn into Zunia. And if she hadn't done *that* . . . well, then it never would have occurred to Thelma to make that little joke about Rose being dangerous, which had landed her in this awful fix.

But that was too far back. How had she gotten into this *particular* fix? It had started innocently enough, with her snooping around like Miss Ariadne Oliver from the Agatha Christie books or, even better, Mrs. Pollifax from the Dorothy Gilman series of books. Now, *that* was a senior on a mission—a *CIA* mission. Ever since she started reading those books she wondered if there really were such things as senior citizen CIA operatives.

A gal could dream, even a gal with an artificial hip. And knee. And gout. She wiggled her big toe, which was hurting something awful.

But *that* was what had gotten Thelma into this particular jam: her curiosity. She had simply wondered if the killer had hidden out in the basement until everyone was asleep before carrying out his dastardly deed, so she had slunk down there and had a look around. That was almost as good as snooping around people's homes when they weren't looking.

The few she had been inside of in recent years were fascinating. Folks would be surprised at what people had in their medicine cabinets and armoires, some things she wasn't even sure what they were for, like pink fuzzy handcuffs. Who would want handcuffs in their bedroom? No criminals there. Or at least she hoped not, because the handcuffs were in the bedroom of the local church ladies guild president.

Anyhoo . . . she had just been snooping around downstairs when that kid, the one who was peeling carrots in the kitchen, suddenly charged out into the hallway to get something out of one of the storerooms. Thelma had nearly fainted and staggered into this room after pushing the door open. But the door had closed after her and now wouldn't budge. She had been imprisoned for . . . how long? Felt like hours. She pushed the little knob on her light-up watch and squinted at the face. It had been a good . . . oh, almost ten minutes.

She had found her own way to the basement when she was taking a look-see at the stairs by the check-in desk. She had discovered that there was even an exit, a back door to the parking lot. She knew that because it was propped open to let in air, and she could practically see the shimmer of heat waves rising from the pavement. She was a little confused; could the murderer have run down the stairs and out that back door? Did that mean it could have been someone from outside? But the door wouldn't be open in the middle of the night; it would be locked. Right? Inn guests had keys to their individual rooms that also opened the front door, which was locked after hours, too.

She surveyed her surroundings in the dim light of one lamp, which she had felt around for and turned on. It was prison-like, for sure, but not bare. There was the cot she was sitting on, as well as some boxes piled against the cinder-block wall. The boxes contained food: canned tomatoes, beans, vegetables, soup and cases of dried pasta. So if she could find a can opener, she wouldn't starve.

But there was no bathroom, and her bladder at that moment decided to warn her that she needed one pronto. Tears welled in her eyes. All alone, and even her granddaughter probably wouldn't notice she was missing until they finally opened this storeroom to get some canned tomatoes one day and found her desiccated body. She lay back on the torture rack that was the cot and resigned herself to her fate.

T he moment they entered the ITCS luncheon, SuLinn took Dana by the arm and went around introducing her to people, ending up near the two sisters, who appeared to be exclaiming over SuLinn's new dress. Dana was smiling and nodding, but she kept stealing glances over her shoulder. Sophie suspected she was looking for Detective Eli.

"Where the heck is Grandma?" Cissy asked as they scanned the convention dining room.

"Let's ask Nana if she's seen her," Sophie said.

The room was poorly set up, Sophie thought, glancing around. The flow was bad from a waitstaff point of view: no room to move all the way around tables, haphazard and inefficient. But she was not here to critique the room; she was here to find her grandmother and godmother.

"There they are," she said to Cissy, who was waiting and following her friend's lead.

Her grandmother and Laverne were at a table with two other older women, all with their heads together.

"My Sophie!" Nana exclaimed, looking up and beaming when she saw Sophie.

She looked tired, Sophie thought, examining her petite grandmother as she squeezed between a couple of tables that were too close together. Nana should have been home by now from her weekend away with her feet up, a cup of tea in one hand and a *Murder, She Wrote* book in the other. Sophie hugged her grandmother and Laverne.

Nana introduced them both to the two other ladies, Mrs.

Littlefield and Miss Benson. They had a moment of polite conversation.

"It is good to see you, Cissy!" Laverne commented. "You look very pretty today."

Cissy's mood improved immediately, and she did look pretty, Sophie thought, glancing at her friend, who wore a sundress and sandals, her hair in a waterfall bun. Since her disastrous engagement a few months before to a man who was now charged with being an accessory to murder, she had come out of her shell some. She was now dating a local police officer, Wally Bowman, one of their childhood friends who had always been secretly in love with her.

She was still the same Cissy, prone to feeling under-appreciated and sometimes self-pitying; however, those were minor character flaws. Sophie worked hard to stay aware of that. Maybe that was why she appreciated the smart, sophisticated and occasionally snarky Dana so much, though they had never been friends as teens.

"We were wondering if you'd seen Mrs. Earnshaw lately," Sophie said, her gaze going back and forth between the two women.

"I haven't. Have you, Rose?" Laverne said.

"I saw her," said Miss Benson, a gaunt, tall woman in her early seventies. She had a sour expression on her face. "I'll *never* forgive myself, Rose, for letting that woman take me in about you. She is a bit odd, don't you think?"

Cissy's pale cheeks pinkened. "My grandmother is *not* odd. She's . . . imaginative."

Sophie glanced over at her in surprise. *Good for you, Cissy!* she thought. Thelma *was* odd, but she was Cissy's grandmother, and family stuck together.

"Yes, well, I was heading to the loo and saw her *imagining* herself down the stairs to the basement," the woman said tartly. "Whatever on earth she would want in the basement I do not know. That peculiar woman has been avoiding everyone since her little charade came to such a bad end."

Laverne stood. She was a tall woman, and though in her seventies, strongly built, imposing in her occasional severity. "That is enough, Faye Alice," she said. "This poor girl is worried about her grandmother, who is our friend." She turned to Cissy and touched the younger woman's arm. "I'll go with you to see if we can find her," she offered.

Sophie stepped in, giving Laverne a grateful smile. She would never have been able to censure the other woman—she had been raised too well—but Laverne, the woman's peer in age, did it splendidly, and Sophie could see that Cissy appreciated it. "It's okay, Laverne," she said. "I'll go with her. I know my way around downstairs since that's how I came in last night."

"Come back after you find her, Sophie," Nana said. "I know Josh wants to talk to you."

Sophie led Cissy out of the convention dining room and toward the door to the basement, but as she started to open it, Bertie Handler popped out from behind the check-in desk.

"Whoa, wait a minute," he cried, flapping his hands at them. "That's for employees only."

Detective O'Hoolihan and a uniformed officer were coming through the front doors of the inn just then, as Sophie explained to the inn owner what they were doing. "We just want to check," she finished. "Someone noticed Mrs. Earnshaw going through this door, and she hasn't been seen since."

"Having spoken to the lady in question, I would say she's

fully capable of not just going downstairs, but getting herself into trouble while there," O'Hoolihan said.

Cissy bridled and was about to respond, but Sophie grabbed her arm and squeezed, since what he said helped them. "I'm sure you don't want to be responsible if she's hurt and unable to call for help. We'll just take a quick look around and be back up in two seconds." Sophie pulled her friend through the door as the detective engaged the innkeeper, asking him a question about something.

A fluorescent light flickered in an annoying jittery beat at the top of the cement stairway as the two descended. She led Cissy to the kitchen. "Hey, guys," she said. The prep cook, chopping onions, did not respond, but the two guys at the stove and grill looked around. "Has anyone seen an elderly lady down here wandering around? She may have poked her head into the kitchen at some point." Sophie knew enough not to say it out loud with Cissy right there, but everyone in Gracious Grove knew that Thelma Mae Earnshaw was a snoop and could not be trusted alone in anyone's home or establishment.

Both shook their heads with identical mystified expressions.

"While we search for her, can you check with your buddy?" she said, indicating the guy who hadn't looked around. She could see earbuds in his ears and a cell phone tucked in the pocket of his apron. He nodded his head in time with the beat in his headphones.

Tugging Cissy after her, she explored the warren of hallways, opening doors, finding the bathroom and storerooms and especially checking the walk-in freezer. She was immensely relieved to find no one in it, because she hadn't put it past Mrs. Earnshaw to get trapped in such a spot. There was one locked door, though. She stopped at it, Cissy at her side, and shouted, "Mrs. Earnshaw? Are you here anywhere?"

"Grandma!" Cissy shouted. "Grandma, are you here?" No sound. Cissy shrugged. "I guess she's not here. Let's go back upstairs. Maybe she went shopping or something."

But Sophie stubbornly held her spot. She had a feeling. "Quiet for a moment," she said. There was a faint scratching sound on the other side of the door, Sophie thought. This was the very room Melissa had jokingly pointed out as Bertie's panic room. She tapped on the door and called out, "Mrs. Earnshaw? Are you in there?"

A weak voice answered, "Help! I've been in here all day. Help!"

"Grandma?" Cissy cried, putting her ear to the door. "Grandma, are you okay?"

"Get me out of here!"

"This is the exact same room I got locked in when I was a teenager!" Cissy wailed, both hands on her head. She began crying, Mrs. Earnshaw was howling, and the two kitchen guys were in the background doubled over with laughter. Sophie shot them a dirty look. "Can one of you guys help? Unlock this door."

One said, "We don't have keys. We're just the kitchen help."

"You're the chef here!" she exclaimed to the older of the two, guessing based on his seniority. "Surely you must have keys."

They shrugged and slouched back into the kitchen. Sophie's ire burned, but she was mostly concerned with Mrs. Earnshaw, who was howling even louder now, repeatedly, *"Get me out of here!"*

"Cissy, stay here by the door and I'll get Bertie."

She threaded through the halls and took the stairs two at a time then bolted through the door to the check-in desk. Pastor Frank was there, and he and Bertie looked to be in some kind of heated discussion, but Sophie didn't have time to wait.

"Mr. Handler, come quick! Mrs. Earnshaw got herself locked in your panic room." The moment she called it that she wished she had said it differently, because his expression changed to anger.

"My *what*?"

She impatiently hopped from foot to foot. "Whatever you want to call it . . . the locked room downstairs."

"The one you locked me in the night Zunia was butchered!" Pastor Frank said, his cheeks bright red.

Sophie's gaze swiveled to the pastor. "He had you locked in that room? Why?"

Bertie glared at him, his gray eyes bulging and bloodshot. "I *told* you not to say anything about that. I apologized for forgetting you, now shut up!"

The pastor backed away from the desk, watching the innkeeper. "I'm sorry, Bertie, but—"

"What's going on here?"

It was Detective Hodge. Sophie turned to him in relief and explained the situation without referencing the conflict between the pastor and the innkeeper, though her mind was going a mile a minute on that subject. Why would the innkeeper lock the pastor in a room downstairs? Was the pastor afraid of Bertie, as he appeared to be?

But back to the matter at hand.

The detective held out one hand to Bertie and snapped his fingers. "The keys!"

"I'll do it. *I'll* unlock the door!" he said, with bad grace, pulling a ring of keys out of his pocket and selecting one.

"Just give me the keys," the detective said, holding his gaze. The innkeeper obliged without another murmur.

Sophie led the way. They found Cissy almost hysterical and Thelma still howling behind the locked door. Detective Hodge unlocked it and Thelma burst from the room, falling into Eli's arms. She looked up.

"Who are *you*?" she asked, righting herself and pulling away, settling her floral muumuu around her ample midsection.

Cissy, weeping, threw her arms around her grandmother. "Are you okay, Grandma? I was so worried!"

Thelma shrugged her granddaughter off and stared at the detective. Sophie introduced them.

"You're one of Laverne's nephews?" Thelma said, eyes wide. "You're a tall drink of water, aren't you?" She turned to her granddaughter. "What are *you* crying for? I'm the one who was locked away."

Sophie stepped into the room, curious, as Bertie Handler hustled down the hall toward them. The windowless room was smallish and lined with piles of boxes, mostly canned and dry goods, as well as some office supplies. But there was a cot and magazines, a lamp, which was on, a flashlight and some rumpled bedding.

"Nothing to see here," Bertie said, entering and trying to shoo her out.

"Is this where you were hiding the evening Zunia was killed? I was told that you were going to hide in the cellar if the storm got bad, and it *did* get bad, bad enough that the thunder and lightning set off the fire alarm, I understand." She met the innkeeper's gaze. "But . . . no, because Pastor

Frank said you locked him in here that night. What was *that* all about?"

"Yes, what *was* that all about?" the detective asked.

"I told the other fellow, Detective O'Hoolihan, what happened," Bertie said, crossing his arms over his chest, beads of sweat erupting on his forehead and balding dome. "Frank got into a tiff with Mr. Pettigrew. I had to separate them and locked Frank in here. I forgot about him for a while, but when the storm hit in the middle of the night I came down here. He was gone, though, and the room was unlocked. He got out somehow, and *that* is the truth! I told the cops everything."

"Pastor Frank was out when you came down?" Sophie said. "How was that possible if you had the key?"

"I don't know, I tell you!" He covered his eyes with shaking hands and moaned, "When is this going to end? Why me?"

"For Pete's sake," Thelma said, making a rude noise, tongue thrust out. "What a crybaby. *I'm* the one who got locked in there. Durned lock must be faulty, 'cause I just fell against the door, it opened, I fell in and the door locked behind me."

So even if Pastor Frank was locked in here at the time of the murder, Sophie reasoned, it didn't eliminate him as a suspect, not if the lock was faulty.

"How long were you in there, Grandma? You said all day, but that's not true."

She shrugged "That isn't important. I need a bathroom, and fast, or you're gonna have to clean up a puddle."

The detective cleared his throat as Cissy supported her grandmother down the hall. Sophie glanced over at him suspiciously, wondering if he was stifling a chuckle; however, his expression was sober and serious. Bertie started to follow the two women, but Eli grabbed him by the sleeve.

"Wait just a minute. Miss Taylor had a good question that you didn't answer. If you didn't let the pastor out, who did? *He* says you let him out; *you* say he was gone when you came down. So . . . was the door still locked when you came down to let the pastor out?"

Bertie paused and looked down at the floor. Whether he was trying to remember or trying to figure out what story would be best for his alibi, it was hard to say.

"I don't remember. I think it was unlocked," he said stiffly. "You heard that woman; the lock is faulty. Now, if you do not mind I am in the middle of a crisis and quite possibly a nervous breakdown." He whirled on his feet and headed down the passageway toward the stairs, and they could hear him clomp up them with a heavy tread.

Chapter 18

"I **know this isn't your case."** Sophie paused, trying to figure out how to say that she'd rather talk to him than one of the others. She didn't want to badmouth the other detectives, but perhaps because of his tie to her godmother she instantly trusted Eli and preferred to tell him over anyone else. "But I have some information that I may as well pass along to you while I have you." In an undertone so the cooks couldn't hear, she told Eli most of what she had thought and imagined and investigated. He listened, leaning back against the wall, looking down at the floor.

She then told him that she was looking into Dahlia Pettigrew's movements that night and he took in a deep breath, shaking his head. "Miss Taylor—"

"Sophie."

"Sophie. I appreciate that you're trying to help, but you just can't interfere in an investigation."

"I'm not interfering." Her phone buzzed just then and she checked it. Jason had just texted her that Dahlia Pettigrew's car had not come back to the lot until three forty-seven in the morning. She showed the message to the detective. "Cruickshank College is about twenty-five or thirty minutes from here."

He nodded and narrowed his eyes, staring down at Sophie. "I know that. And you did *this* after I basically told you to butt out."

Sophie didn't reply; she was too busy working out the timeline. Nana had said that the body was found at around three thirty. It seemed that Dahlia was out of contention as the murderer, then, but where was Emma? Josh had said that Emma came into the inn while they were all gathered in the convention room, and that was well *after* the murder. If she had been with her mother, where was she in the meantime? "Sorry . . . what did you say, Detective?"

"Look, we appreciate the information. I'm not sure O'Hoolihan is aware of the Dahlia Pettigrew angle, so I'll bring it to his attention."

"Josh Sinclair told me that Emma Pettigrew came into the inn early in the morning after the murder in the same clothes he'd seen her in the night before, so she could have been with her mother, I guess." She'd let him figure out the timeline himself.

He was silent for a long moment, but then said, "I've read through all the statements, but I can't share that stuff with you. We'll take it into consideration. Thank you for your information; now leave it alone."

"But can't you—"

"No, Sophie, leave it alone!" he said sternly. He paused,

watching her, then said, "You seem like a reasonable sort, so I'll tell you why you must let it be. You could seriously damage the case if you interfere. Don't endanger yourself out of some mistaken sense that you can find the truth before we do."

"Okay," she said, subdued by his demeanor. "I haven't been asking around because I think I can solve the case." For some reason his opinion mattered to her, and it concerned her that he thought she didn't have confidence in the police's ability to solve the murder. But she had a vague feeling that he had manipulated her to feel that way, and it irritated her. "I was just trying to help. I'm mainly concerned for my grandmother."

"I don't mean to be harsh," he said gently, his serious blue-gray eyes holding her gaze. "I'm concerned for your safety. In my experience murderers find it easier to kill a second time. And they get paranoid; they'll kill just to cover their tracks."

Reality-check time, Sophie thought, with a shiver. She touched his arm. "Thank you, Eli. You're absolutely right. I'll take your advice and be careful. All I want is to get my grandmother home safe and sound."

"That's my focus, too, getting my Auntie Lala back to GiGi."

Dana's smitten expression and hyped-up awareness came back to her; her friend hadn't had a lot of luck in the romance department. In fact, the girl hadn't dated in over a year, she'd told Sophie. She complained of a list of losers in her dating past and stated her determination not to date again unless the guy was marriage worthy. "Detective, you seem like a really nice guy," she said, on impulse.

"I hope I am," he replied, taking her arm and leading her toward the stairs. "Some men think 'nice' is an old-fashioned concept, along with manners and honor. I don't hold with fellows who think that to be cool they have to be bad boys."

"Are you single?"

She felt a jolt of surprise go though his body and he looked down at her.

"Uh, yes. Yes, I am." His expression was uncertain.

It took her a moment, but she got why he looked that way; she smiled. He thought she was coming on to him! Wow, that was so far from her modus operandi. He was giving her points for guts she didn't have. She couldn't even talk to Jason about their relationship, whatever it was. "Just curious. Thought I'd let you know, my friend Dana Saunders is not only gorgeous but one of the smartest woman I've met in a long time and nicer than she pretends to be."

"Why does everyone in my life think they have to fix me up?"

She chuckled at his plaintive tone as they wound back through the hallways. "I have a feeling it's because you're a really nice guy. Take it as a compliment! I'm just saying . . . she is worth going out of your way for." She stole a glance sideways, but his expression was impossible to read. "I won't say another word, I promise."

Once upstairs the detective went to find his colleagues, so Sophie took a seat in the lobby alcove to text a thank-you for the information back to Jason. She finished that and got her notebook out as a shadow fell over her.

It was Rhiannon with a box in her arms. "I have Rose's Tea-riffic Tea Blend order," she said.

"Okay," Sophie replied. She waited a moment, watching

her friend's face. "You look like you have something more to say," she said.

"I do." Rhiannon set the box down and sat in one of the alcove chairs across from Sophie, the leather crackling and squeaking as she shifted. "Is Detective O'Hoolihan here?"

Sophie nodded.

"I need to talk to him."

Sophie remembered what Detective Hodge said about Rhiannon lying about being home all night. "What's up?"

Rhiannon paused, but then looked down and scuffed at the worn carpet with one toe of her sandals. "I wasn't home that night like I told the cops."

"Where were you?"

Rhiannon let the silence stretch for a while. When she spoke again, it was not in answer to Sophie's question. "I work hard to make my business a success. It's my mother's, after all, and I don't want to bring shame to it." She paused and shook her head. "Geez, that sounds so lame."

"It's *not* lame. I get it, Rhi, I really do," Sophie said. "I feel the same about Nana's tearoom."

"Friday was hard. I had a rotten day here, for reasons I won't go into."

Sophie knew some of it and could imagine more. Rhiannon was being sidelined by the ITCS leadership and it was affecting not only her personal life, but also her business, if what Sophie had heard was correct. Nana said that Zunia was trying to get Rhiannon removed as official tea supplier to the ITCS New York division. But Rhi was also faced with her former lover Walter Sommer, his new lover Zunia, and everything else. It's no wonder that she had that fight with Zunia at the inn that evening.

"Instead of going home after that argument with Zunia, I headed out—I didn't care where I was going. I ended up at a bar on the highway and met Mike, this guy I know. He's the courier driver who brings my packages." She shook her head and sighed. "I went home with him."

Gently, Sophie said, "Don't beat yourself up. So you had a night with a guy you know; it's not the end of the world and it's not like you picked up some stranger."

Rhiannon sighed. "I don't handle stress very well. I've done that before and it's no way to behave. I need to get my act together."

Sophie reached out and took Rhi's hand, ducking her head to meet her friend's green eyes. "Stop being so mean to yourself. You're a good person. Nobody's perfect."

"I hate the regrets I have the next day, you know?"

"The things we do that we regret don't define who we are."

"Maybe not, but if Nora Sommer ever gets wind she'll make sure Zunia's aim is finished. She and Zunia have a lot in common, like two peas in a pod."

"But that wouldn't be any of her business, would it?" Sophie asked, wondering if Rhiannon was being just a little paranoid. Maybe her experience from the year before had made her hypersensitive.

"She wouldn't see it that way, I can tell you that."

"So Nora doesn't like you, either?"

"Let's just say that both Zunia and Nora have a good reason not to be too fond of me."

Sophie tried to think of a way to ask about her and Walter's relationship but was tongue-tied. There were just some things you couldn't ask, but her self-confessed tendency to have flings explained a lot. "Rhi, did you notice anything else going on that evening when you were here arguing with Zunia?" Sophie asked, thinking of the confrontation between Orlando Pettigrew and Pastor Frank, and Bertie Handler's "jailing" of Frank in the panic room.

"What do you mean?" Rhiannon said, standing and tugging her shorts down.

"Was there anyone else around?"

"I came here to confront Zunia. I had phoned her, wanting to clear the air. She had some . . . uh . . . mistaken ideas about me and Walter." She shifted from foot to foot and looked off into the distance. "I don't want to go into that. Anyway, I met her here in the lobby and we argued, then I stormed off. I didn't see anyone else, but there probably could have been a dozen costumed clowns here and I wouldn't have noticed, I was so angry."

"What time was that, anyway?"

"About ten thirty or eleven. It was late. I had been stewing about it, so I texted her and then called her, saying I wasn't just going to slink off and let her ruin my standing with the ITCS, not when my mother worked hard to build that darned organization to what it is today." She stared at Sophie. "Why are you asking all these questions?"

"No reason. Just curious," Sophie said.

Rhi took a deep breath. "Well, that's off my chest to you, and now I have to go talk to that detective. It was so stupid of me to lie to the cops about where I was, but I just . . . I felt like an idiot. Can I leave the box of tea with you?"

"Sure. Nana will send you a check when we get back to GiGi." She hesitated a moment, but then said, "If you don't feel comfortable talking to O'Hoolihan, look for Detective Hodge. You might find him more simpatico."

"It doesn't really matter who I talk to, but I don't want to have to explain myself all over again to a new detective, so my fellow Irishman will do. Talk to you later, Soph."

"'kay. Keep your chin up. It'll all be okay."

Rhiannon walked away, but just before she reached the check-in desk, presumably to ask Bertie where the detective was, Walter Sommer emerged from the dining room and saw her. He strode over to her. They chatted for a moment, and then he took her in his arms and hugged her. He glanced around with a guilty start and released her. She clung to his arm and they walked away together.

It was odd that Rhiannon had referenced her relationship to Walter, said that Zunia didn't need to worry about it, and yet there she was hugging him in an intimate manner. Maybe Nora and Zunia did have the same reason for not liking Rhiannon. Maybe Walter was still fond of Rhi in a way he shouldn't be, as a married man.

But it all came down to the facts: If Rhiannon was telling the truth then she could not have been Zunia Pettigrew's killer. That was good—one person knocked off the list, but many more to go.

She paused to marshal her thoughts and glanced down at her notebook. What had she established so far? The teapot was not the real weapon, so the teapot was stolen just to make Nana look guilty. That meant there was another weapon out there, and if they hadn't found it readily, then it had been disposed of, either nearby or somewhere else. But it would pretty much have to be nearby, because the killer, if it was one of the inn guests, had to be close at hand.

She remembered the Dumpster in back and the yellow police tape floating from it. That was the most likely location of the real murder weapon, and it meant that the killer did indeed nip through the downstairs, out the door and likely back in again. The killer had to have known their way around the inn, but she knew it pretty well already herself, and she had just arrived the day before. For all Bertie's antsiness about her going down there, if even Thelma Earnshaw could slip down to the basement unnoticed, then anyone could.

The basement made her think of Pastor Frank's assertion that Bertie had let him out of the locked room, and Bertie's adamant statement that he had *not* released him but had come to the room and found Frank gone. Was it possible that the killer, with the master key in hand, had turned the key in the lock to free the pastor and then escaped back upstairs before he emerged?

It *was* possible. If it was dark down there, as it likely was in the dead of night, it would be easy to disappear before Frank got out into the hall. He would think Bertie had let him out when it was really the killer, who wanted yet another potential suspect free. But if that was so, then where did the pastor go? If he went up to his room and Zunia was already dead by the elevator . . . But who said she was already dead?

Ah . . . that is true. The alarms had gone off in the wee hours of the morning, about three, according to Nana. The killer could have let him out, he would have gone up to his room, which he shared with no one, and *then* the murder was committed!

However, it was also possible that either Frank or Bertie was lying and was actually the killer. Bertie would release Frank to add him into the mix of suspects, though there was no reason why he'd do it secretly, if that was the case. Frank could have let himself out of the room if he had the master key from stealing the teapot out of Nana's room. She took out her notebook, jotting down a note to find out from the pastor what time he was released, if he knew, and where he went. In concert with that, she needed to know what time Bertie went into the panic room.

It occurred to her that she was doing exactly what the detective had warned her not to do, but surely it wouldn't hurt to just speculate. She wouldn't actually *do* anything and would turn over any information to him. And she wouldn't take any chances.

But still, she had kind of promised. She considered that for a moment. It had seemed that in Eli Hodge's presence the detective had some kind of hold over her; she understood perfectly what he was saying and felt deeply that she must not interfere. It was like hypnotism, those cool blue-gray eyes and their fixed magnetic gaze. Weird. Out of his sphere of influence, she knew that she would keep discreetly trying to figure out the mystery.

If what she speculated was true, though, one or the other could be lying, but both Pastor Frank and Bertie could just as well be telling the truth. One thing still puzzled her; Pastor Frank legitimately thought Zunia was going to run away with him, that she was sure of. And if that was the case, Zunia likely led him to believe that. She pondered, and the answer came to her in a flash: It was a smoke screen. She was using the pastor to conceal her real plans, which involved Walter Sommer.

But were she and Walter really planning to run away together? Would he leave Nora? Sophie didn't think so, but it was possible that with Zunia getting pushy, he told her whatever he thought she wanted to hear just to shut her up temporarily.

Something Thelma had overheard came back to her: Orlando Pettigrew said that Zunia was afraid of her lover, and that she was trying to get rid of him. It might be a lie, or it could be true. Perhaps Walter Sommer was hiding a side to his character that fit with that fear. From all reports, Nora was asleep in her room that night. Walter said that she took sleeping pills, which would explain why she hadn't emerged from their room until, according to Nana's recitation of the events of that morning, the police woke her up. So Walter could have stolen the key to the basement room, stealthily let Pastor Frank out so he would provide another possible suspect, lured Zunia from her room with a promise to either talk or actually run away, killed her, then gone back to his room, showered and gone to bed like an innocent person.

The storm was a complication no one could have foreseen, pinpointing the time of death to some extent. It apparently set off the alarm—if that was true and it wasn't set off by someone else—bringing everyone out to find Zunia dead. But she hadn't been dead long. Surely it would have been better for the killer if the body was cold and time of death less certain, as it would have been if the body had not been discovered until someone rose for breakfast at six or seven.

She pocketed her phone and notebook and was standing to go into the dining room when the doors opened and some members flooded out. Josh was in deep conversation with Malcolm Hodge and Horace Brubaker, but when he saw Sophie he said a quick farewell to them and darted over to her.

"Sorry I didn't catch up with you," Sophie said. "But I've been looking into things, and then I had a couple of conversations."

"That's okay. But I do have news."

Just then Emma Pettigrew slunk in through the front door of the inn and took off her sunglasses. Josh called to her. She strolled over to them. They exchanged greetings as Sophie examined the girl, who had dyed her hair a weird patchy pink shade sometime in the last few hours. She looked sullen, but she may just have seemed that way because of her down-turned full lips and unsmiling demeanor.

"Tell Sophie what you told me about what you were doing the night your stepmom was killed."

"Why?" She turned to Sophie. "What's it to *you*?"

"Nothing, really," Sophie replied.

"No need to get tragic," Josh said to the girl, looking exasperated. "Sophie's cool. She's trying to figure out where everyone was . . ." He paused, probably aware of how accusatory that sounded. "Uh . . . you know, to find out if they could have seen anything or heard anything that would help. Her grandmother was accused of the crime, you know."

There was just enough truth in Josh's statement that Emma nodded and then shrugged. "It's no big," she said. "I had a fight with Zee and left the inn."

Zee . . . Zunia? "What was the fight about?"

She eyed Sophie, and Sophie could feel herself crossing over into enemy territory with that question.

"Why?"

Step back. It probably didn't matter what the fight was about anyway, since they apparently fought all the time. "No reason. So, you left the inn," Sophie prompted.

"Yeah. I left and called my mom at Cruickshank. We met at the all-night coffeehouse and talked for a while, then . . ." She drifted off and looked thoughtful, her gaze unfocused. "We, uh, we drove around for a while."

Sophie wondered why she suddenly seemed evasive. Josh noticed, too, and they traded a skeptical look.

"You said you guys talked all night, until she dropped you off out front," Josh said.

"What is this, like freaking Nancy Drew and Whoever Hardy Boy?" Emma exploded. She whirled and strode toward the elevator, but then she stopped and turned back to them. "Neither of you had better tell the cops what I . . ." She trailed off and glanced around. "You just better not." She strode off toward the elevator and punched the up button with a vicious stab.

Josh, his eyes wide, said, "I swear, Sophie, she told me she and her mom had spent the night talking in a diner until her mom brought her back to the inn."

"I believe you. I think she lied to you about some part of her story. In fact, I'm sure of it," she said, explaining what she had learned from Jason about Emma's mother returning to the parking garage by three forty-seven. "Where was Emma after that?"

"And why did she need to lie?" Josh asked.

"That's a good question. I just don't know how to get an answer."

Chapter 19

Sophie and Josh went back into the dining room, where some of the ITCS members lingered. Laverne was arguing with Nora Sommer, an arresting sight since Laverne was tall and imposing, where Nora was short, stubby and red-faced, her habitual steely calm dissolved.

"You clearly don't understand how these things work, and how difficult it would be to coordinate a chapter-wide vote on such short notice," Nora stated.

"I do understand," Laverne said levelly. "However, I still do *not* see why we are having Frank Barlow foisted upon us as president simply because you feel sorry for him. How can you appoint him division president, given the behavior we've witnessed?" She glanced over at the pastor, who sat alone chewing his fingernail. "No offense, Pastor. I truly mean no disrespect."

Nana had a half smile on her face but stayed out of it.

Sophie joined her at her table and scooped up a sandwich from a pretty flowered plate, since she hadn't had anything since breakfast. "What gives?" she asked, then sank her teeth into a tuna salad sandwich that was surprisingly good.

Her grandmother told her about the Sommers' plan to appoint Pastor Frank to the position left vacant by Zunia's death. Sophie chewed, swallowed and asked, "Does he even want to do that?" She watched the argument go on. Frank still sat on the sidelines, as Laverne and Nora squabbled.

"I don't know, honey. He hasn't said no, anyway. He's already been doing a lot for the chapter. Zunia even had him creating and mailing out the chapter newsletter. He's the only one who knows everyone's addresses and e-mails. I suppose he's a natural fit, in a way."

"How does Orlando Pettigrew feel about it?"

"He didn't show up at the meeting. I understand he's down at the police station. Some folks are saying he's there trying to get information about Zunia's murder, and others say the police asked him to come down to answer more questions." Nana shrugged. "Your guess is as good as mine."

Sophie finished the rest of her sandwich, washed it down with some weak tea and crossed the room to join Pastor Frank. She sat down opposite him. "How are you doing?"

He smiled, but it was a weepy version of a happy grin. His eyes watered and he dabbed at them with a paper napkin. "I don't know."

She studied him for a long minute. "I can't stop thinking about your story earlier. If you don't mind my asking, you're *sure* you don't know if Bertie let you out of the room downstairs?"

"*Someone* let me out, and that's all I know."

"Didn't you see the person?"

"Uh-uh. I was sitting there feeling crummy. I didn't even have ice for my eye," he said, touching the still-purplish puffiness under the frame of his glasses. "Then I heard something. When I tried the knob, the door opened. I assumed it was Bertie because he'd said he'd be back for me."

"And what time was that?"

Frank shook his head. "How am I supposed to know? I went up to bed."

"You took the elevator?"

"How else? Why would you even . . ." He paused, his mouth hanging open. "Oh, of course. There was no body. Poor Zunia! She wasn't dead yet."

"Presumably," Sophie said absently. As she'd already figured out, if Frank was telling the truth, there were only two options: either Bertie let him out but didn't want him to know about it for some reason—like, he was the murderer, but wanted to add one more possible suspect to the mix—or he didn't let him out and someone else did. In that case that person had to be the murderer. Who else would be wandering around the inn with a key in the middle of the night? How could she figure out if her third possibility was the right one, that the pastor was lying and had an easy way out of the locked panic room, having stolen the key earlier? "Pastor, who do *you* think killed Zunia? You know all these folks; I'd be interested in your opinion."

He glanced around, a jumpy nerve near his bad eye revealing his stress. "I've been trying and trying to think. Who wanted poor darling Zunia dead?"

Sophie squinted and stared at him. His devotion to the division president seemed so over-the-top. From all accounts

Zunia Pettigrew was an unpleasant woman. He even acknowledged that she was difficult at times. Why had he been so devoted? Was it all a ruse to divert suspicion? "You *must* have some ideas."

"I do have some concerns." He leaned across the table, his sour breath coming in puffs. "I haven't told a soul this—well, no one but the police—but Orlando wanted out of the marriage."

Sophie held her breath, both because of the pastor's halitosis and to hopefully not dam the stream of his gossip. When he fell silent—lost in thought, it appeared—she prompted him by saying, "Did he tell you that?"

"We were friends once, you know, Orlando and I, while he was married to Dahlia. We started talking again lately and he broke down two weeks ago after one of our local collectors meetings. He was desperately unhappy." He looked around and lowered his voice even more. "I know for a *fact* that he even called Dahlia while he was here to see if she'd take him back if he left Zunia."

"Really?" Sophie said. If that was true, it opened a whole new realm of possibilities. She may have ruled out Dahlia, but she could certainly imagine Orlando in the role of the killer, in that case. Or . . . She pondered some new thoughts about how to get Dahlia Pettigrew's car into the garage at Cruickshank, about twenty-five minutes away, and yet have her still be available to commit murder. Did Emma drive? There was a possibility there, though it was a long shot.

However, common sense would prevail. "But he could just divorce her, right?" Rational people did not resort to murder to solve their marital difficulties, and Orlando Pettigrew seemed a rational sort.

"You would think so, but maybe Orlando was worried about how another divorce would affect the bottom line. Zunia was smart," Frank said, tapping the side of his head with his index finger. "She figured it all out. Orlando has money, though you'd never know it to look at him. Zunia told me all about her plan. She was going to tell people he abused her, run away with me and tell him she'd sue him for alimony unless she got a nice settlement."

"And you were going to go along with this?" She kept her cool as best as she could, though the whole thing disgusted her. Pausing to reflect, she turned things around; she had only his word for all of these allegations, she realized. What if the pastor was really the murderer? He could say whatever he wanted about their private conversations because Zunia Pettigrew was not alive to refute them. But Orlando could certainly confirm or deny that he wanted out of his marriage. But would he, even if it was all true?

"It would never have come to that," he patiently explained. "Orlando wanted out, too. I knew that, even if Zunia didn't. I figured she'd tell him what she wanted and he'd go along with it, just to get out of the marriage."

"Why didn't you tell Zunia, if you knew Orlando wanted out?"

He folded his hands together in a prayerful manner and blinked, owl-like. He touched his still-puffy eye under his glasses again and said, "You had to know Zunia. If she thought Orlando was regretting their marriage and wanted out, she'd hold on. She was tricky."

That was one way to describe her. "But you weren't sure near the end that she was really going to run away with you, were you?" She watched his eyes as she said that, and he shifted his gaze away, looking off to Nora and Laverne, who were still discussing his fate as division president . . . or not. "Did she *tell* you so outright?" Sophie pressed. "Did you argue with her about it?"

He looked alarmed. "That's the same thing the police asked," he said, blinking rapidly. "You're working for them, aren't you? I saw you taking to that tall fellow, the new detective."

"I'm not working for them. Mr. Barlow, are you saying you think Orlando killed his wife?"

He shivered. "I don't know, I tell you, I don't *know*! Somebody did this awful, *awful* thing."

"Pastor, Mr. Pettigrew was overheard on his cell phone telling someone at home about Zunia's death. He told them that she was having an affair and he knew about it, but that she was afraid of the man she was having an affair with."

"On his cell phone?" His gaze was riveted on her now, and there was honest puzzlement in his expression. "But Orlando told Zunia that his phone wasn't working. I was right there when he said it; she asked him to call for a car rental and he said his phone was kaput. Not just low in charge, not working at *all*! How could he . . ." He shook his head. "That doesn't make any sense."

No, it doesn't, Sophie thought. It led her to believe what her grandmother had postulated, that Orlando Pettigrew timed his "phone call" to coincide with a gossipy old lady listening in, sure that she would spread what she heard. Why would he do that unless he had killed his wife? "Mr. Barlow, who do *you* think killed Mrs. Pettigrew?"

"I don't know, I don't know! But I won't let *anyone* pin it on me!" Barlow stood and stepped backward, knocking into an older lady and causing her to spill tea all over her flowered blouse. As a convention attendee came to the woman's rescue, Pastor Frank whirled, mumbled an apology, then headed out, stumbling between the tables. A middle-aged blonde woman with frizzy hair—Penelope Daley, if Sophie recalled correctly—darted a poisonous glance Sophie's way and hustled out after him.

She watched them leave the dining room knowing there was no point in going after the pastor. His panic was interesting, though: Why so defensive and afraid that she was working with the police? She'd gone at him too aggressively, perhaps, but they were coming down to the wire. She wanted to leave with Nana in the morning. Given that they were only an hour away, the police would let them go, she was sure, but if they left without knowing who had killed Zunia Pettigrew it would weigh on Nana's mind. She needed to think about Orlando Pettigrew's actions. While it was possible that he had deliberately misled Thelma, knowing she was lurking and feeding her what he wanted spread around, it was also possible that he had lied to his wife about his phone not working. It could be a lazy man's way out of doing what she asked and calling for a rental car.

Sophie rejoined her grandmother. Detective O'Hoolihan entered the room again, sought Nana out and asked if he could have a word. She nodded with a weary look and stood. Sophie rose to go with her, but Nana stayed her with a hand on her arm. "It's okay, sweetheart."

"But I want to come with you," she said.

"Don't worry about me," Nana said.

"I just need your grandmother for a few minutes," the detective said. He looked as tired as Nana, his eyes pouchy from lack of sleep. "We have her bag, and I want her to verify that the rest of the contents are hers, that's all."

"Go find the girls," Nana said.

Sophie did just that. Cissy and Dana, having decided to stay the night, were making themselves comfortable in Thelma and SuLinn's room. SuLinn was driving back to Gracious Grove that evening, now that Cissy and Dana could take Thelma back in the morning, so Dana was going to use her bed, while Cissy shared with her grandmother.

They were chatting when someone tapped on the door. Dana called out for whoever it was to come in, and Josh sidled into the room, but didn't advance beyond the doorway. He looked relieved to see Sophie.

"What's up?" she asked.

"I heard something. I was sitting in the alcove by the front door waiting for a call from my mom and one of those detectives, the red-haired older man, was on his phone with someone. He wouldn't have known I was there because I was sitting cross-legged in one of those chairs, and I was behind one of those big palmy kinda plants."

"That's an excellent spot for eavesdropping, it seems. And?" Sophie prompted.

"You were right; Mrs. Pettigrew wasn't killed with your grandmother's teapot."

"Yes!" Sophie exclaimed, fist pumping the air. "What else did you hear?"

"They think they've got the weapon; it was in that Dumpster out back. I guess they took away the full one and have been searching it somewhere."

"Eww!" Cissy exclaimed. "Gross."

"Shush, Cissy," Dana said. "Go on, Josh. What was the weapon?"

"A hammer! That was what the ME thought, or that's

what I got from the detective's conversation, anyway. And a hammer was found in the Dumpster, so they're testing it for blood, trying to get prints off it and trace it."

A hammer. What a completely ordinary weapon, one you could find anywhere, one that would even have been ubiquitous in the inn, if you knew where to look. Something you could buy at any dollar store or hardware store. "Did you hear anything else?" Sophie asked. "What kind of hammer? New or used?"

He shrugged. "That's all I heard. He finished with the call and walked away toward the dining room."

"That must have been when he came in looking for Nana," Sophie said.

"It had to be a guy, then," Cissy said. "No woman would kill with a hammer!"

Sophie shook her head. "Not true. A few years ago a woman killed her husband while he was sleeping, with a hammer."

"He was sleeping with a hammer?" Dana said, with a sly look.

Sophie rolled her eyes. "You know what I mean. She killed him with a hammer while he was sleeping. And I've heard of other cases, too; a Newark woman just last year attacked her elderly mother with a hammer."

"Wow," Cissy said, and shivered. "Why do people have to be so mean?"

"More to the point, why do you know this stuff?" Dana asked, eyeing Sophie.

"I watch TV," Sophie said loftily.

"Anyway, I gotta go," Josh said, heading to the door. "Another meeting is starting in a few minutes."

"Aren't you bored by all these old folks and meetings?" Dana asked, watching the teenager.

"Not really, especially not the old people. I think Mr. Brubaker and Mr. Hodge are two of the coolest fellows ever! Did you know Mr. Brubaker was in army intelligence in World War Two? And Mr. Hodge played jazz piano with Count Basie once. I'm going to interview both of them for my school newspaper this year. They're better than half the lunkheads in my school."

"You're a rare bird, Josh Sinclair," Dana said.

He shrugged, his cheeks turning red. He couldn't even look at Dana, and Sophie figured that was because looking at Dana was kind of like looking directly at the sun: dazzling. Even on a normal day she was gorgeous, but she was paying extra attention to her appearance now that Detective Eli was in the mix. *Good luck resisting, Detective*, Sophie thought.

"Anyway, just thought I'd tell you about the hammer, Sophie," he said, heading to the door.

"Thanks," Sophie said. He left and closed the door behind him.

"Well, what do you think?" Dana asked.

"I think it will help the police, but it doesn't really tell me anything," Sophie replied.

"Why not?" Cissy asked.

"The police will be looking at where the hammer is from, if any of the suspects bought one recently or if it's from the inn's stash of tools." Each of those possibilities had potential to point to one person more than the others. "But I won't know any of their conclusions. If we're going to figure this out it will have to be from what we already know, can find out or can deduce."

"Look at you, Stephanie Plum!" Dana said.

Sophie laughed. "I only wish I were half as gutsy!"

"Detect away," Dana said. "I'm taking Cissy to see a stylist friend of mine who has a house just outside of town, close to the lake."

"A stylist?"

"Fashion stylist, darling," she drawled. "I'm getting Cissy a makeover. We are going to tip Wally over the edge from boyfriend to fiancé."

Cissy blushed but nodded, looking determined. "Wally is the one. I want to get married."

Since her last engagement had turned out to be disastrous—being engaged to a guy who considered matricide the price of business did not bode well for her choices—Cissy Peterson was entitled to some happiness and Sophie wished her well. Wally was a much better choice, and he adored her, always had.

"You could use a makeover yourself," Dana said, eyeing Sophie's clothes and hair. "For a rich girl, you don't look so hot."

"You can't offend me, Dana, so don't even try," Sophie said with a smirk. "My mother has said it all and worse. Right now I have bigger fish to fry. I am going to figure out who killed Zunia Pettigrew and hand him—or her—over to the police wrapped in a bow."

Chapter 20

It was late afternoon, and the street outside was shadowed by a thick ceiling of dark clouds, though the day was at its hottest. The convention was meeting again behind closed doors, then they would break for dinner and meet again for the last time that evening. Sophie had gone outside briefly to sit in the garden but it was far too hot and humid, the air so stifling it was even too much effort to think. Also, there was a foreboding sense of a storm building. The whole hotel and everyone in it seemed to be clouded by an aura of fear as the detectives worked on methodically, always there, rarely speaking. They had finished with Zunia and Orlando's room, finally, and the tape was off. Was Orlando nervous at all, Sophie wondered, about going back into the room that he had shared with his wife?

"What took the police so long to clear it?" Sophie had asked Detective Hodge, who had told them the news—more because it was already evident by the seal coming off the door than by any wish to share information—but he wasn't willing to go into it. It was a procedural issue, he claimed; O'Hoolihan was a good and thorough detective and left nothing to chance. She was left with the feeling that the older man was not handling it how Eli would, but Laverne's nephew was not going to criticize.

A rumble of thunder rattled the window in the alcove where Sophie was sitting. Bertie Handler, alone at the check-in desk, jumped and looked around fearfully. Whatever else she wondered about his version of events on the fateful night, his fear of storms was real. She just couldn't believe he would be out and about during a storm, and so his story of cowering downstairs while the storm raged had to be true.

But still, he was hiding *something*, Sophie felt. That wasn't the kind of thing you could say to a detective, though. She texted Jason and watched Bertie futzing around with the check-in desk computer. She decided to stay where she was to wait for a reply.

Josh slunk out of the meeting room, guiltily looking over his shoulder.

"Caught you sneaking out," Sophie said, loud enough to make him jump.

He rolled his eyes and looked down at his phone, tapping the screen. "Mrs. Earnshaw keeps giving me the shifty eye every time I look at my phone. What's she got against texting?"

"She doesn't need to know or be personally affected by something to be against it. If I listed all the things she's ratted people out for over the years I'd be talking into tomorrow. I was afraid of her growing up, but she's harmless enough."

He perched on the edge of a chair, and grumbled, "Except for her laser vision. It's like a superpower."

Sophie slipped her sandals off and tucked her feet up under her. "Josh, I'm still worried about Emma. She seemed so vague when we asked her what she was doing that night. I have a feeling her mother dropped her off but she didn't go right up to her room. But where else would she go? You don't think she's involved with the murder, do you?"

"I don't think so. She acts tough, but it's all a put-on." He glanced around and leaned closer. "I think I might know where she was. I was talking to one of the kitchen guys when we went out for a smoke—"

"Smoke?"

"Not me, them!" he said, exasperated.

"Sorry, just a knee-jerk reaction."

"Do you think I'm nuts? Anyway, he said he was hanging out in this all-night café and saw her there with her mother. They left, but a while later she came back alone. I think she likes him and wanted to hang out with him more."

Sophie was relieved. "Okay, good. So it's likely that her mother dropped her off outside the inn but instead of coming in she went back to the café."

He nodded.

"But she doesn't want her mom knowing that, and no one would have been the wiser if it wasn't for the murder."

"That's what I would guess."

"I wonder if she saw anything."

He frowned down at his phone. "Aha!" He jabbed the screen and read something. "You know what, I wondered the same thing, so I just texted her. She's out back. You want to talk to her?"

"Let's go."

They headed toward the door to the stairs down to the basement but Bertie gave her a look, so she turned and led Josh out the front door. The air was like trying to breathe through a wet electric blanket, it was so muggy, and thunder vibrated in the distance. She and Josh scooted around the side of the building as it got gloomier.

Emma was out back with a couple of guys. She sat up on the closed Dumpster smoking a cigarette. She wore jeans, even on a hot August day, and her eyes were made up with dark rings of eyeliner; along with the newly pinkened hair, it was an interesting look. She watched them approach with an uncertain expression. But Sophie had found a few moments during the day to make friends with the kitchen help, and the two guys welcomed her with smiles and nods.

"Hey, Lenny, Gord, Emma. What's up?" she asked.

They chatted for a moment because Lenny, the older of the two guys, was actually interested in becoming a better cook and kitchen manager but didn't know how to go about it. She gave him pointers about training and offered to show him some tricks and give him some basics to work with, then turned to Emma. "What about you? Have you decided what you want to do in college?"

She shrugged. "Like it matters?"

"Of course it matters," Josh said, leaning back against the cobblestone wall. "You can do anything you want in life, but it starts now. May as well get some of the education over with first, I figure, then I can go and do whatever I want."

She cast him a pitying look.

Domenico Dominguez came through the basement door

with two heavy trash bags and then stood looking up at Emma on the Dumpster. She just sat and puffed on a cigarette.

"Come on, Emma, give the guy a break. He's just trying to do his job," Lenny said. He was a tall, slim fellow and strode over to her, helping her down.

She was blushing. Aha, so *this* was the knight in shining armor, Sophie thought, the one she was interested in. He was hipster, with a small neat beard and long hair tied back in a ponytail, but he was smiling and polite. He didn't seem interested in Emma—she was probably too young for him—but he wasn't a bad choice for a teenage crush.

As Lenny helped Dom by opening the Dumpster lid, easier for him to do because of his height, Sophie said casually, "What an awful thing this was, the murder in the hotel. Lucky you were nowhere near the inn when it happened, right?" she said pointedly, looking at Emma.

"Right."

"You and your mom were talking?"

She nodded.

"Yeah, her and her mom were at the coffeehouse where some of my friends and I were hanging out. It's called the Poor Relation," Lenny said, helping the night cleaner lift the heavy bags into the bin. "They have an all-night open mic on Friday nights."

"Open mic?"

"They host kind of a poetry slam," he said. "Emma competed!"

Sophie gazed at her, trying to imagine that and failing, but it was interesting to say the least. "Do you like poetry?" she asked the girl.

"Sure."

Dom ducked his head and said thank you. Lenny clapped him on the shoulder and the new cleaner shuffled back through the door.

"And you write it?" Sophie prodded.

The girl shrugged.

Lenny said, "She's pretty good, actually. Better than me. When she came back to the Poor Relation she laid a cool one on us—what was it called?" He looked to Emma, who tossed her cigarette down and stubbed it out.

Forced to answer by his expectant look, she grudgingly said, " 'Stepmother of Invention.' "

"Was it about Zunia?"

She rolled her eyes and sighed deeply, the ritual of the misunderstood teen. "It wasn't a *literal* poem."

Lenny's gaze switched back and forth between Emma and Sophie. "It was more like, she talked about family and how messed up everyone is," he helpfully supplied.

"So your mom dropped you off at the inn but you didn't actually go in, you just went back to the coffee shop and did the poetry slam. And *then* you came back," Sophie said.

"How long did that take?" Josh asked. "Is it far?"

Sophie was grateful he chimed in, because it was beginning to sound like an inquisition coming from her.

"She was only gone a few minutes before coming back to the Poor Relation," Lenny said. "We hung out, then I walked her back here," he added. He ducked his head in embarrassment. "I didn't want her getting in trouble."

Sophie smiled at him. It was funny how an old-fashioned guy often popped up in the most unusual places. Old-fashioned by some standards, she supposed, but good manners never went out of style. Increasingly Sophie thought

Emma showed good taste in her crush. "Must have been late."

"Yeah, it was morning, like five or so? I didn't think much about it, but there were a couple of cop cars here already, so . . ." He shrugged and looked away, not wanting to bring the topic back to Zunia's death.

That probably let Emma out of contention as the murderer, and Sophie was happy about it. From what Lenny said, there was only time for her to walk back to the coffeehouse after being dropped off at the inn, certainly not enough time for her to commit a murder and hide the weapon.

He looked at his watch. "Crap, I've got work to do. Dinner service is in two hours." He paused and looked at Sophie. "Uh, do you think you could come down to the kitchen and show me some stuff right now?" he asked.

"I don't know how Bertie will feel about that."

"He ought to be grateful," the other kid, Gord, mumbled, the first time he had spoken, other than casting longing glances at Emma. "Anything that would make the Lenster a better cook would be good news."

She descended to the basement kitchen with the two fellows, as Josh and Emma went back into the inn. After washing up, donning a hairnet and pulling on an extra chef's jacket that was two sizes too big, Sophie explained *mise en place*, the proper way to coordinate a cooking and prep area, then moved on to knife skills and a lot of general information that Lenny had vaguely grasped before his training was ended by the inn chef quitting in a fit of pique over not having proper creative control.

She then swiftly helped him set up for the evening's dinner in the dining room, rustling around in the fridge and storeroom and finding enough fresh food to create some new entrees. She showed him how to properly assemble a bulk salad—they had been doing it, but adding garnishes like croutons and bacon too early, so they became soggy—and make side dishes that would hold until service, like roasted Parisienne potatoes and green beans amandine.

She then found a chalkboard in the storeroom and some colored chalk, and wrote the day's specials in flowing cursive. That was for just inside the doorway of the dining room, she explained, mostly to help the waitstaff remember. Whether he'd be able to follow her instructions was another thing, but she had given him the basic tools. Lenny was energized, practically bouncing off walls in his excitement, and he set to work on all the prepping.

Gord shyly expressed some interest in pastries, so she gave him a rough run-through on the chemistry of baking, explained leavening ingredients and the differences among baking soda, baking powder and double-acting baking powder. He caught on fairly quickly once she made it into a science project; this was just his summer job, as he was still a student going into his last year of high school in September.

"I can't believe you guys have been dealing without any of this. How have you been cooking? Where are the recipes you used to use?"

"Chef took them with him when he left two weeks ago," Lenny said gloomily, wriggling his chin under this beard net. "Since then we've been barely staying above water."

Above water? Sinking like the *Titanic*, in truth, judging by what she had eaten the night before. "I hope this helps." She turned to Gord. "Okay, let's get you making some pastries." She thought a minute, then got together all the things to make a simple rustic apple tart. He caught on fast and in quick order there were several baking to be served as dessert that evening.

"I'm impressed," she said, watching the two fellows work. "You guys are going to be okay."

"That's because you're a great teacher," Lenny said.

"I appreciate that," she said, dusting flour off her hands. "I always tried to communicate with staff and fill in all the holes left in their training. Len, I'll give you my e-mail address and phone number and you can e-mail or text me anytime with questions, but you're obviously going to need more help in the kitchen beyond Mr. Headphones over there," she said, hitching her thumb in the direction of the third guy, who was bopping to the tune of the music in his ears as he worked. He, at least, had good knife skills and chopped or sliced whatever was put in front of him with dispatch.

"Especially once *you* go back to school," she said to Gord. "Anyway, let me help get you ready for tomorrow morning." While the kitchen team worked efficiently—dinner service was in a little over an hour—she found the ingredients and worked up a quick scone batter and a couple of cookie doughs that could be stored in the fridge and baked up as needed. She wrote down times and temperatures, then set to work with one of the chilled cookie batters and produced a baking sheet full of Cherry Blossoms, an almond-flavored cookie that had a maraschino cherry–and–slivered almond "flower" in the center of each. She made them regularly for Auntie Rose's, and they were a hit among kids and adults alike. She baked them off and left them to cool.

As she peeled off her chef's coat, stuck to her skin by

sweat because of the heat in the kitchen, she realized that she felt better—clearer of mind and more relaxed—just for having spent a couple of hours cooking and baking. She missed the comradery of working in a kitchen with other cooks. She checked her phone, but there was no message back from Jason yet, then she threaded her way through the passages and up the stairs. She cautiously opened the door to the lobby but was met with a howl of pain or horror.

She bounded out of the passage to find Bertie Handler sitting on the floor behind the check-in counter holding his hand out and covering his eyes with the other. From his hand there dripped crimson blood.

"Help me, someone!" he wailed.

I n the meeting room after a brief discussion about the next year's convention, when it was overwhelmingly decided to again hold it at the Stone and Scone Inn, the debate raged on concerning the chapter presidency. They had taken a straw poll to see who thought what, but it was fairly evenly split, with a slight majority favoring holding a mail-in ballot to vote a new president and reinstate the two-year term, rather than appointing Pastor Frank to serve out Zunia's term.

Frank sulked in the corner. Nora was making the rounds of the tables, haranguing individuals to try to get a majority to vote her way. Horace eyed Orlando, who sat alone at a table. "Now, Rosie, girl," he said reflectively, "why do you think Orlando didn't notice that his wife wasn't in bed with him?"

"I don't know," she said. "Heavy sleeper?"

"When my wife was alive I couldn't sleep if she wasn't in bed with me, near enough to touch. Maybe I'll just mosey on over and ask him. You coming, Malcolm? You can be my wingman, as the young fellas say."

"Now, Horace, don't you go stirring up a hornet's nest!"

"Why, what do you think's going to happen?"

"You just might say the wrong thing to the wrong person and get yourself killed!"

"Rosie, I'm almost a hundred." His rheumy eyes sparkled as he went on, "Reminds me of my days in the intelligence service. Worst that can happen is I'll cheat the Grim Reaper by a year or two. Or maybe more." He then winked and, leaning on his cane, toddled off with Malcolm so they could grill the grieving widower, who sat mopping his nose and sneezing.

Rose joined Jemima Littlefield and Faye Alice Benson, who were anxious to discuss the murder. Having all read a fair amount of Agatha Christie novels, they fancied themselves experts, Rose thought, though she knew that the dark passage of a murderer's mind was a much more intricate highway than she had encountered in any Christie novel. The great dame had a set notion of how evil worked. In Rose's experience there was no such thing as a wholly evil person, but more a broken one who had let evil seep in through the cracks like rising damp, as the Brits called the moisture that leads to rot in foundations. Like that rot, it didn't always show until you did some digging.

"I'd call it *Murder at the Stone and Scone*," Jemima said, working on a crocheted baby blanket in Christmas colors, a snowflake the center of each square with a border of red or green. She had a great-grandchild due in November and wanted to be ready.

"We have a cast of characters," Rose said, deciding to play along. "We have the nervous innkeeper who seems extra jumpy this year, as opposed to the past."

Jemima paused in her crocheting. "That's true, isn't it? Bertie is all over the place, jittery like a long-tailed cat in a room full of rocking chairs. Why do you suppose that's so?"

"He was convinced that Zunia was going to talk us all into holding the convention somewhere else next year. He counts on this as a revenue boost."

Faye Alice, who had run a bed-and-breakfast in the past after a career in the navy, nodded sagely. "No one event could sink him, but once word got around that we were not coming back, speculation would be rife. It could have been the beginning of the end."

"But he knows now we'll be back, so why is he still so jumpy?" Rose said.

"Can you blame him?" Faye Alice said, looking down her nose at them, her gray brows arched. "The police are ever-present and he's had to postpone and move bookings for tonight. I believe Bertie is close to a nervous breakdown."

"Go on with the cast of characters, Rose," Jemima said, her eyes gleaming. "This is like watching a good episode of *Murder, She Wrote*."

"Okay, we've got the wealthy patrician pair, Walter and Nora Sommer, dilettantes. He's a playboy, she's a club woman."

"Oooh!" Jemima cooed, finishing a square and directly starting another, chaining for the center of the next snowflake. "He cheats with the dead woman and she's a jealous harpy! Nora did it!"

Faye Alice said, "I'll bet you always think you know who

did it in the opening scene of the *Murder, She Wrote* episode, too, right?"

Jemima paused to count out her chain, but then said, "The kids gave me a box set of DVDs for my birthday, so I *do* always know who did it."

"Then there is the wretched husband," Laverne said. She cast a look at her father and Horace, chatting with Orlando and Walter, who had joined them. "I sure hope those two don't get themselves in trouble. Eli would not be happy if his grandfather interfered in the investigation."

Jemima shivered. "I just can't look at Orlando when he mops his nose like that; it's so . . . ick!"

"He can't help having allergies," Rose said.

Thelma stomped over to the table and stood glaring at them. "I say you're all missing the point," she said. "No one listens to me. You're all gib-gabbing away, but don't see what's right in front of your nose."

"And that would be?" Rose asked, smiling up at what Sophie called her frenemy.

Thelma leaned over and said, "That Nora woman, Mrs. Sourpuss . . . She and the innkeeper are having a fling. Told you I saw her coming out of his office!"

"Even if that was true—which I doubt—what has that got to do with anything?" Rose asked.

Thelma harrumphed and plunked down in an empty seat. "Don't know yet, haven't gotten that far."

"Anyway, we were going through the suspects," Faye Alice Benson said, shooting an irritated look at Thelma. "Who else?"

"Well, the husband, of course," Rose answered. "He's always a suspect."

"Poor Orlando," Jemima said, softly. "I feel sorry for him with that nasty daughter, Zunia getting herself murdered and Dahlia creating all kinds of trouble for him."

Rose took a deep breath as Laverne watched her and bit her lip. "Orlando had an affair, from what I understand, and then deserted his daughter and wife, getting a quickie divorce and marrying the other woman. Given Zunia's character, I think we can agree that he was headed in the wrong direction. Don't you think if Emma is nasty it is her father's behavior that is at least partially to blame? It can't be easy on the child, being dragged to this dull convention with the stepmother she loathed, all to put on a display of fake family solidarity."

"Having to put up with Zunia could not have been a picnic," Laverne added.

Jemima's cheeks colored pink and she bent to her crocheting. "I was just giving my opinion." She finished the loop to start another square, then gathered her crocheting, stuffed it in a cloth bag and rose. "I think I'll go up and have a nap before dinner." She flounced off.

"What bit *her* bum?" Thelma griped, watching her leave the room.

Faye Alice stood and straightened her beige slacks. "It's this heat and all the nastiness. She's touchy. I think I'm going up, too, for a bit."

When she exited Rose heard a cry of shock through the open door, and Laverne did, too. They both headed to the lobby, where they saw nothing, at first, until Rose spotted Sophie bent over on the floor. "Sophie!" she cried, stumbling.

Laverne grabbed her arm to keep her from taking a tumble. "Slow down and take it easy! Sophie's okay; it's Bertie who's in trouble."

They approached and found that Sophie was kneeling by Bertie Handler, who was shrieking like a banshee. Her granddaughter was wrapping his hand in a tissue while she tried to soothe him.

"Mr. Handler, it's okay. Yes, there is blood, but it's just a small cut, really! Nothing major."

"What's going on?" Laverne said sharply.

"He cut his hand on a letter opener," Sophie said over the wailing cry of the innkeeper. "I can't get him to shut up!"

Domenico, the new cleaner, bolted toward them. *"Te puedo ayudar?"*

"Sabes de primeros auxilios?" Laverne asked.

"Sí. Soy una enfermera."

"What did you say?" Sophie asked, looking up at Laverne.

"He asked if he could help and I asked if he knew first aid. He said, yes, he's a nurse!" Laverne answered, looking bemused.

Domenico dashed into the office and Rose could see him locating the first-aid box mounted on the wall. He rapidly sorted through it and came back with alcohol, peroxide, ointment and bandages. As Sophie sat cross-legged on the floor by them he donned plastic gloves, then crooned in Spanish and tossed the bloody tissues aside as he examined the wound.

"Will you help?" he asked Sophie, with a thick accent, looking up at her. "Is not so bad, but he nervous."

"Of course."

Bertie had calmed somewhat but still looked away. He had some kind of revulsion to blood, Sophie guessed. As Dom worked efficiently, cleaning the wound with alcohol, dabbing with peroxide, then applying ointment, she looked up at her grandmother and Laverne with raised eyebrows. She had wondered about Bertie as the culprit, given his run-in with Zunia about moving the convention and her threat and false lawsuit. But surely a man who couldn't stand the sight of blood would not kill someone by bashing them over the head.

Dom finished up and Sophie gingerly disposed of the bloody tissues and disposable gloves, then helped the nurse to his feet. "Thank you, Dom," she said, patting his shoulder.

He ducked his head, then examined Bertie closely. "You okay now?" he asked. He put one hand under the innkeeper's elbow and helped him up.

Bertie nodded. "I'm all right. I just can't handle the sight of blood, even my own!" He shuddered. "Uh, Domenico, thank you! You have the job, if you want it; it'll be wonderful having you here."

He nodded.

"Sophie, could you help me into my office?" Bertie plaintively whined. "And get rid of that garbage bag with the bloody tissues, please!"

"Sure, Mr. Handler." She cupped her hand under his elbow.

Thelma, panting heavily, joined them and eyed the innkeeper. "Why don'tcha get your girlfriend to help you out?" she loudly asked.

"Girlfriend?" Sophie asked.

"Yeah, that Nora Sommer. She's your girlfriend, right? I saw her comin' out of your office that night, the night that woman got herself murdered."

"I don't know what you're talking about, you horrible . . . you . . . You're mistaken," he finished, his voice breaking. "Sophie, please, *help* me!"

Laverne grabbed Thelma's arm, and said, "Just let them be, Thelma. You're making a scene."

Indeed, the folks from the convention room were buzzing, whispering and watching. Bertie's face was blanched and he wavered on his feet.

"Sophie, you help Bertie into his office. We'll get Thelma out of here," Nana said.

Bertie leaned on her heavily as she helped him into his office and sat him down. She knelt by him, looking up into his watery eyes. "Don't let Mrs. Earnshaw rattle you," Sophie said.

He whimpered but then said, his gaze darting around, "She's right, though."

"What?"

"She's right about me and Nora," he said, his voice a little loud. "We've been working together so closely over the years, and this year she was so upset about Walter and Zunia that she came to my room and we had a drink, and . . . we . . ." He trailed off and shrugged.

It defied her imagination to think that fireplug Nora and weepy Bertie could be passionate, but maybe she was just seeing the world through thirty-year-old eyes. Nana always told her that though young folks believed love was only for the young, you never truly got too old for romance.

"You won't tell anyone, will you?" Bertie said, a pleading look on his face. "We were together. That's . . . that's why I forgot to let Frank out of the room downstairs."

"But *someone* let him out!"

"I don't know who. Nora and I were together, that's all I can tell you."

"But Walter claims his wife was in her bed and slept all night."

A sly smile tilted one corner of his mouth, as he said, "He sleeps like a log, Nora told me. And why do you think she slept through all the commotion? By the time she got upstairs and into bed, she was exhausted."

A shudder of revulsion shivered through Sophie, but she chastised herself, saying just because Bertie wasn't for her, it didn't mean he wasn't for somebody. However, none of this cleared either of them of the murder if Nora returned to her room on the second floor before the body was found by the elevator. "Are you feeling better now?"

He nodded and caught her hand. "Thank you, Sophie. I feel better just for having told someone. I didn't know what to do, what to say."

"You haven't told the police this?"

He shook his head. "Should I? I don't want to get dear Nora in trouble with her husband. I don't know if we'll ever be together again," he said, and looked pensively down at his hand, joined with Sophie's.

"I think you should most definitely tell the police," Sophie said.

He nodded. "I will."

There were still a few people in the lobby, and Sophie had the uneasy sense that some of them must have overheard Bertie's admission of an affair with Nora Sommer, but that was not her problem. She went upstairs in a thoughtful frame of mind. Bertie's confession hadn't changed much for her because she hadn't considered him a real suspect anyway.

The only thing that made her suspect him was his evasiveness about where he was that night and why he didn't let Frank out of the locked room, and now that had been explained.

She was beginning to wonder if they would ever figure out who killed Zunia Pettigrew. And did it really matter as long as the police didn't pin it on Nana? She tried to tell herself no, but yes, it did matter. It mattered because whomever did it had tried to make Nana look guilty, and Sophie was not going to stand for that. Whoever did that should pay. She went upstairs in a determined mood.

Chapter 21

The evening meal in the dining room was interesting. As much as Sophie tried to concentrate on looking around at the other convention goers to figure out who killed Zunia, she was too involved with the food and wondering how the fellows were doing in the kitchen. Service was still slow, but when she ordered the special she had helped them put together, a salmon steak with a simple maple Dijon sauce and the green beans amandine, she was thrilled with the result and so were the diners around her. She had warned Lenny to keep the entrees simple while they were shorthanded and figuring things out. Salmon, so delicate and fragile, could be overcooked in minutes, but hers was perfect.

The beef special looked good. Laverne marveled over it. "It's as if they got a new cook between last night and tonight," she said.

Sophie smiled inwardly, a glow of satisfaction warming her. Lenny, though relatively inexperienced, was an engaged and interested cook, which meant he could become a great chef if he wanted to. The other two fellows were good helpers.

But after the first edge of her hunger was sated, her mind inevitably returned to the mystery in which they were embroiled, and Bertie's confession. She eyed Nora and Walter, who sat alone, silent and ignoring each other. Josh was eating with Emma and Orlando Pettigrew, while Pastor Frank sat with the two sisters and Penelope Daley, who all but cut his steak for him. Jemima and Faye Alice dined with Nana's group.

"I'm staying tonight but leaving in the morning," Faye Alice said. "And I don't know if I'm going to stay with the ITCS."

"Don't quit the group because of this," Nana said.

"Oh, it's not Zunia's murder," the woman replied, forking up the last of her maple salmon with gusto. She chewed, swallowed and continued. "It's the Sommers. It just seems no one has their head screwed on straight. What is Nora thinking, foisting Frank Barlow on us as chapter president? That man is a wreck. I wasn't here last year or I never would have let them rush Zunia through as president. I would have run myself just to avoid it. Zunia Pettigrew got on my last twitchy nerve."

"She got on everyone's last nerve," Laverne said. "Which is why it's so hard to figure out who killed her."

The topic rested as everyone finished their food.

Nana had been speaking with Malcolm and Horace through part of dinner. The two gentlemen had decided to eschew dessert, since neither was much into sweets, and stated their intention to take another walk, long and slow, now that the day was beginning to cool a bit. Laverne fussed over her father, making sure he had his wrist gadget on, the one that let him call for help from wherever he was. He sighed but let her fidget, then made his way out with his old friend, arm in arm. It was nice that the two gents had each other, Sophie thought.

Nana beckoned to Sophie when dinner was done and the dessert course about to be served. Sophie joined her at her end of the table, taking Horace Brubaker's empty chair. "What's up?"

"At the end of the meeting this afternoon, Malcolm and Horace spent some time with Orlando and Walter. Horace told me just now that Walter admitted that he wouldn't really know if Nora was out of the room or not. They sleep in separate beds."

"Ah. Well." Sophie paused for a moment, but then divulged what Bertie had told her about his affair with Nora, and their rendezvous that night.

Nana looked stunned, her creased face frozen in an open-mouthed expression of disbelief. "I would never have guessed that in a hundred years," she finally said.

"I don't believe it," Laverne said flatly, leaning into the discussion.

"Me neither. I've known Nora for a few years and it just doesn't fit," Nana added, her palm flat on the table, patting as she did when thinking deeply. "She's too . . ." She paused as she lined up her silverware. "She's just too *dignified* to cheat with an innkeeper."

Laverne nodded. "Exactly! I was trying to think what I

meant, but you hit it on the head, Rose. If she was going to cheat, it wouldn't be with Bertie."

Thelma, who was leaning across the table, ear toward them, listening in, snorted and said, "Don't put it past her! These women going through the change . . . They'll do anything to feel young again."

"Thelma Mae Earnshaw, you don't even know her!" Laverne said.

"Human nature," she said, settling back in her chair. "My father always said never overestimate human character and never underestimate how low folks can sink."

"That explains a lot," Laverne said, exchanging a look with Sophie and Nana.

Dessert arrived and effectively stopped conversation. The rustic apple tart with locally made vanilla bean ice cream was an enormous success.

An hour later Dana, Cissy and Sophie were holed up in SuLinn and Thelma's room while those two ladies were downstairs with Laverne and Rose at the last formal meeting of the convention. Sophie checked through her purse, then took out what she needed: her cell phone, lip gloss and Nana's room key.

"So tell me again why you called Jason and why you're meeting him to go for a drive in the middle of trying to solve the murder?" Dana was lying back on SuLinn's bed, her bare foot in the air, examining her toenail polish, which she was touching up.

Cissy, who sat on her grandmother's bed, turned her back as she continued to talk to Wally. She had called him ostensibly to ask him to check in on Gilda Bachman at La Belle Époque, but her friends knew it was really so she could exchange telephone kisses with him. A text saying *"I love you"* and a string of hearts just wasn't enough. Sophie was happy for Cissy, who had finally woken up to the good guy right in front of her who only wanted to love her and take care of her.

"I just figure an outsider's perspective might help me figure this out some. I want to bounce ideas off him."

Dana smirked. "What else do you want to bounce off him?"

"Dana Saunders, you be quiet or I will begin to ask why you felt it necessary to dab extra perfume on your neck before going into the coffee shop, where you knew a certain detective was having his dinner." They had briefly joined Eli Hodge for coffee after dinner, Dana sliding into the booth seat next to him, but he had kept it strictly professional, except just before they parted ways he asked for Dana's cell phone number "in case he needed to get in touch."

Dana laughed out loud. "Busted. Go on, have your talk and be sure to park somewhere dark so no one will see if your chitchat involves more than just lip service."

Sophie swiftly wound her hair up in a messy bun, eyed her makeup in the vanity mirror and slid her feet into sandals. She said good-bye and slipped out of the room. As she ambled down the hallway she came across Orlando Pettigrew at the door to his room. He was fumbling with the key and sneezing repeatedly.

"Can I help you, Mr. Pettigrew?" she asked, rushing over to the poor man.

He took a tissue out of his pocket and sneezed again, giving up on the key but leaving it in the lock. "Darned allergies!" he groaned, mopping at his nose. "I was at the meeting, but my sneezing and hacking was disrupting things. Besides, I just didn't feel like being there. I need to take my pills and lie down; I'm not good for anything once I take those things."

She turned the key in the lock and opened the door for him. He shuffled into the room, so she took the keys out of the lock and followed. "Can I get you anything? A drink of water to take your pills?"

He dropped onto his bed and fished a bottle of scotch out of a bag, looking around for a glass. She went to the sideboard, where the hospitality tray was, and retrieved one for him.

"I don't understand why the police keep asking me the same questions over and over. I've been down at the police station three times trying to find out what they think, but they just keep . . ." He sighed deeply and passed one hand over his face. He grabbed a bottle of pills from the night-stand and opened them, shaking two out into his palm and looking around.

She handed him the glass.

"Do you mind getting me some water?"

Either Melissa or Dom had been there, so the room was spotless, and there was a fresh thermal carafe of water on the hospitality table. She crossed the room again and poured some cold water into the glass and brought it back to him.

"*What* do they keep doing, Mr. Pettigrew?" Sophie asked, as he took the glass, poured a large shot of scotch into it and then downed some, swallowing the pills. She picked up the bottle of allergy meds and looked at the warning label. It distinctly said not to take it with alcohol, but it appeared to be something he did all the time.

"They keep asking how could I not notice she wasn't in our room. I told them I sleep soundly."

There was a faint hum from the television and Sophie picked up the remote. It was not turned off properly. She wondered how long it had been like that, as she clicked it off. "Do your allergy meds make you sleep even more deeply?"

"I suppose."

"Did you take your meds with alcohol that evening?"

He nodded.

"Was that after the fight with Pastor Barlow?"

He nodded again. "Zunia was in the room at that point, that's all I can say. But she was pretty peeved at Frank by then. Told him she wasn't going to run away with him; it was all a little joke on Zunia's part from the start. Frank's got no sense of humor."

"Did you tell the police that you take your allergy meds with scotch?"

He shook his head, turning his dull gaze to her. "Do you think I should?"

"If that contributed to you sleeping so soundly that you didn't notice Zunia had left the room, I would, if I were you." She sat down on the other bed opposite him. "Mr. Pettigrew, it's just such a puzzle. Who do *you* think killed your wife?"

He shrugged. "She was always making someone mad. In the time we were together I never did figure out how to keep her happy."

She hesitated, but then plunged ahead. "I met your ex-wife, Dahlia. What a coincidence that she's in town right now."

"It's no coincidence," he said, slipping his watch off and setting it aside on the nightstand. He loosened his tie. "She made darn sure she was close by. She didn't trust Zunia and Emma stuck together for three days."

So clearly the trip to Cruickshank had been planned by Dahlia ahead of time. "Why was that?"

"Those two hated each other. This weekend was supposed to be about building a stepmom-stepdaughter bond."

"Was that something Zunia wanted?"

He yawned. "I don't know. Emma wouldn't give Zunia a chance, and Zunia just made things worse. Then there was my ex . . . Dahlia tried to get Zunia in trouble just after we got together. She was so bitter about our divorce! I tried to be generous, but no amount of money was enough to get her to leave us alone."

Well, duh! It wasn't money she wanted; she wanted her family back. "What do you mean, she tried to get Zunia in trouble?"

"Emma told her mother that Zunia slapped her in a quarrel."

"Did she?"

"Of course not!" He slumped and shook his head, knitting his brow. "Or . . . Zunia told me she didn't. And I believed her." He paused. "At first."

"I heard someone say that Zunia hit *you* sometimes."

"She was such a little thing, but a spitfire. She didn't mean anything by it."

"So she *did* hit you."

"Well, yes, but it didn't hurt."

"Did you hit her back?"

He turned bloodshot eyes on her. "Why would you ask that?"

There was a trace of anger in his tone, and she thought

carefully before she went on. She got up and moved toward the door, turning the knob. "Just wondering," she said. "You said your ex-wife tried to get Zunia in trouble. Did Dahlia report Zunia to the police?"

He nodded, watching her, his eyelids getting heavy. He yawned. "Zunia was fiery, and she and Emma butted heads all the time, but my daughter is a bit of a fibber, Miss Taylor. I would not believe anything she says."

A bit of a fibber? Since Sophie had already established where Emma was it didn't seem possible that she was the killer, but there were ways she could have fiddled with the time a bit, she supposed. They only had Len's word for it that Emma was where she said she was at the time she said. He might not be the most reliable guy when it came to watching the time. Was Orlando throwing his daughter under the bus by implying she was lying about where she was at the time of Zunia's murder? Hard to tell. Cautiously, she asked, "Do you often call your daughter a liar, Mr. Pettigrew?"

He shook his head but seemed confused. "I'm so tired."

"Mr. Pettigrew, I was told that you were talking about leaving Zunia. Is that true?"

Again, he shook his head. Sophie couldn't tell if he had heard her and was saying no, or if he just was getting so sleepy he didn't understand what she was asking.

He glanced around. "How odd to be back in here, but without Zzzunia." He was beginning to slur his words. He used his toes to push his dress shoes off, kicking them aside, then he slumped down on the bed, flinging his arms out. "I need to go to sssleep."

She wasn't going to get anything more from him just then. She watched him from the door. He took the second pillow on the bed and cradled it in his arms. "You must miss her," she said.

"Pain in the keester," he mumbled. "Maybe now I'll get some rest." He started snoring.

She tiptoed from the room, wondering just how sad he was, or if he was dissembling for the benefit of the police, making himself into the bereaved widower when really Zunia's death was the answer to a prayer. Or the result of active malevolence on his part. Had he really taken meds and booze that night, or was he putting on an act for her benefit, worried that she suspected him? On the whole, though, she thought he really did sleep through his wife leaving his room and getting murdered.

Police work must be difficult, she realized, with a new appreciation for how much surmise, character study and filtering through conflicting stories must go into an investigation, alongside the mechanical testing of alibis against each other and the collection of evidence. After the murder of a prominent local woman in Thelma's tearoom in May, Sophie had become fascinated by true crime and watched every true crime show on TV. But as Eli Hodge had said, those were edited for entertainment purposes, and the details had already been figured out and assembled into a logical story line.

She rode the elevator down and strolled through the lobby. The whole thing was still a bit of a jumble in her mind, but she felt that she had eliminated a few people, at least: Emma because of her quick walk back to the coffee-house, Dahlia Pettigrew because of the parking lot evidence of when she had arrived back at the campus and Bertie because of his revulsion toward blood. Orlando was *likely* out of it because if he had been taking his medication with alcohol, as he appeared to have done, he was probably sound asleep.

Who did that leave? The Sommers, together or individually. Interesting. She had long thought that Walter Sommer would not want Zunia to make a scene. Dead, she couldn't threaten his lucrative marriage and position in the society anymore. If she believed Bertie that he and Nora were together, then maybe the solution was as simple as the lover, all along. It was getting tangled in her mind, who was where when, and if she could eliminate them or still consider them a suspect.

She glanced at her phone; it was eight, and Jason had said he'd be there shortly after the hour. She heard another rumble of thunder and hoped it wouldn't begin raining. Would Jason be borrowing Julia's convertible again? She hoped not. She was still uneasy at how chummy he seemed with his married colleague. Maybe it was silly, but he and Julia were so perfect for each other, while Sophie and Jason were so different in a lot of ways.

She went around to the side of the building to wait, lingering in the dark shadows, idly thinking of Jason and pondering how to get him to acknowledge what she felt they both understood: that the past years had seen them both grow emotionally to the point that they could talk about beginning a new relationship. Not that she could even figure out how to raise the topic.

She noticed movement out of the corner of her eye from the back of the building. *What was that?* She flattened against the wall in the shadows not touched by the parking lot lighting and watched. She spotted a figure creeping out the basement door. The person—a woman, judging by the outline—paused, then slunk across the parking lot to the shelter of the shadowy trees that lined the edge of the property. She scooted along the tree line until she got to the sidewalk, then she scurried onto the sidewalk and down the street.

It was Nora Sommer! Why would she be sneaking out of the inn? Curious, Sophie followed, hanging back until she knew which street Nora was turning down. To keep following or not: What was the right decision? She made up her mind and texted Jason, saying that she still wanted to meet him but she was taking care of something. She'd let him know where she was so he could meet her there, instead of at the inn. Then she set out in the direction Nora was going.

The night was still, and the sound of Nora's heavy step on the sidewalk drifted back to Sophie; her own sandals were leather-bottomed and fairly silent. She felt at times like someone was following *her*, but it was probably just a weird echo of Nora's footsteps. She was unfamiliar with Butterhill, so she only had a vague sense that they were leaving what passed for a downtown district in such a small town.

She would not have thought twice about Nora going for an evening stroll except for two things: First, she should have been in the evening meeting. There the final decision would be made about the now-vacant presidency of the New York State chapter of the ITCS. Adding to that, Nora had been moving in a stealthy manner. That was not the behavior of someone going for an innocent evening stroll.

Sophie became more and more nervous as they moved past anything she recognized, and entered a part of town she had never seen. It was residential, a neighborhood that had no streetlights, depending instead on lampposts on each lawn. Trouble was, many folks either didn't turn them on or had let the bulbs burn out, so there were long stretches that were darker and darker, as twilight became dusk, which rapidly deepened into night.

And still, she could hear footsteps behind her somewhere. Ahead there was a side street. She ducked down it and hunkered behind some bushes, feeling ridiculous but unnerved by the little follow-the-leader game she had become a part of. She quickly texted Jason, asking if he was in Butterhill yet. She was about to rise but heard another set of footsteps—was this who seemed to be following her?

She peeked out. It was, of all the people she did not expect, Bertie Handler. She hid back behind the bushes and the innkeeper passed by, his heavy tread echoing in the night.

Where could those two be going? Was it a lovers' assignation? Or a coconspirators meeting?

Chapter 22

There was only one way to find out. She slipped out of the bushes and went back to the street. She could hear the faint echo of footsteps so she followed and spotted a park in the distance, lit with pathway lanterns. Two figures stood by a swing set.

Sophie looked around. How could she get close enough to hear their conversation without being seen? There was a brick building near the edge of the park, so Sophie slipped along the dewy grass and behind that building, following the shadows until she got closer to the play equipment. From there she scooted across an open swath of grass to another outbuilding. She slipped along the nubbly brick wall, trying to quiet her breathing.

They were not going to be able to hear her, anyway, she concluded, as she got closer. They were talking loudly. She didn't know what preceded it, but Bertie was protesting.

"I didn't do it! Why would I kill Zunia?"

"I know she was threatening you with taking the convention away from the Stone and Scone. And I heard from Walter that she had some ridiculous fake lawsuit cooked up."

There was a pause, then Bertie said, "The lawsuit was because she said I sent you an e-mail telling you about her and Walter."

Nora's responding bark of laughter cut through the humid air. "She was just getting my husband to toe the line, or so she thought. She figured I would toss him out on his butt."

"She *swore* you got an e-mail from my e-mail address."

"And I did. But I knew right away that *she* sent it; I told Walter that. He was getting fed up with Zunia's little tricks and stratagems, but she really thought she could get him to leave me."

Sophie inched closer.

"The lawsuit was a fake," he said weakly.

"Of course. I'm never going to let Walter go, but Zunia didn't *know* that. When she heard that I knew about them, she was frantic to do damage control. She was an idiot, too stupid to reason with."

Bertie replied, "But Zunia couldn't have sent you that e-mail from my e-mail address."

Nora was silent for a few seconds, then said, "If she didn't, then who did?"

Sophie thought for a moment, as did they, judging from the silence. The e-mail to Nora could have had a couple of motives; it could indeed have been intended to force Nora to acknowledge the affair and so release Walter from marriage. Or . . . it could have been calculated to get Zunia in trouble. Given Walter's reliance on Nora's money and the unlikelihood that she'd leave him, it was most likely going to result in Walter breaking it off with Zunia, and who would want that?

Pastor Frank, for sure. If they were both telling the truth and neither of them had sent the e-mail, nor had Zunia herself, then it had to be Pastor Frank. But he was the one person who did not have a motive to kill Zunia. Or *did* he?

Bertie suddenly said, "When did you get that e-mail?"

Nora abruptly said, "Why does that matter? Look, Bertie, the other thing I wanted to talk to you about was, why did you tell that stupid girl we were having an affair? I heard all about it, and I was *humiliated*!"

"Who did you hear that from?"

"Good Lord, I heard it about from *everyone*! You apparently shouted it out loud enough for everyone to hear."

"I didn't set out to do that!" Bertie whined. "You have to believe me, Nora. It was that wretched old woman, the new one, what is her name?"

"Thelma Mae Earnshaw," Nora said. "What has she got to do with anything?"

"She told people she saw you coming out of my office and that we were having an affair."

"And if you'd just kept your mouth shut no one would have believed her! She's crazy. Everyone knows that after that stunt she pulled, telling everyone Rose Freemont was a dangerous murderer. Ridiculous. No, Bertie, it's your saying it was true that made folks believe. Why'd you do it?"

"I don't know, I don't *know*. It just seemed like an alibi for both of us, to get the police off our tails."

"You're a fool, Bertie Handler. How could it be an alibi

if I supposedly went back up to my room before Zunia was killed?"

So there really was no affair. Just another dumb lie. Had every single person in the case lied about something? Sophie went back to working on the Pastor Frank angle; she remembered it being mentioned, when they were talking about making Frank the new chapter president, that he had been working on the newsletter for the ITCS, and that he had coordinated the e-mail list for Zunia. Was he the source of the e-mail after all?

She sagged against the nubbly brick wall, wondering how anyone was ever going to sort through all the lies and misleading statements to figure out the truth. Was there one thread she wasn't getting? One thing that tied it all together?

"But what were you doing in my office, Nora?" Bertie asked, his whiny voice cutting through the misty night as a rumble of thunder rolled across the sky. He whimpered. "I gotta go, but tell me why you were in my office."

"Never mind, Bertie. Just leave it alone."

Sophie's mind teemed with ideas, but one possibility suddenly struck her: Nora was in his office and Bertie wasn't there at all? She could easily have stolen the key at that moment, gone up to get the teapot from Nana's room and put the key back with no one being the wiser. Nora had ample reason to want Zunia dead. She would obviously not want word to get around about Zunia and Walter's affair. Or would it matter to her? According to Nana, she was fine with her husband's cheating as long as he was reasonably discreet, so she certainly wouldn't kill to conceal it.

"Tell me. I want to know!"

"Look, Bertie, just go home and forget all about it. Just leave ITCS business to us, and everything will be all right."

"No, Nora, I'm so *afraid.*" There was a weird emphasis in his nasal tone on the word "afraid." "*Some*one killed Zunia, and if you all leave they're going to pin it on me, I just know it!"

"Keep your head and let it go," Nora warned again. "All I wanted in your office was to figure out if you had actually sent me that e-mail or not. I didn't want to accuse you outright. But it doesn't matter now, does it? Zunia was out of control. She was trying to force Walter into divorcing me. She actually said she'd expose their affair and send an e-mail to every member of the ITCS."

"And you couldn't allow that, could you?"

Sophie gasped as a new voice entered the conversation. She peeked out, and there was Pastor Frank Barlow, his hands bunched into fists. "Admit it, Nora. *You* did it. *You* killed my Zunia!"

"Are you out of your mind? Where did you get that idea?" Nora shrieked. "I don't have to stand for this, Frank. Maybe I'm looking at the guilty party right this minute!"

But Frank Barlow was not Zunia's killer, Sophie was sure of that. Neither was Nora. Her mind had been sorting through the threads, and there was only one logical solution. In a high school critical-thinking class she had been taught the principle that if you have competing theories, you should select the one that required the fewest suppositions. In this case of the murder of Zunia Pettigrew, the answer to many questions came down to one person.

Who had the simplest access to the housekeeping key?

Who had access to Bertie Handler's e-mail account, and

thus to send the e-mail telling Nora about Walter and Zunia's affair?

Who could move about the inn with impunity and knew it better than anyone else?

Whose whereabouts for the pivotal time were questionable, and/or had no witness, now that it was clear he had lied?

Who had she eliminated based solely on his own behavior, which would have been an easy fake? The scene with Bertie and the blood aversion had been calculated to put an end to any supposition on her part.

Thunder rolled across the sky as a shot rang out, the sounds mingling and competing. Frank shrieked, in fear or pain, and Sophie darted from cover, anxious to prevent another murder. Without a second more to spare, Sophie tackled Bertie Handler, who now was pointing a handgun, taking aim to get another shot off at Frank. They tumbled to the ground together.

"Call nine-one-one," Sophie screamed as she wrestled with the wiry innkeeper. She threw her cell phone to Frank Barlow, who appeared to be unscathed even as he shrieked and hopped from foot to foot in a frightened dance. A dog barked and thunder crashed, building in crescendo. Someone in the distance shouted.

Sophie had all she could handle, grabbing fistfuls of the inn owner's short-sleeved shirt, the fabric ripping and sliding from her grasp. "Call nine-one-one *now*! What are you waiting for?" she yelled. "I don't know how long I can hold him."

Bertie was writhing beneath her, cursing and threatening, his body odor intensifying into a sour stench. "Get off me, you stupid little witch!" he screamed. The gun went off again, thunder crashed and the rain began.

Sophie put her hands over her ears and screamed in terror, but she hadn't been hit. Her ears rang, but whether it was the gun's report or her own fear causing it, she didn't know. Bertie heaved her to the side and she rolled in the wet grass, rain spattering into her eyes.

"Stop!" Nora screeched as the pastor wailed and began to babble into Sophie's cell phone. "Why, Bertie? Why'd you do it?"

"Why do you think? Zunia Pettigrew was out to ruin me!" Bertie skidded as he tried to stand.

Sophie rolled onto her back and managed to kick at his wrist, connecting. He yelped in pain or surprise as the gun flew out of his hand and away. He didn't stop to retrieve it and ran, staggering and wailing, into the bushes as sirens filled the air and police descended on them. There was no way Sophie was going to follow him. It was one thing to tackle him when someone's life was at stake, but another to be stupid and imagine she was Kinsey Millhone.

As Sophie babbled her story to a uniformed officer, more police arrived and, with guns drawn, they searched the bushes. An officer escorted Sophie, Nora and Frank to separate cruisers, but Sophie was close enough to the edge of the park that she could still see the flashlights as they scanned the groves of shrubs. In five minutes they had located Bertie, squatting in the bushes judging by how filthy and wet he was, with leaves sticking out of his soaking wet hair. Two Butterhill officers led him away in handcuffs to another police car. He shot a malevolent look at her as thunder rolled overhead.

Once he was secured in the cruiser Sophie ducked out and retrieved her cell phone from the wet grass, where Frank had dropped it as the police arrived. She hopped back in the backseat of the car and wiped it off, then thumbed the button along the side; it glowed, and as she swiped the screen, a string of text messages came in just then.

One was from Dana. *"Bertie NOT afraid of blood, Melissa/ housekeeper says,"* it read.

If only she'd known that a half hour before.

The next was from Jason: *"Where are you??????"*

"Meet me at the Butterhill police station," she texted back to Jason.

Then to Dana, she wrote a short *"Case solved: Bertie guilty. Tell you all soon."*

Three hours later she emerged from the Butterhill police station with Eli, who wanted to make sure she got back to the inn all right. But Jason was there waiting. She introduced the two men, who shook hands.

Eli regarded them both in the yellowish light of the police department parking lot, the wet pavement gleaming, the air scrubbed clean of the muggy heat by the vigorous thunderstorm that had roared for an hour or more. Detective Hodge turned to Sophie and said, "I'd appreciate it if you'd tell my aunt and granddad that I will see them in the morning, after which I hope they will head back to Gracious Grove."

"Sure will. Anything else?" She watched him, her head tilted to one side.

He smiled. "And tell Dana I'll give her a call. I'll be coming to GiGi next weekend, work permitting. Maybe I can see her then."

Sophie nodded and let Jason take her in his arms. A close hug felt so good, even though she was still damp and muddy from her experience. "I think she'd like that," Sophie murmured. "Maybe we can all get together." A triple date: Wally and Cissy, Dana and Eli, and her and Jason—it sounded wonderful, but just then she wanted home and quiet and sleep in the worst way. However, she had to go back to the inn.

Jason drove her there, but though she could feel his desire to ask questions, as he glanced over at her again and again, she didn't want to talk about it until they saw everyone. The place was a bustle of police who were tearing apart Bertie Handler's office as well as his private quarters, looking for evidence. Melissa, the housekeeper, sat on a stool behind the check-in desk, her expression glum, shoulders slumped.

"What are *you* doing here?" Sophie asked, heading to the counter and leaning on it. Jason followed and put his arm around her.

She shrugged. "Dom called me to check in after he was done this evening. I wanted to go over things with him, just to make sure he had gotten to everything on the list. When he told me about the blood and Bertie's claim that he was blood phobic, I didn't know what to think. I came over to talk to him, but he was already gone. That's when I saw Dana and the others in the coffee shop and asked what was going on."

"How do you happen to know he's *not* afraid of blood?"

"Sophie, Bertie was an EMT before his aunt left him the inn," she said. "He wasn't very good at it; in fact he had lost his job because of something that happened, some negligence on his part, and a guy died in his ambulance. I know there was some lawsuit, and a judgment against him. He's got to keep paying it, so if he lost the inn, he'd be bankrupt. But anyway, the upshot is, he could *never* have been afraid of blood, not on that job, not for seven years. I couldn't think why he was pretending otherwise."

"I don't suppose anyone but you would have known that," Sophie said. She'd had some time to think about things while waiting to be interviewed, and she knew how Bertie had timed it so that she'd be the one to find him with the bloody gash, crying and wailing about his fear of blood, too. She had been downstairs, and he must have known that; he had security cameras trained on the kitchen, after all. When she headed toward the stairs he must have been right there, ready to gash himself. Why? The only reason she could think of was that her questions and intent to get to the bottom of things must have unnerved him.

"So let me get this straight, the innkeeper was setting it up to look like he couldn't be guilty of bashing the woman over the head because he couldn't stand the sight of blood," Jason said.

Sophie nodded. "He couldn't leave well enough alone. It was the *one* thing over the line among all the tricks he used to cast the blame on different folks. If I'd heard that—what you told the others, Melissa—I would have known immediately, but I was so sure for a while that it was Nora. She had been seen in Bertie's office—she was apparently trying to figure out if Bertie really did write the e-mail to her—and I knew whomever was guilty had to have access to the key, so she made sense to me. Plus she had ample reason to hate Zunia. Of course, Bertie was the one person who *always* had access to the key." She paused. "But what about the thunderstorm fear?"

"Oh, *that's* real enough," Melissa said.

"I suppose he really was hiding in his panic room while the thunderstorm raged, but he first let poor Pastor Frank out without letting him know it was he who unlocked the door."

"Why would he do that?" Melissa asked.

Sophie shivered as the air-conditioning finally got to her wet skin and clothes. Jason hugged her close, using his body heat to warm her up.

"He wanted to cast doubt on Frank's story," Sophie said. "He could always tell the police that Frank must have had the master key and let himself out, if he decided to lay the blame on him. He made his decision to steal and use Nana's teapot to point the blame at her as soon as he heard the story of Zunia and my grandmother's argument, but he was hedging his bets. It was like he was using a scattershot to put the blame on lots of different people, figuring he'd muddy the waters, I suppose. It sure worked for a while. I was so confused I couldn't figure out who was telling the truth and who was lying."

"I just don't know what to think," Melissa said, tears in her eyes. "Bertie and I got along all right. I can't believe he's a killer! Why'd he do it?"

Sophie shook her head. "Fear. He was losing his grip on everything, including this inn, and coming unglued. Zunia was threatening to take the convention away, and he was scared it would be the nail in the inn's coffin. With her gone he hoped everything would return to normal." She had a feeling he followed Nora and Frank intending to kill one and frame the other.

Melissa, calmer, sniffled and said, "His aunt, the one who left him the inn, was a lovely person—my godmother, actually." She grabbed a tissue and mopped her eyes, taking a deep trembling breath. "I guess I'll take care of things here until the police tell me what to do. I feel like I owe it to *her* more than Bertie. She loved this old place."

In a thoughtful mood, Sophie accompanied Jason upstairs and led him to her grandmother's room. Nana, her lined face weary, jumped up as quickly as any octogenarian could when Sophie entered the room to a chorus of her friend's voices, chattering and asking if she was okay, and what had happened, and was she sure she was all right! Nana stiffly toddled across to Sophie and enveloped her in a hug, trembling. "Thank the good Lord! I was so worried when I heard what had happened. We stayed together; they all kept me from going crazy. How could you do something like that, heading out after folks when there was a murderer among the group? Young lady, I ought to tell your mother!"

"Nana, it's okay," Sophie said, hugging her hard. "I'm all right."

After some chatter and crowding around, and satisfying them all that she really was okay, Sophie changed her clothes and washed up, then joined her friends and Nana. Sophie sat beside Jason cross-legged on a bed in Nana and Laverne's room with a mug of tea. The room was crowded, but it was hours yet before the coffee shop would open, and everyone wanted to hear what had happened.

She told them all how she had been waiting for Jason, but when she saw Nora slinking out of the back door and staying in the shadows, she felt the need to follow. At that point she was still vacillating as to the identity of the killer. She had first settled on Nora, because Thelma had seen Nora coming out of Bertie's office; it was a perfect opportunity to snag the key, she figured. But her alternate was Pastor Frank. His evasiveness over where he was that night, his uncertainty over who had let him out of the locked room, his weird obsession with Zunia: it had all contributed to her thinking that he must have done it.

"It was only at the last minute that I decided it just had to be Bertie. There were so many conflicting stories and lies told for a variety of reasons, I was confused . . . still am. So let's figure this out," Sophie said, taking in the room at large. "There were several people who *could* have done it. If I'd gotten the text about Bertie not being afraid of blood, I would have figured out he was the guilty one earlier. I mean, otherwise why the sham?"

"So many people were lying about so much," Nana said.

"I know . . . so many lies, I had trouble keeping track of them all." The e-mail outing Walter and Zunia's affair that Bertie claimed he did not write, Orlando lying about being on the phone and claiming he knew all along about her affair and that it wasn't serious, Bertie lying about having an affair with Nora, Emma refusing to explain where she was all night . . . so many lies, large and small. She glanced around at the gathering. Nana, Thelma and Laverne occupied straight-backed chairs by the little table. Jason sat on Sophie's cot with her, his back against the wall, while Dana, Cissy and SuLinn—who had not gone home after all—sat on the two double beds. Sophie had been informed by Laverne that Josh was downstairs with the two elderly gentlemen, learning to cheat at gin rummy.

"So . . . what really happened? Are we clear yet?" Nana asked.

They went over the evening before the murder. "What gave us pause," Laverne said, "was Frank Barlow coming to the Pettigrews' door and confronting Orlando. Where was Zunia at that point?"

"I have to imagine she was in bed or getting ready for bed," Sophie said. "She didn't come to the door at all, right?"

"No," Nana said. "And Walter was at *his* door, so he wasn't with her. She must have been in their room, probably fed up with Frank and not willing to talk to him."

"But when she was found dead she was still in the same clothes she had been in earlier," Sophie said.

"True," Nana said. "She either never changed out of them, or put them back on before she went out."

"I don't think the police ever found her cell phone, but it's probably safe to say she got a text or call saying Bertie wanted to come clean about the e-mail, so she went out to meet him." Sophie explained to the others about the e-mail to Nora Sommer that Zunia believed Bertie had sent, the very e-mail that it seemed he really *did* send, hoping to get Zunia in trouble so deep she'd be thrown out as ITCS New York State chapter president, no doubt. How could he know that she'd pretty much call his bluff with a fake lawsuit? That was likely when the scheme to kill her had occurred to him.

Laverne said, "But her body wasn't found until three thirty A.M. or so. Surely she would have been in her pj's by then."

"I wondered, what would I do if I was at an inn, already in bed or ready for bed, and got a text or e-mail asking to meet someone? I'd put the clothes back on that I'd worn that day. Orlando fell into a deep sleep—the scotch and allergy meds made sure of that—so he didn't even know when she left the room."

There was a tap at the door just then. Sophie bounced up and crossed the floor, flinging the door open.

Rhiannon Galway stood in the doorway, a smile on her face. "Can anyone join this party?"

"You're welcome, of course," Sophie said, and crossed

back to the cot. She introduced Rhiannon to Jason and brought her up to speed.

Rhiannon took a deep breath, clasping her hands together in front of her. She glanced around at the gathering. "I can add to the conversation. First, you were wondering about Walter Sommer, right? Where he was when the murder happened?"

Sophie watched her. "Well, yeah, that's *one* of the things we wondered about."

"He was out looking for me," she said, her pale cheeks pinkening.

Sophie felt bad for her, having to admit to that. "But you were with your . . . uh . . . friend."

"Mike," she said, with a faint smile. "He called me last night," she said to Sophie. "He wants to go out for real."

"Do you want to go out with him?" Dana asked, watching her face.

"I do; he's a great guy. But about Walter . . . I messaged him about the fight with Zunia, and he wanted to talk to me in person, to reassure me that I didn't have to worry about losing the ITCS contract for tea supplies. He'd see to that. I didn't know that then, of course. But he was out looking for me some of the night and got back after the murder. He's had a rough go of it because the cops have been grilling him."

"So he lied to us all when he said he was in his room in bed?" Sophie asked.

Rhiannon nodded again.

Dana said, suddenly, "He's your father, isn't he?"

"Dana, don't—" Sophie was about to tell Dana the subject of Rhiannon and Walter's relationship was off-limits, but she stopped in midsentence when she saw Rhiannon's nod of affirmation.

"He is?" a chorus of voices asked.

"Can't you see it?" Dana asked, watching Rhiannon. "She has his eyes and his hands, and the same way of talking. I've only met the guy briefly, but I can tell."

Suddenly a dozen little things fell into place: Rhiannon's attachment to him, the way he had hugged her—fatherly, not in a lover's fashion—the fact that Lacey Galway had been among the first members to start the ITCS more than twenty-five years ago along with the Sommers.

"That's why my mom didn't stay in the ITCS and why she moved to Arizona when she got married. She just couldn't handle being around Walter anymore, not with him not willing to acknowledge me openly for so long. And that's why Nora doesn't like me."

"Because you're a constant reminder of his . . . uh, his behavior."

Rhiannon shrugged. "I tried to creep around and pretend my feelings weren't hurt. Nora held it over him all these years, since he had the affair with Mom, and he felt he owed it to her to just keep our relationship on the down low. Zunia picked up on our vibe and figured we were having an affair. That's why she hated me so much and wanted me out of the ITCS; she was going after him hard, and didn't want me in the way."

"Wow. She was quite the piece of work," Dana said, brows arched high.

"She sure was. I guess she was disillusioned with Orlando and was moving on. Dad did have a fling with her, but said she was an awful person, just spiteful and mean-tempered.

He was trying to ditch her, but she was holding on and threatening to expose their affair. Not that any of that excuses murder," she added hastily, looking around the group. "She didn't deserve to die, and we would have sorted it all out eventually. Anyway, Dad and I finally had a real discussion, and I'm not hiding our relationship anymore, and he isn't, either. He's told Nora she can shove it, or something to that effect."

Nana got up and went to the girl, hugging her. "I'm happy for you, dear," she said. "You're a good girl and didn't deserve the way you've been treated."

"I'm sorry things went the way they did. As much as I disliked Zunia, she didn't deserve what Bertie did to her," she repeated. "I still can't believe it, but I guess I have to."

"I could have told you it was that innkeeper. I always said he had fishy eyes," Thelma said.

Cissy rolled her eyes and said, "Oh, Grandma!"

Chapter 23

Everyone scattered to try to get a little sleep. The next morning they had coffee in the coffee shop with some of the other convention attendees. The convention itself had been abruptly terminated with no real decision made as to the chapter presidency. Nora and Walter told everyone at the quick meeting they called that they would consider the matter and give everyone their opinion, after which it would go to a mail-in vote.

Pastor Frank was out of the running. He was still in the hospital after his run-in with Bertie, his nervous system completely collapsed, Penelope Daley claimed. She was staying to see him though his crisis, and Laverne was taking bets that she would soon be Mrs. Pastor Frank. Most of the others simply packed up and left, including Emma Pettigrew, whose mother had come to get her. Josh's mother had arrived at the crack of dawn and packed him up, offering Malcolm and Horace a ride back to Gracious Grove as well.

Faye Alice and Jemima had coffee with the remaining Silver Spouts crew in the coffee shop. SuLinn, Cissy and Dana had all headed back to Gracious Grove early so they could open both businesses: Cissy's bookshop and La Belle Époque. Thelma was going back with Laverne, while Nana would travel with Sophie.

"We'll see what happens with the ITCS now," Laverne said. "I say Rhiannon should take over this chapter. She's Walter's daughter, after all, and tea runs in her blood!"

"I'd second that," Nana said.

Faye Alice harrumphed. "We'll see. If I'm to stay with the ITCS, I think we'll need some changes made, and I may just run myself!"

"I'd vote for you," Jemima said.

"I wouldn't," Thelma croaked. "You're as shifty as that Bertie Handler fella."

"Says the woman who caused all this trouble in the first place with her lies," Faye Alice shot back.

"Now, that's not quite fair," Nana said. "Thelma pulled a prank, but Bertie intended to kill Zunia anyway; that's why he had planned it all out ahead of time. It's just that with so many folks not liking Zunia, it was too easy to find suspects. Including me!"

Her blue eyes sparkled, and Sophie giggled softly. "My Nana, chief suspect in a murder investigation! Wait 'til Mom hears."

"Young lady, you are to tell Rosalind nothing!" Nana said.

"I said all along that Zunia woman was a murder waiting to happen," Thelma growled.

The group broke up and they packed their vehicles, ready to go. Before they left, Melissa told them the inn was closing, for the moment, until Bertie was either out on bail or had made arrangements for who was going to take care of things. He had no family, Melissa said. The aunt who left him the inn was the last of his line, besides Bertie himself.

Their arrival back in Gracious Grove was tumultuous, since Gilda was weepy and clingy, and the cats, both Pearl and Sweet Pea, meowed and demanded to be a part of the celebration. They opened both tearooms that day and managed to muddle through.

After a couple of days they learned that Bertie Handler had not yet been arraigned because they were doing a psychiatric evaluation on him. Sophie suspected that he would eventually be found fit to stand trial. He was an emotional sort, but he hadn't seemed truly imbalanced or incapable of knowing right from wrong.

As for the teapot that had been used to point the finger of blame at Nana, shortly after they arrived home Sophie got an e-mail from a specialist who confirmed that the vessel she had sent him a photo of was indeed a Tibetan holy water vessel and not a teapot at all. Of course, the pot was still in the possession of the Butterhill police department, as it was evidence in the murder case against Bertie Handler. Nana shook her head when she heard, and told her granddaughter that she had no desire to ever have the pot back. If it was offered to her after the trial, if there was one, she'd have to figure out what to do with it then.

Finally it was Saturday, the end of the long week. The day had been hectic, with a couple of bus tour groups, a baby shower, a wedding shower and lots of drop-ins. La Belle Époque had been busy, too. Sophie was looking forward to Sunday because she and Jason were going to go to the lake for a picnic. She was intent on telling him how much she regretted the way they had parted as teenagers, and how she hoped they could become more than friends again.

The bell over the door indicating another customer entering rang and Sophie whirled, ready to tell the newcomer that they were just closing up for the day. Instead she stood openmouthed. "Mom!" she yelped, skipping across the tearoom and throwing her arms around the slim, blonde, well-kept woman.

"Sophie, let me look at you!" Her mother held her away from her and turned her around. "You need a manicure and a proper haircut. Who has butchered your ends?" she exclaimed, grabbing a handful of her daughter's hair. "And what conditioner are you *not* using?"

"It's so good to see you," Sophie said, staring at her mother. She hadn't realized how much she had missed her in the last four months. "Let me lock up. Come see Nana."

Sophie locked the front door, then tugged her mother back to the kitchen and hopped up and down in delight as Nana turned and saw her daughter standing by the door. "Rosalind!" she cried. "Oh, my dear, it feels like forever!"

"Mama, I saw you not that long ago; wasn't it Christmas?"

Rose enfolded her in a long hug, and Sophie saw a tear on her grandmother's cheek. Rosalind didn't like Gracious Grove much, though she did visit her mother at least once a year.

"Not Christmas. It was Thanksgiving last year. I've missed you so very much."

When the hug ended, mother and daughter stood and

stared into each other's eyes as Sophie watched. For all their differences, Sophie could see so many similarities in her mother and grandmother.

"I've missed you too, Mom," Rosalind said.

Nana was tired, so though her mother would have liked to go out for dinner, Sophie insisted on cooking, and they ate in Nana's apartment with Pearl sitting on Sophie's lap, much to Rosalind's chagrin. Her mother was going to stay in Nana's guest room on the second floor, but Sophie wanted to talk, so her mom joined her in her apartment for a glass of wine before bed.

Mother and daughter chatted for a while but eventually the subject came around to Sophie's plans, as she knew it would.

"You can't mean to stay here in Gracious Grove indefinitely, darling?"

Sophie watched her mother. A lot of people thought her mom was a typical wealthy man's wife, and in some ways she was. Sophie loved her father, but he was not cut out to be a dad. He enjoyed work and little else. Rosalind Freemont Taylor had gracefully found a life of her own to keep her occupied. She traveled, shopped and saw the world with the occasional presence of her husband when he was forced to take a vacation.

"I'm really enjoying being here, Mom. You know how much I love this town, and being with Nana."

The woman smiled and sipped her wine, making a little face and setting it aside. She curled up and said, "What about your goals? You wanted to get back into a really good restaurant, last I heard. You're such a good chef, darling. Dinner tonight was delicious. Are you going to waste your talent making scones and cupcakes?"

Sophie narrowed her eyes. This was the first time her mother had ever talked about her ambitions with such enthusiasm. "It's not so bad. I've been experimenting with soups and pastas, light lunches. They're going well."

"But you're a chef, not a tearoom cook."

"What are you getting at, Mom?"

Rosalind uncoiled and leaned forward, setting a few things on Sophie's coffee table at right angles. "Do you remember Bartleby's on Shinnecock, darling?"

"Of course." Bartleby's was a lovely old restaurant near the Taylor house in the Hamptons, where Sophie spent a few weeks at the beginning and end of every summer when she was a teen, whatever time she could spare from Gracious Grove. "We used to have dinner there every Labor Day, just before you took me back to school."

Those dinners had always been fraught with so many emotions: sadness, anger, resentment, excitement, but most of all, confusion. Sophie had never been sure whether she most longed for or feared the parting at the beginning of the school year, when she knew she wouldn't see her family again until Thanksgiving in November. But that restaurant was where she had become familiar with and gained a love of truly fine food. They were legendary for their oyster and lobster dishes. "What about it?"

"They're under new management. The most darling man has bought it, a gift to his son, who is a fabulous designer."

A pause, and time ticked. Sophie could feel her stomach churn. "And?"

"And he knows of you from In Fashion, darling." She flicked a glance up at her daughter, then returned it to a chrome teacup that sat on the table. "It seems your food made quite an impression on him. When I told him you were my daughter and that In Fashion had closed, he was aghast. You weren't cooking? he asked." She shrugged elegantly, her pale blue silk pajamas rippling, shimmering softly in the low lighting. She sat back again, watching her daughter.

Sophie waited.

"He has a chef, of course, but it seems they are in desperate need of a sous chef de cuisine, someone who understands New York palates." Rosalind fished in her purse and brought out a letter, which she handed to Sophie. "He asked me to give you this."

Sophie took it and tore it open. In florid, expressive language, Hendriques Van Sant begged her to consider coming to work at Bartleby's. He named a staggering wage. He told her his vision: to reconnect the restaurant to its seafood origins, from which it had strayed. The job was hers, no application nor audition needed. He had eaten her food and was satisfied.

"That would mean leaving here," she said numbly.

"You could stay at our house in the Hamptons, darling. It would be so much fun! We could spend time together."

Sophie eyed her mother. "Did you have anything to do with this?" she asked, flapping the letter around.

"The offer? Of course not! As if I would."

Did it matter even if she did? Sophie regarded her mother. This was the first time she felt like her mom was taking her ambitions seriously, and it meant a lot. "What does Daddy think?" Sophie asked.

"You know your father, he hardly heard me. I swear, I could say I was running away with a gondolier from Venice and he'd just tell me to have a nice time."

Sophie felt a twinge of remorse. She was sometimes

guilty of tuning her mother out, too, but her mom told the same stories over and over or talked about stuff that just didn't interest Sophie. She'd have to listen better. "I'll think about this. Can I call him to talk to him before accepting?" Sophie said. This was a test. Definitely a test.

"You certainly can. Oh, I hope you take it!" She clasped her delicate hands together and held them in front of her face, the pearl pink of her nail polish glowing softly. "It's such a beautiful place, and they are getting ready to open in a month. You'll not keep him waiting, will you?"

"No, I'll phone him tomorrow morning." Just before going on a picnic with Jason. Her stomach clenched yet again. What to do? She had been having budding romantic feelings for her teenage love, but if she was not going to stay, was it fair to reignite the flame that she still felt was banked in her heart?

She wasn't sure. She just wasn't. She'd see him tomorrow. Rosalind rose and stretched languidly, very much like Pearl would.

"Good night, Mom. Thank you for this," Sophie said, folding up the letter as she stood. "It means a lot to me that you believe in me so much."

"My darling girl, I've always believed in you. You just never gave me a chance."

"I promise, I'll give you a chance from now on," Sophie said. She hugged her beautiful mother, feeling the sharp angles of her shoulder bones sticking out. "I'll *always* give you a chance from now on," she whispered.

Cherry Blossom Cookies

Yield: 48 cookies

1 cup butter or shortening
3 ounces cream cheese, softened
1 cup sugar
1 egg
1 teaspoon almond extract
2 ½ cups all-purpose flour
½ teaspoon salt
¼ teaspoon baking soda
1 cup finely chopped pecans or almonds
    (optional)
Slivered almonds and maraschino cherries to
    decorate

Cream the butter or shortening and cream cheese together, then add the sugar, egg and almond extract.

Sift the dry ingredients together and stir into the creamed mixture, then add the chopped nuts, if desired.

Chill the dough thoroughly, then form chilled dough into 1-inch balls.

Cherry Blossom Cookies

Place them on an ungreased cookie sheet, flatten slightly and with your thumb make an indentation in the center.

Press a cherry half into the indented center of each cookie, and use slivered almonds to form petals around the cherry center.

Bake at 350° for 10 to 15 minutes.

A Cup of Enlightenment

A Brief Explanation of Types of
Tea and How to Steep Them

by Karen Owen, aka Karen Mom of Three

The popularity of tea has been steadily gaining ground since tea was introduced in England in the 1660s. Tea first arrived in what is now the United States of America in the early 1700s, brought over by the Dutch. It later came to Canada in 1716 via the Hudson Bay Company. Today you can find tea and tisanes in almost every restaurant and grocery store. If you find yourself overwhelmed in the tea aisle of your local grocery store or in one of the ever popular tea shops, here is an explanation of the types of teas and tisanes which are the springboard for all the "new flavor" teas offered today.

Black tea: Black tea is the most popular of all the teas. Black tea is a leaf from the Camellia plant that is fully fermented before drying. It brews a full-flavor, high-caffeine tea. Some of the most popular and well known black teas are Earl Grey and English Breakfast. Earl Grey is a black tea that has been flavored with oil of bergamot. English Breakfast tea is a blend of black teas that is rich in flavor and usually enjoyed with milk and sugar. Black tea originated in China but is now produced in many countries all over the world. Known for its antioxidant properties, stress relief and ability to lower the risk of stroke and diabetes, black tea is sometimes flavored with citrus, caramel flavors and fruit. It is offered in both tea bags and as loose leaf as tea shop blends. Black tea should be steeped once for two to three minutes and served fresh.

Pu-erh tea: Pu-erh tea is a variety of fermented dark black leaf tea from China. It has a beautiful dark color and at first glance may remind you of a cup of coffee. Pu-erh tea should be steeped two to three minutes and can be re-steeped up to three times.

White tea: White tea comes from the buds and leaves of the Chinese Camellia Sinensis plant, and is lightly oxidized, which means the leaves are browned in a chemical process that exposes them to moist oxygen-rich air for a short time. Grown and harvested primarily in China, this tea has many health benefits. White tea is the least processed tea and is full of antioxidants. It is believed that white tea can lower blood pressure and blood sugar, that it can help protect the body from heart disease and stroke and can strengthen the circulatory and immune systems. White tea should be steeped four to five minutes and can be re-steeped up to three times.

Green tea: Green teas are un-fermented Camellia leaves and usually from China or Japan. Black teas are by far the most popular tea consumed around the world but green tea is gaining in popularity. Green tea has been shown to improve brain function and help with fat loss, and may lower the risk of cancer in those who consume green tea regularly. Green tea is high in antioxidants and L-theanine, an amino acid that can help with lowering anxiety. Green tea does contain caffeine, however not as much caffeine as black teas. Green tea should be steeped two minutes and can be re-steeped up to three times.

Matcha tea: Matcha tea is a powdered green tea. It is made with a whisk and hot water to produce a frothy tea. This tea is very high in antioxidants.

Rooibos tea: Rooibos tea is from an evergreen tree in South Africa. This is a tisane, a name given to a tea that is herbal and not from the Camellia Plant family. They are caffeine free, contain powerful antioxidants, have a high mineral content and aid in digestion and the absorption of iron. Flavored Rooibos teas are very popular. You can find flavored rooibos in both loose and bagged teas. Lemon and vanilla Rooibos are some of the most popular tisanes today. Rooibos tea should be steeped four to six minutes and can be re-steeped up to three times.

Fruit tea: Fruit tea is a herbal tisane. Fruit is dried and then chopped or shredded for loose-leaf or bagged tea. Fruit can be added to a caffeinated tea but on its own is a lovely way to enjoy the best that summer has to offer year round. Fruit tea should be steeped four to five minutes and should only be steeped once.

Mint tea: Mint tea is a herbal tisane created by drying the leaves of mint plants. Peppermint tea is very popular for aiding in the relief of stomach problems and stress and even as an appetite suppressant. This is an easy tea you can find in both loose-leaf and bagged teas or even a tea you can make from the mint leaves you grow in your own garden. To make mint tea, tear up fresh mint leaves and pour boiled water over the leaves, then steep for three to seven minutes and enjoy. Mint tea should only be steeped once.

Visit Karen Owen at her cozy mystery and tea blog: acupofteaandacozymystery.blogspot.ca.